SUZANNAH ROWNTREE

Dark Secrets

Miss Dark's Apparitions, Vol. VI

First edition

ISBN: 978-0-6454668-9-8

Cover art by MiblArt

This book was professionally typeset on Reedsy.
Find out more at reedsy.com

Chapter I.

If you ever happen to be in Germany on a cold December afternoon just a few days short of Christmas, there is nowhere nicer to be than curled up before the fire with a good book and a cup of tea and a tidy little packet of *pfeffernüsse* to munch upon. That the book should be by Anthony Trollope goes without saying.

Schnuckelig, is the word I'm looking for. One *ought* to be *schnuckelig* at Christmas, and also *gemütlich,* and absolutely *heimelig.* On this particular afternoon, I was none of these things. I was standing in a narrow street of the little university town of Heidelberg—down which the icy December wind rushed with a pained moan—knocking upon the door of a tall, forbidding, red-brick house.

The door opened to reveal a short, plain little woman with a rather anxious-looking face. "Yes?" she asked, blinking up at me in an obscure panic.

"Good afternoon," said I, in my best German. "I am Fräulein Dark, the new governess. Will you inform Dr Schwab that I have arrived?"

As I spoke the words I gave an inward sigh. To think that barely a week ago I had been dancing with a Grand Duke at Maxim's Restaurant in Paris, wearing not only a Worth gown in red silk velvet, but a garnet necklace worth hundreds of pounds! And to think that I had been congratulating myself upon having once and for all escaped the dreary life of a spinster governess!

Of course, I was now no *mere* governess. Today my motley crew of philanthropic thieves and I were in Heidelberg upon a frightfully important bit of business, upon which the fate of all Europe might depend.

Not that the eminent Dr Schwab, Chair of Chemistry at Heidelberg University, was aware of this. Thank heaven!

The name of the doctor wrought powerfully upon the timid little woman before me. "Oh," she stammered. "The Herr Doctor is expecting you? Come in, come in. I will fetch him at once. —Have you travelled far?" she added, as she led me into the drawing-room and offered to take my coat.

"I have come by train from Nuremberg, via Darmstadt," I told her, which was stretching the truth considerably. In fact my journey had brought me from Paris on the previous evening. Today I had travelled only from the house next-door, which was to serve my confederates and me as a general staff headquarters for the duration of our Heidelberg campaign. I thought with a pang of the scene I had left behind me: the cosy drawing-room; the side-table spread with spiced and sugared biscuits; the cups of fragrant tea; the roaring fire; and the comfortable murmur of voices as we planned our mission.

Dr Schwab's house, by contrast, had the look of a place that was reverting into bachelordom and perhaps poverty. As the housekeeper withdrew to find the doctor, I gazed about me with a sinking heart. The drawing-room smelled horribly musty, and there was no fire in the grate, so that with every breath a puff of white fog drifted from my lips. The rugs were threadbare and there were empty spaces on the walls where the patterned paper was a little brighter, suggesting that pictures had been taken down and sold. Even the gas remained unlit, despite the thick clouds that smothered the sky and the tiny windows that further restricted the entrance of daylight. Altogether it was a rather austere house, bare and comfortless; which I was unaccustomed to in Germany. For this I was prepared: the doctor I heard, had lost his wife a year or two past. But somehow the most ominous thing of all was this: there was not even a Christmas tree.

A house with children, and no Christmas tree!

Hearing soft scuffling sounds from the hall, I opened the drawing-room door and ventured out into that equally cheerless thoroughfare. Absolute silence greeted me. For a moment there was not a sign of life. I fancied that I saw white faces and staring eyes peering at me between the balusters on the stairs, but when I ventured a step nearer, I found that I had been deceived by some splotches of ink on the peeling wallpaper.

Just then, a fleeting movement caught the tail of my eye. I turned. A little girl of nine or ten years, with dark hair and very pale skin, stood poised in the doorway from which I had come. In the same absolute silence that had reigned since I opened the drawing-room door, she regarded me with enormous, solemn blue eyes.

I put a hand to my heart, for there was something eerie about the child's sudden and soundless appearance.

"Good day," I said politely. "And what is *your* name?"

She made no answer.

There was another scuffle above me, and I turned to see that now in truth a small face was gazing down at me from the

3

stairs. Then the face moved and doubled.

Two above, and one below! That was not right. The hair prickled upon my scalp, but before I could turn to look again at the silent girl behind me, there came a piercing whisper from above.

"Are you the new governess?"

"I hope so," I said, attempting to arrest the creepy feeling tiptoeing delicately down my spine. (This was the strict truth. I might be here on false pretenses, but I drew the line at telling untruths to children.)

"Do you want to see Aunt Dete?"

This question dragged me back to the moment. Aunt Dete! thought I, with alarm. Who was this? I was *quite* sure the children had but one aunt, and that she lived comfortably far off in Nuremberg. I did not know how my nefarious plans would survive a second aunt, and one who was present in the house!

"Indeed I would," said I cautiously, after an awkward moment. The children on the staircase got up and rushed down into the hallway. One of them was a boy, and the other was a girl whose hands were clasped together at the knot of her sailor collar. The two of them had the strong familial resemblance of twins, as well as dark hair and eyes that accentuated the extreme, unhealthful pallor of their skin. The little girl, in particular, gave me a shock of recognition. I turned to the drawing-room, but the silent little girl behind me had vanished.

I stood for a moment quite speechless. What had I seen? Never before had I known a shade or imprint to be abroad during the *lifetime* of its original.

"Hold out your hand," said the little girl in the sailor-dress.

With the unreal feeling of a dream, I did so. I half expected her hands to go through mine without touching. If she was a shade—that is, a spirit still clinging to life after the death of its mortal rind—then this might explain her instantaneous flitting about from drawing-room to upper stairs.

Her clasped hands settled on mine. They were chilly and bloodless; but they were quite real—they had the weight, the heft, the undefinable pervasive stickiness of a real child's hands.

I soon ceased altogether to worry about the apparition that had appeared to me. A delicate pressure fell onto my gloved hand. The child drew her hands away and I beheld an enormous house spider, as large as my palm, so large that I might have counted the hairs on its slender brown legs.

I was rendered entirely speechless. I merely looked at the creature; and the creature, with far too many eyes, gazed back upon me with placid interest. Its mandibles twitched, but that was all.

"I think she *likes* you," said the little girl, with mischievous glee. The little boy giggled.

I opened and closed my mouth in silence. It is not that I am particularly averse to spiders, mind you. I have seen much worse things. Not only am I gifted with the ability to see the shades and imprint-memories of the recently—and often violently—departed dead; but, far more to the point, I have spent *quite* a number of years as a governess.

No; it was merely the unexpectedness of the spider that rendered me speechless.

I was about to recover and say "Aunt Dete, I presume?" when a door opened with a sound like a cannon going off, and the children's father emerged from the recesses of his study, trailed by the meek little housekeeper.

"What's all this?" he puffed. "A governess? I don't require the services of a governess, thank you, Fräulein."

A change had come over the children at the appearance of their father. The little girl turned even paler, if that were possible. The boy edged nearer to me.

At that involuntary movement I felt as though a spell had broken—a spell which had begun imperceptibly to bind and deaden my reactions the moment I had entered this peculiar house. There was a cheap-looking Japanese ginger-jar on the credenza to my right. With the utmost economy of movement I lifted the lid, deposited Aunt Dete within, and handed the jar to the little girl.

"Herr Doctor," I said in my most pleading tones, "I beg you to cast an eye over my references. Perhaps you received a telegram from Fräulein Schwab, in Nuremberg, recommending me for a position?"

The mention of his sister did nothing to endear me to the doctor. He turned red, and his jowls quivered with emotion. "No," he said, as though the mere suggestion was offensive. "I've told my sister that the way I raise my children is *my* business, not hers."

Well, this was a blunder. Had we taken a little more time to prepare ourselves before attempting to smuggle me into the doctor's household, we might have known of the quarrel between the doctor and his Nuremberg relative—but there. We had been pressed for time; and besides, with every minute that passed, I was getting a better idea of Dr Schwab's weak points.

"Please," I said, clasping my hands, and deploying the large, melting blue eyes that had stood me in such good stead over the years. "Herr Doctor, I need the position. You don't know how grateful I would be. I am an excellent governess. I would be of great assistance to you."

The doctor hesitated. "The children are very troublesome."

"Perhaps they have too much time on their hands."

He looked tempted. We had, of course, ascertained from Dr Schwab's University colleagues that the children had no governess and did not attend school. Their father saw to their education, we had been told—but as a busy lecturer, I did not see how he found the time. And now that I had seen the children, I was almost certain that he had *not* found the time.

"No," the doctor repeated, with renewed resolve. "I have no money for a governess. Good day, Fräulein."

I played my final card and burst into tears.

"Don't turn me away," I sobbed into my handkerchief. "I have nowhere to go—nowhere—if I cannot find a place. Indeed I don't know how I will live."

"I am not a charity, Fräulein."

"You need not pay me," I said. "Only give me food and board and that will be enough."

The doctor hesitated. "If you are such an excellent governess, then you will find work elsewhere."

"But I cannot," I said, wringing my handkerchief. "I am in trouble with the law. In Nuremberg I was fined forty marks for improper use of a perambulator, and where am I to find forty marks? And how was I to know that it was against the law to obstruct traffic with a perambulator?"

This was ridiculous, of course. One can hardly take care of children in Germany without a thorough grounding in the laws governing the uses of *kinderwagen*, as they are called. There is a booklet for the purpose. But I was willing to wager

7

that considerations of this sort had never troubled the doctor's mind.

"You are in *hiding* from the *police?*" Dr Schwab inquired, censoriously.

"Yes," I whispered. "So you see that I am hard-pressed to find respectable work."

There was a long silence. I saw the calculations being made, slowly but surely, in the doctor's head.

"Very well," he said. "You may remain for a week. After that, if I am happy with your services, you may consider this a permanent position, so long as you take care to break no more laws. Fräulein Angermeyer, please prepare a room. Sine, Cosine," he added, turning to the children, "you are not to give Fräulein—"

"Dark," I supplied.

"Fräulein Dark," he repeated, "*any* trouble whatsoever. And put that spider back in its box!"

With that he vanished, once more, into his study. Fräulein Angermeyer, with a spiritless sigh, trudged upstairs to fulfil her orders. I was once more alone with the children.

"Sine?" I asked, hesitantly. "Cosine?"

The children gazed up at me, looking as doubtful as I felt.

"Are those your names?"

"Yes, Fräulein," they said, but not as though they believed it themselves.

Yes, I am afraid that Dr Schwab *had* named his children after mathematical functions. That this ought to be a hanging offence was an opinion I kept to myself.

I smiled. "Well! Why don't we take Aunt Dete upstairs, and you can show me your nursery-room?"

Obediently—for they still seemed somewhat cowed by the

weight of their father's warnings—the children led me upstairs. I followed them, feeling rather more relieved than worried. There was something not quite right about this house and these children. Still, I was ensconced within the family as I had wished; and could now set about my true mission.

Chapter II.

Here it may behoove me to say a few words about the mission which had brought me and my friends to Heidelberg, and had required me to inveigle myself into the house of Dr Schwab.

All the world knows of the horrible revenant policemen—revivified corpses, prized by the world's empires for their unquestioning obedience to orders, and for their brutality when crossed—which had until a bare two years previously terrorised the streets of Europe nearly as much as the bomb-flinging anarchists had done. (To the surprise of many, the anarchist bomb threats had subsided notably since the puzzling disappearance of the revenants. Possibly setting dreadful undead watchers to hound the poor with unsparing ferocity had never been a very good idea to begin with.) At any rate, one bright summer's morning we had all awoken to find the streets full of lifeless corpses in the brass buttons of the gendarmerie. There had been no sign of struggle or violence: the animating spark had simply fled. The remains were quickly gathered up and carted away, but from that moment the revenants were no more; the powers of Europe being thenceforth obliged to recruit their policemen from among the ordinary, human variety of monster.

Such was the state of things until barely a week ago, when my crew and I unearthed a revenant who had been lurking in the cellars of the Paris Opera and terrorising the corps de ballet. Yes, I am aware that this seems tremendously unlikely, but for a fuller vindication of these events I will refer the interested reader to the fifth volume of these memoirs. At any rate, the news was electrifying—not only to the Parisian police, who could not be prevented from learning of the creature's existence, but also to my crew. Someone, it was clear, had rediscovered the secret of revenant-making. And we had among us, by a strange quirk of fate, two people who had assisted at the Heidelberg laboratory at which the revenants had first been created.

Our gifted but kindly pugilist, Alphonse Schmidt, who had been more deeply concerned in that dreadful business, had no memory of his life before the decommissioning of the revenants. Whatever he might have remembered from his Heidelberg days had been removed by the authorities as a means of preventing any single Great Power from attempting to recreate the revenants without the knowledge of the others. But our sagacious inventor Miss Nijam, having escaped the notice of the authorities, remained fully in possession of her own memories. According to Nijam, the master-mind behind the creation of the revenant policemen was Stefan Schmidt, Alphonse's elder brother—now, alas, deceased in the same event which had put an end to the revenants. But the Schmidt brothers had had a teacher. The late Dr Auberlen, the former Chemistry Chair at the University of Heidelberg, had survived the revenants by a couple of weeks, and succeeded in creating one more before his death—the one we had unmasked in Paris.

To Heidelberg we had come, therefore, on a mission not

only to restore Alphonse's memories, if possible—but also to discover what had become of Auberlen's knowledge after his death, and to arrange for the destruction of any papers and journals he may have left behind him.

Yes—their destruction! Indeed it was our purpose to put the revenants forever beyond the reach of all Great Powers. I imagine my readers shaking their heads and saying that they should expect nothing better from a gang of international scallywags, comprising a burglarious ballerina, a half-Indian inventor, a pugilistic former valet, a renegade Grand Duke— and me, that conniving female, Molly Dark! But to those of you inclined to think so, I shall say only this: *you*, dear reader, did not face that monster in the catacombs of the Paris Opera. You did not view the corpses of his victims, nor witness the unholy malevolence that animated his dead carcass. You, who know the revenants only as efficient public guardians, cannot imagine the terror and cruelty which they might inspire within those unfortunate enough to be made their targets; nor the bitter regret with which Schmidt and Nijam regarded the creatures they had assisted to make.

Myself, it has always been my opinion that the dead ought to be left in peace, and neither called back nor revivified for the convenience of the living. Therefore, as I say, we had come to Heidelberg quite determined once and for all to destroy what was left of the secret to revenant-making.

Dr Schwab having replaced Auberlen as the Chair of Chemistry at the university, Nijam thought it likely that Schwab had inherited his predecessor's papers and perhaps also his fascination with the revenants. It was this probability that had brought me into the doctor's household as governess to his children.

"I don't mind admitting that it was touch and go for a moment, there," I whispered to my little transmitter a few hours later. I had spent the afternoon with the twins, inspecting the nursery, the terrarium in which Aunt Dete passed her days, and the children's workbooks. (These, between you and me, were in a disgraceful state; for the children were behind in arithmetic and barely literate in their own native tongue.) Now, tucked up in bed with the day's final cup of tea, a little packet of *pfeffernüsse*, and my well-thumbed third volume of *Can You Forgive Her?* which I *still* had not finished, I was at last enjoying a quiet word with my suitor, the aforesaid renegade Grand Duke.

Vasily had given the *pfeffernüsse* to me as a parting gift. "Something to remember me by," he had said mournfully. As though I could forget him, when he had planted himself in the house next-door and was in constant communication by transmitter!

I wondered whether he had yet discovered a little surprise of my own. Not wanting him to forget how much I loved him, I had in a quiet five minutes before quitting the house thoughtfully sewed up the legs of his pyjama-trousers. I hoped that when he attempted to retire for the evening, this trifling inconvenience would make me feel very real and near to him.

"Touch and go? It was bound to be," said Vasily now. "We didn't have the time for proper observation. But the main thing is that you got *in.*"

"Oh, yes," said I. "It was simple enough, once I saw how Schwab had the children and the housekeeper so utterly cowed. He needed to feel that he could control me; so I burst into tears and told him a wonderful story all about how I had broken the perambulator laws in Nuremberg and was in

13

hiding from the police. That pulled the wool right out from under his eyes."

"I think you mean *over his eyes,* my dear."

"At any rate, he believes he can pay me a pittance and terrorise me the way he does everyone else in the house; and that's the main thing. Tomorrow, when he's away lecturing, I'll try to have a look into that study of his. The children say he spends most of his time at home shut up there, very close. And I'll try whether I can slip away for half an hour or so, and you can tell me what you and the others have found."

"You might see me sooner than that," Vasily answered.

An imperious rap at the door interrupted me before I could ask what this meant. I heaved a sigh.

"I'm wanted," I whispered, and quickly switched the transmitter off.

The room was chilly; it took me a moment to summon up the nerve for the shrinking slither out of the warm bed, and the belting of the sensible dressing-gown. The knock was repeated, more urgently this time.

"What is it?" I asked, opening the door. Then, upon recognising the rotund figure without as that of my employer, I added, "Oh, it's you, Doctor. I thought it was one of the children."

Dr Schwab had his hands thrust into his pockets like a man who resents being kept waiting. "I'm holding a scientific gathering downstairs," he told me brusquely—that, I thought, explained the formal academic robe and hood he wore over his shabby tweeds—"and I shall require the presence of my son. Bring Sine downstairs and make sure his face is clean."

With that he departed, not even waiting for my assent. I heaved a second sigh and closed the door in order to dress myself. Although I might not find the learned doctors of the ancient university town of Heidelberg to be bursting with masculine appeal, I could scarcely appear among them in my dressing-gown. I had to pin up my hair and then lace myself into my corset and the old grey skirt and jacket of which I was now thoroughly tired. Then with one last longing look at the *pfeffernüsse* awaiting me upon a little chipped Dresden saucer, I departed.

Of course the two little Schwab children had already been undressed, washed, and put to bed. I went down the corridor and softly opened the nursery door, whereupon I found that the narrow little beds opposite the fireplace were empty. Aunt Dete sat tidily folded in her cage, chewing placidly upon a bluebottle from the collection of insects which the children kept for her sustenance. Of the young miscreants themselves there was no sign, although I flashed my lamp here and there and peered beneath the beds. Nor were they giggling behind the curtains, nor lurking in the washroom.

"Sine! Cosine!" I called.

There was no answer. I turned towards the door and saw a little girl in a sailor-dress, who stood beholding me in grave silence.

"Cosine!" I said, putting a hand to my heart. "What have you done with your nightgown? Come to bed before you catch your death. Where's your brother?"

The little apparition gave no reply. On the contrary, she whisked about and darted into the shadows of the corridor beyond just as silently as she had come.

I felt that creepy feeling again, like cold prickly spider-feet running down my spine. None of this made any sense.

I ventured into the corridor. Down one end of it was a

silvery gleam as the rising moon peered in at the window. Down the other was a golden glow arising from the front hall, whence came a hum of indistinct voices and the sound of the front door opening and shutting. There, two little figures were silhouetted against the light, their noses peering through the balusters.

I was thankful to have spotted my quarry so easily. I had not been in the place six hours, and while I certainly intended to ransack the place for clues that might aid me in my mission, I did not think that now was the ideal moment to carry out my search.

"There you are!" I murmured, descending upon the fugitives. The children made no reply; but, seeing that they were caught, got up and hurried back to the nursery. I followed more slowly, with a detour to my room, where I pocketed the packet of *pfeffernüsse.* A moment later I found them in their beds, giggling and pretending (badly) to be asleep.

I set down my lamp and turned on the gas. That made them sit up and pay attention.

Following the prank with Aunt Dete, the twins had been angelic all afternoon—a sight *too* angelic, if you ask me. It is not good for children to be too well-behaved. Their naughtiness now had come almost as a relief; but now they were solemn again, and watched me with huge dark eyes that seemed like blots of ink against the papery whiteness of their faces.

It occurred to me to wonder what, precisely, the doctor wanted his son for.

"I'm afraid I have bad news for one of you," I said, feigning brightness. "Papa has asked me to bring Sine downstairs, and I suppose that means Cosine must remain above. But if you

16

are good, Cosine, and stay in bed, I shall give you a *pfeffernüsse* from the Night Market."

My heart sank at the sight of their faces when I delivered this news. Sine turned even paler than was his wont, and scuttled sideways onto Cosine's bed where he could hide behind her. Cosine's lips trembled.

"What's the matter?" I asked, trying to sound jolly. "Don't you like *pfeffernüsse?* I'd be very happy to eat them all myself, you know!"

Not even the promise of spiced and sugared biscuits, however, could wring a smile from the children. Sine peered over his sister's shoulder. There was something pinched and terrified about his face. I found that I could not continue speaking.

I had *suspected,* of course, that the children could not be very happy, or very safe, in this house. But this felt like confirmation of something worse than I had feared. At the same moment it struck me that Cosine was in her nightgown, and the little girl I had seen in the doorway just now had been wearing a sailor-suit.

A cold hand clutched my heart.

"I'll tell you what," said I, suddenly. "Papa can wait. Let's *all* have a *pfeffernüsse.*"

I took the little packet from my pocket. The children accepted the delicacies gratefully, and I sat next to Cosine on her bed.

"Now, then," I said, "You aren't really twins, are you, my dears?"

Sine did not answer, but Cosine shook her head: "No—we're *triplets.*"

Then my worst fears were true. I took a deep breath. "Don't

17

tell me. You once had a sister named Tangent."

There was a shimmer in the air and there softly faded into view the solemn, silent little girl I had glimpsed twice before. She seemed to be looking at my *pfeffernüsse* with a rather woebegone expression.

"We call her Clara," Sine said defiantly, speaking for the first time that evening. He pointed at his living sister. "She's Heidi. I'm Peter."

"Those are *much* more sensible names, Peter. I approve. I'm so sorry poor little Clara is no longer with us."

Peter and Heidi exchanged glances. Then Heidi brushed away *pfeffernüsse* crumbs and declared, "She isn't gone! Peter can see her! We play with her *all* the time!"

The solemn little face of the girl in the sailor-suit broke into a smile, and she ran to the bed and settled beside her brother. Peter broke a *pfeffernüsse* in half and offered it to her to sniff, which she did with every appearance of enjoyment, closing her eyes and looking both wistful and rapturous.

Finding that I had left my mouth ajar, I closed it. Not only was Peter able to *see* his sister, but apparently the shades of the dead can smell, if they cannot eat. Poor child! to be able to see the treat, and smell the treat, and never to eat the treat! and at Christmas, too!

"Clara, my dear," I said, very gently. "You know that I see you, too, don't you?"

It was time for Heidi's mouth to hang open. "That's not fair!" she proclaimed. "Why am *I* the only one who can't see her?"

"I'm afraid it isn't always a happy thing, Heidi, to be able to see the dead," I said gravely. "Is it, Peter?"

He shook his head.

The three of them watched me closely. The poor little dead

girl; the little boy, who had something of my own gift, which had been such a frightening thing to me; and the living girl, so full of energy and determination. I was overcome suddenly with the ferocious desire to gather all three up in my arms and protect them from everything that might harm them. What had happened to poor Clara, and how long ago? What about their mother? Was there any possibility that Clara, like Mimi's friend Anna, might still be alive somewhere?

But of course I could not overwhelm them with questions at once. Nor could I stand between them and their father, who after all had the law on his side—unless I was to steal them away entirely; but I did not know enough yet to commit to such a course of action. I drew a deep breath.

"Do you *want* to go downstairs, Peter?"

He shook his head. So did Clara; and she nestled a little closer to her brother, as though comforting him.

"Very well, then," I said. "Why don't I go downstairs and tell Papa that you aren't feeling well and mustn't be disturbed?"

All three heads nodded, and Peter said fervently, "Yes, please."

"All right. Into bed with you, quick-smart! And don't jump out again, or Papa will know that I'm fibbing!"

I shut the nursery door and ventured downstairs.

The front hall was as dingy and cold as ever, the gas having been turned up only so far as would serve to ruin your eyesight, if you should linger there for very long. But there was a line of gold shining beneath the study door and a convivial hum of voices within. I knocked, and when no one answered, I opened it and ventured inside. I noted with interest that the study, unlike the rest of the house, was well-stocked with books and bookshelves—all of them with impossible German titles printed upon the calf-leather spines. It struck me that here might be the best place to commence my search for what we were looking for. Then a sharp voice called my name and Dr Schwab swept me out of the study again with a rush.

In observing the bookshelves, I had not neglected to note that gathered within the study was a crowd of more than a dozen academic German gentlemen, all of them wearing their academic robes and hoods. As Dr Schwab hurriedly pulled the door shut behind him, I could not help laughing.

"Dear me!" I said. "You all look frightfully sinister! Like something out of an Edgar Allen Poe story!"

There was a gleam of spectacles within the shadow of Dr Schwab's hood. "And *who*," he said suspiciously, "is this Edgar Allen Poe?"

Surprise had led me to blunder. "No-one important," I reassured him with a resumption of my meek demeanour. "Forgive me for intruding."

The doctor's cold scrutiny did not abate. "Fräulein Dark," he said, with impressive gravity, "this is not a house where you may enter any room at will. This is the headquarters of the Order of the Black Temple."

My apologies died on my lips. "The what?"

"The Order," Dr Schwab repeated, "of the Black Temple! A secret society dedicated to the scientific advancement of mankind. We insist upon having our privacy, fräulein!"

They did not seem such a *very* secret society, if meek little Fräulein Dark was to be told all about their existence. But I was not here for my own amusement. "What sort of scientific advancement, Doctor?"

"That's a secret," he snapped. "Where's Sine? You ought to have brought him down with you."

"Poor lad, he's feeling poorly," I said. "His dinner must have disagreed with him, for now it's all coming up again."

The doctor muttered angrily beneath his breath. "Bring him down when he's finished, then."

I was growing to dislike the doctor more by the moment. "That would be cruel. He's not fit to stand."

"I didn't engage you to argue with me, fräulein!"

"No, indeed not," I said, as contritely as I could. He was evidently not going to back down; but neither, for once, was I. "You engaged me to care for your three children, and that is what I am doing. I believe I might be of assistance to you in Sine's place."

"Excuse me, I have two children," he corrected me, in a somewhat calmer tone, as though I had said something to make him cautious.

"You have now," I acknowledged. "But it's a shame about little Tangent. I saw her shade just now in the nursery—a solemn little girl with a great resemblance to Cosine. In truth, Doctor, I think you'll find me every bit as helpful as Sine. Perhaps more."

It was, of course, complete madness to let anyone else know of my unnatural abilities—let alone a person as repellant as Dr Schwab, towards whom I ought to have been behaving with the utmost caution. But I was in a reckless mood. Also, it behooved me to find out what these—Black Templars—were up to.

What kind of professorial gathering requires the mediumistic services of a child?

The doctor watched me, and although I could not see his face very well within the shadows of his hood, I saw his jaw bulge like a cow chewing its cud. Then he shrugged. "Very well," he said. "Wait in the hall until you're called for."

Just then there came another knock at the door, and the doctor himself went to open it. In came two or three more gentlemen in academic robes and hoods that were pulled over their heads, swallowing their faces.

"Herr Dunkel!" the doctor boomed, greeting the tallest and most lissome of the newcomers. "How good of you to come!"

Something about the newcomer attracted my attention. For one thing, he was by far the handsomest of the men in the room. For another, his beautifully-trimmed beard made him look as dashing as a stage-magician beneath the shadow of his hood. Drawn by some ineffable magnetism, I ventured towards him.

Dr Schwab was busily introducing the theatrical newcomer to the others. "Brother Otto, have you met Herr Basileus Dunkel? He has a keen interest in our work with the revenants, and means to provide finance."

"He's not one of us," muttered Brother Otto, with a resentful sideways glance at Herr Dunkel. Otto was a young man with a fine, vigorous figure. But his features were marred by a jagged scar that ran almost vertically up his chin and lower lip, all purple and livid as though it was barely healed yet.

"Herr Dunkel will be admitted to the Order tonight," Dr Schwab said, testily. "He has only to take the oath, and—Fräulein! What are *you* doing here?"

"Waiting in the hall, as you asked," I said, turning upon him my most innocent, blue-eyed look.

Beholding me, Herr Dunkel gave a start. "Why, Dr Schwab, who is this angel—this vision of loveliness?"

"That's the governess," Dr Schwab said, icily. "Step into the study, gentlemen, where we shall have some privacy."

The other gentlemen followed him, but Herr Dunkel lingered. "Fräulein," he murmured, "you are the most ravishing creature I have ever beheld. Will you pardon my youthful impetuosity, and consent to be my wife?"

"You know very well you're not a day under thirty-seven," I said, "and I've already told you, I refuse to be proposed to in such a flippant manner!"

"Rejected again! At this rate, Nijam and Schmidt will be married before us."

"You forget that Nijam and Schmidt have been engaged for *years*," I told him. "What are you doing here? 'Dunkel?' Really?"

"It means *dark* in German," Vasily said, adoringly. "But for that matter, I could ask the same of you! What are *you* doing here?"

"You know *quite* well," I protested. "I told you all about it on the transmitter just now!"

"Well, I know why you're in the house," he acknowledged, "but this meeting is supposed to be secret!"

"So is the Okhrana, and yet everyone knows about *them*," I said, referring to the Russian tsar's secret police. Vasily, who together with Schmidt had been hounded across half the globe by these persistent servants of his cousin Nicky, gave a conceding nod.

"It turns out that one of the children has abilities like mine," I continued. "Dr Schwab wished to make use of them, and I persuaded him to substitute myself.

"Excellent work," Vasily said. "But, *Schwab!* My dear, what a name!"

"You ought to hear what he named his children," said I. "Don't try to distract me! What are *you* doing here, Vaska?

Surely there are other avenues of inquiry to follow!"

"That's what brought me here," he said, casting a glance towards the study door. "I told you I meant to introduce myself to the Rector of the University, and ask about revenants. The Rector introduced me to Schwab, and Schwab asked me to join his little brotherhood. *I shall show you the future!* said he. Intolerable man! So I have come to be initiated."

"He evidently knows something about the revenants, and wishes to recover them," said I.

Vasily snorted. "If he knew anything of any importance about the revenants, he would be keeping it quiet, and not advertising his secrecy to the whole of Heidelberg."

"All the same," said I, "we had better investigate. I'm not quite easy in my mind about Herr Doctor Schwab. You'd better get after him before he comes looking for you. I shall go upstairs and reassure the children."

We parted, Vasily kissing my hand furtively as we did so. As I ascended the stairs, I reflected that I was indeed loath to leave Dr Schwab to his own devices—at least, not until I knew precisely why his children, living and dead, were so terribly frightened of him.

Chapter III.

The triplets were *not* in bed, which was of course merely a sign of things to come. All three were once again lolling on the floor at the head of the stairs, watching the proceedings below with great interest.

I sent them a very serious look and pointed towards the nursery, and once again they got up and retraced their steps. But this time Peter put a confiding hand in mine.

"Now, children," I said sternly, having closed the door, "what did I tell you just now about getting out of bed?"

"That Papa would know Peter wasn't really sick," Heidi declared. "But we didn't know whether you would convince him! He might have sent that horrible ugly Otto von Entzen after us!"

"Now, Heidi," I protested. "You cannot say that a man is horrible and ugly, only because someone has been cruel enough to hurt his face. That is not kind!"

"I'm *not* being unkind!" Heidi said. "He *is* a horrible man! He is always duelling the other students—our old governess, Fräulein Pfeiffer said so—and cutting up their faces! And Fräulein Pfeiffer said that he nearly killed a man just last year!"

I had been in Heidelberg scarcely two days, and Brother Otto was not the first scarred man I had seen. Later, when I asked

Nijam about it, she told me that the wealthier of the University students attend perhaps one or two lectures a day in their chosen specialty, and spend the rest of their time idling about the town with their corps-fellows, drinking at beer-gardens or shooting in the forest. Twice a week, to relieve their boredom, they gather together and fight duels using sharp swords; the duel ending only when one or both is streaming with blood from the wounds dealt to his unprotected head. A nice way for men of birth and education to carry on!

"I don't like Otto," said Peter in a very small voice. "Whenever Papa wants us, he always sends *him.*"

I made an internal note not to bother correcting the children in future, should they describe Otto as horrible and ugly. As regards character, they were likely better judges than myself.

"Well," I said, "you are safe from him tonight. Now you *must* stay in bed, or all my hard work persuading Papa to let you go will be for nothing. Otto will come upstairs to get you, and there will be nothing I can do."

"All right, but stay and tell us a story," Heidi demanded.

If one cannot spend a winter's evening in bed with a cup of tea and a good book, the natural alternative is to spend it in a children's nursery telling them the tale of *The Black Bull of Norroway* or the Princes in the Tower or some other, equally interesting history. Alas! this, too, was not to be. Instead, I was obliged to go and infiltrate a secret society of monster-creating academics in funny robes. By way of consolation I reminded myself that Vasily would be there—and he was perhaps the only man alive who could give those robes such an air of distinction.

I ruffled Peter's hair. "No, my pets, I can't. I have an appointment to keep with your papa. So it is very important that you stay in bed and let me go."

Peter clutched my arm. "No! You mustn't go downstairs for experiments!"

"Clara went downstairs for experiments!" Heidi said, very earnest. "And I *never* saw her again!"

Clara stood before me, her childish form limned in the darkness with the faint light that hung about shades of the dead. She looked at me with pleading eyes and made a gesture of supplication. I felt my stomach turn over.

"My darlings," I said after a moment, very softly, "you do not know what I am. I am a good fairy who has come to look after you. If your papa tries anything with me, I shall simply snap my fingers. Do you know what will happen then?"

Clara shook her head, wide-eyed. So, too, did her siblings.

"Then Mephistopheles shall appear with a twirl of his moustache and a sweep of his jet-black robes!" said I. "And he shall carry Papa away to—to a bad place where he will feel very sorry. So you are absolutely not allowed to be afraid for me. All right?"

"All right," they said. I tucked them in for the third time, Clara nestling beside Peter, and kissed all three of them good-night. I lingered, looking at the little ghost-girl.

"When was the last time you went downstairs for experiments, Clara?" I asked.

She shrugged.

"It was a *long* time ago," Heidi volunteered. "Not long after we came to Heidelberg for the University."

Dr Schwab had been Chair of Chemistry at Heidelberg for a little over two years. This made Clara's shade the most long-lasting I had ever known; a curious fact, about which I wished I knew more. "And what about your mother?" I asked. "Is she dead, too?"

"Oh, no," said Heidi. "She's in gaol. Papa said it was wicked of her to try to take us on the train to France without him knowing. But *I* wanted to go. Papa never takes us *anywhere.*"

"It's wicked of *Papa* to send her to gaol," Peter muttered darkly.

I could not have agreed more. Privately, I resolved not to leave Heidelberg until the man had been forced to drink the cup of his misdeeds to the very dregs. But this I did not tell the children.

I ventured into the corridor, meaning to hurry downstairs, but at the head of the stairs, a furtive sound arrested my steps. For a moment I thought that it was the children climbing out of bed again. Then the sound recurred and I knew that it came from a room nearby, at the front of the house.

Good heavens, thought I—was it really possible that some-one should have chosen *this* moment to commit a burglary?

Then I went back and thought that thought again.

In a trice I flung open the door and found myself in a large front bedroom, doubtless the one belonging to the doctor himself. The window stood open onto the night, and there in the muffled light of her dark-lantern stood my dear friend and colleague, Mimi Laine, clad in dark-red knickers like those worn by circus-performers. She gazed at me with parted lips, looking rather like Dian surprised while bathing.

"Mimi!" I exclaimed, reproachfully. "Not you, too!"

"Dark!" she hissed, hurling a cushion at me. "You made me jump! Next time, why not just hit me over the head with a log?"

"What are you doing here?" I was in no way abashed. I am justly proud of my capabilities as an investigator of bad men, haunted houses, and sinister goings-on. There is an air of golden-haired, blue-eyed helplessness about me that makes the bad men very foolish, and it seemed hard that my friends could not trust in me to do my job without barging in and breathing down my neck. "I thought that you were meant to be helping Nijam and Schmidt search the Library!"

Mimi shrugged. "I was bored. I prefer forests when they are made of living trees, not dead. And there was no sign of Auberlen's books in the chemistry section, or among the anatomy books, or anywhere else Nijam could think of. I asked her if there was anything I could burgle, and she said to come here."

"Well, Dr Schwab wouldn't keep any of that sort of thing in his bedroom," I said, testily. "It will be downstairs in his own study, and that's just where we can't go—not tonight, at any rate. He has a great number of very important academic men down there at the moment, all of them dressed up in robes and hoods. They call themselves the Black Templars and pretend to be frightfully secret."

"Robes and hoods," Mimi repeated thoughtfully. When I entered the room, she had been standing before the doctor's big wardrobe. Now, from one of the shelves, she whisked two long black gowns and, a moment later, accompanying hoods. "Like these?"

I fell silent. It struck me that a scholarly robe was quite capable of concealing all the modest bloom of Mimi's figure and possibly also that of mine. The hoods, meanwhile, were being worn low over the eyes just at present; in the dim, old-fashioned gaslight of the study I had not seen a single face.

"Surely those will be too long for you," I said.

Mimi threw one of the gowns about her shoulders and

thrust out her arms with a gracefully theatrical gesture. Indeed, the hem of the robe merely brushed the carpet. Dr Schwab, as I have mentioned, was not a tall man.

It was at this interesting juncture that we were interrupted.

"Who are *you?*" a voice demanded from the direction of the open door. The reader may guess who it was. The reader ought to be getting the idea by now.

I sent the miscreants a long-suffering look. "You *promised* to stay in bed, children!"

"We heard noises," Heidi protested. "Peter thought it might be a burglar."

Mimi and I looked at each other.

"Do you remember that I told you I was a good fairy?" I asked them.

Mimi bared her teeth. "Well, *I'm* not," she said with mock ferocity. "I'm Mother Flog, here to find and punish the naughty children! No Christmas presents for *you!*"

Peter looked worried, but the little girls were immensely pleased. Clara clapped her hands, and Heidi giggled. "Tell her we've been good, Fräulein Dark!" she protested. "We got nothing for *Sankt Nikolaus,* either!"

"Nothing for *Sankt Nikolaus!*" Mimi repeated, astonished out of her character.

"Papa doesn't believe in it," Peter said, for a wonder managing to speak before Heidi.

"Yes, he says that if we eat too many sweets we will get sick and never become immortal," Heidi added.

Mimi sent me an inquiring look. I was equally at a loss.

"Immortal?" I asked.

"Papa says that when the men of science rule the world we shall all be immortal," Peter said earnestly. "But only if we don't eat anything nice, or waste our money on toys."

None of this made any sense to me. But I could see that Mimi was now experiencing some of the same sentiments I had, earlier this evening.

"There is some mistake," she said firmly. "No child can ever be naughty enough to deserve no toys and no sweets, either for *Sankt Nikolaus or* for Christmas. I, Mother Flog, give you my word of honour that there *shall* be presents for Christmas."

I wished she would not say such things. Now I would *never* get them to stay in bed.

"I'll be back," was all that I said to Mimi, and then I flapped my hands at the children. "Let's get you back to bed," I told them. "And don't intrude on Mother Flog again, or she might change her mind!"

There was a lock on the nursery door. I felt rather tempted to make use of it—but although the children had been difficult to settle, they had not been foolish enough to venture downstairs. Besides, I did not know where to find the key. Leaving the children where I hoped they would stay, therefore, I went back to Mimi. We quickly disguised ourselves, stole downstairs, fell in behind another small group of Black Templars who had just entered by the front door, and stole in after them to the forbidden study.

By this time the gathering had swelled to perhaps thirty or forty gentlemen, all of them very convivial over enormous glasses of brandy or tiny glasses of port. All this bounty could not have done much for their chances at immortality, but I am not an expert on such matters. The room, as I have already noted, was crammed full of books on shelves that reached from floor to ceiling. Only a narrow space between two windows remained clear; and here a banner had been hung, bearing curious symbols. One I recognised as a white shield bearing a black cross, which I knew to be the emblem of the Teutonic Knights. This puzzled me. On the one hand, these people called themselves the Black Temple, not the Teutonic Knights—doubtless because the *real* Teutonic Knights would have something to say about the appropriation of their name. On the other hand, not only was the emblem of the Templars a *red* cross, but *that* Order had been defunct since medieval times.

Moreover, all these Knights were, as they always had been, *Catholic* Orders, under Popish authority. If Dr Schwab had ever in his life had anything to do with the Roman See, I would eat my hood.

This careless appropriation of medieval imagery rather heightened my enjoyment of the ridiculous situation than otherwise. It was not lessened by the fact that beneath the banner in a massive wooden chair of antique make, Dr Schwab sat enthroned with his hood drooping over his face, like some ominous personification in a Symbolist painting. I found myself suddenly quite able to believe everything the children had said about their father's ambitions towards immortality. He certainly had the necessary fatness of head.

Vasily stood to one side of the throng with a solitary brandy. Mimi and I had already warned him via transmitter that we would be joining him in the study, and now we sidled up to him.

"How is the cognac?" I murmured.

"Execrable," he sighed. "These people are all dreadful bores and I don't understand half of their talk. What is *consciousness-transference,* anyway? We ought to have brought Nijam."

The transmitters crackled in our ears. "Speak quietly,"

hissed a familiar voice. "I can hear you from here!"

Vasily, Mimi, and I turned to find another of the hooded Templars watching us from behind a pair of glinting pince-nez, a bushy black beard and an open book. Where Nijam had found a false beard at such short notice I could not say, but it was certainly she. Those pince-nez were quite familiar to me.

With an inward groan I touched my own transmitter. "Nijam! Not you, *too!*" Was there *anyone* at this gathering who was *not* part of my crew?

Nijam turned towards the bookshelves and spoke in a low voice. "I was at the University Library and old Zangemeister, the librarian, recognised me. He introduced me to Schwab as Stefan Schmidt's former assistant. Schwab asked me to work in his laboratory as a bionic chemist. I began asking questions, and that led me here."

"All roads lead to Dr Schwab," I murmured. "No doubt he has all our answers about the revenants."

"Not necessarily," said Nijam, with her customary tiresome exactitude. "He spoke to *me* about consciousness-transference, not revenants."

"There's that word again!" Vasily muttered. "What does it mean?"

"Consciousness-transference," Nijam informed the book-shelf, "is exactly what it sounds like—the goal of transferring human consciousness from an old body to a new one; whether natural or, preferably, artificial. In this way its proponents hope that they may be able to cheat death, and go on living as machines long after their first bodies are worn out."

"Immortal life!" Mimi murmured, no doubt recalling what the children had told us.

"Immortal life!" Nijam repeated, with withering scorn. "It's preposterous. Science and willpower can achieve a great deal, but immortality isn't a science; it's a fairy-tale. We don't even know how the human mind works, much less have a way to transfer it to a prosthesis."

This made me think at once of my former fiancé—that rebarbative American, Warren Vandergriff, who had already replaced several of his limbs with prostheses. "I wonder if Griff knows about all this. It sounds precisely like something he *would* like."

And I returned silent thanks to Heaven that Griff, at any rate, was far away from Heidelberg; no doubt still trying to set up his San Francisco-to-Hong Kong trading empire.

"Vandergriff has all the time in the world to waste on such things," said Nijam with irritation. "I should go home. There are none of old Auberlen's journal here, and I have a case of siren-induced amnesia to reverse."

"Oh, don't go away," I said. "We're all here now; the only person missing is Schmidt, and I'm sure he'll be along in a moment."

Nijam sniffed. "I certainly hope not!"

"Speaking of dear old Schmidt," Vasily interposed, "when are you making an honest man of him, Miss Nijam? Have you set a date?"

Nijam sent him a withering look; although whether this was a commentary on Vasily's frivolity on the job, or whether it was merely the shock of hearing Schmidt's honesty impugned, I found myself at a loss to say.

"Alphonse is doing his own job," she said. "We found him a familiar old text at the Library, and he has gone home to look at it in the hope of recovering some memories. He takes this very seriously."

We were all silent a moment. Not so very long ago, Schmidt had been desperate to avoid restoring his memories; now, it seemed odd that he was equally bent upon restoring them.

"What caused this change?" Mimi asked, voicing some of my own questions.

Nijam returned a book to the shelf with unnecessary force. "Alphonse still imagines himself guilty of some terrible wrongdoing," she muttered. "I don't know what they did to him at that place—the *Akbar,* or the *Shah Jahan,* or whatever it was called—the prison where they put him after taking his memories. But something has convinced him that he is the one to blame for what was done to him. Now he feels that it is his duty to find out, and he will not rest until he has thoroughly punished himself for it."

"He'll come around," I told her. "Once you restore his memories, he will find that he never did a bad thing in his life."

"Would that it were so simple," Nijam muttered. She stood gazing unseeingly at the shelves. In a very low voice, she said, "It isn't just that his memories were taken by the sirens. There's also the sigil carved into his chest."

"The *what?*" Mimi demanded, a little too loudly. One of the nearby Black Templars sent her a curious look. She cleared her throat and repeated the question in a lower tone.

"He showed me last week before we left Paris," Nijam said, in a voice so utterly devoid of emotion that I knew the sight must have been painful for her to contemplate, let alone to speak of. "Someone carved a revenant-sigil into his chest. The Dunwich Signature, as they called it. I have seen the mark, and the slashing blow that marred it. I cannot think—*why* would Stefan Schmidt do such a thing? What did he hope to achieve by it? It is said that one must carve the sigil upon the dead, not upon the *living*."

From the faces of my companions I could tell that they, too, found this item of news to be inexpressibly sinister. In Paris we had all of us had the chance to view the revenant-sigil. This, when marked upon the body of the dead, was commonly believed to be a necessary component in the revivification process that created revenants. I knew that Nijam did not believe in the sigil; for to her mind, the process of revenant-making must be a purely scientific one. There was nothing scientific about that sigil, which combined crude occult imagery with what appeared to be hieroglyphs in an unknown and unlovely script.

Nijam had said of consciousness-transference that it was not science, but fairy-tale. If we spoke of revenant-making, I thought a good word for it might be *sorcery.*

I wondered, too, whether the dead Dr Auberlen had been involved *only* in making revenants, and not also in consciousness-transference.

But the thought of that sigil marked into Schmidt's flesh made me shudder. "I can guess why it is there," said I in a low voice. The thing suggested, to my mind, a desire for mastery over the subject's will. And I wondered whether that, perhaps even more than the theft of poor Schmidt's memories, had made him so reluctant to assert himself, and so ready to believe the worst of himself.

But then, to everybody's surprise, Vasily spoke. "I need not guess at all, for I know the answer quite well."

Nijam forgot herself so far as to turn from the bookshelf in astonishment.

"You *knew?* And you never *told* me?"

A hush had fallen over the room as Dr Schwab raised a hand

for silence. There was now a stir as the gentlemen present lowered their glasses and turned attentively towards their master.

"I'll tell you later," Vasily murmured, and Nijam retreated within the shadow of her hood.

"Brothers, our guest of honour has not yet arrived," the doctor announced. "Let us call the roll. Herr Dunkel, you will step out of the room until this sacred ceremony is completed."

A roll-call! My blood ran cold. In that case, were we not sure to be discovered? As Vasily withdrew I looked at Mimi, and then at Nijam; but neither of them moved. Well, thought I, doubtless we could not rush the door in a body at the calling of the roll. That would certainly invite suspicion. We ought to have departed sooner. Indeed, I ought certainly to have done so; for at some point in the proceedings the doctor would send for the governess, Fräulein Dark, and not find her!

The door closed behind Vasily. Brother Otto stood up at the doctor's right hand and opened a large leather-bound book, which had been decorated with more of the same occult symbols which adorned the banner. Then, in a resonating voice, he began calling names.

"Brother Cornelius!" he trumpeted. "Brother Ernst! Brother Max! Brother Leopold!"

With each name called, a hand rose. Nijam left her shelves and drifted towards Mimi and myself. I edged away from them. If all three of us were discovered to be interlopers, let alone females, then I should be let go on the spot, and the triplets would be left to their father's tender mercies.

We were getting towards the end of the list. "Brother Theodore!" Brother Otto proclaimed, and a man who had kept to himself all evening raised his hand. This seemed to be the end of the list; yet no one spoke. Otto scrutinised the room with narrowed eyes. Then, suddenly—"We have an imposter among us!" he declared.

In my agitation, I reached out to grasp Nijam's arm.

"Stop it," her transmitter whispered in my ear.

"You aren't Brother Theodore!" Otto declared in a thunderous voice. In a trice the brother in question was seized and dragged before the throne. His hood was jerked from his head and the grinning face of a young man was revealed to the company.

"Hermann Kappelmann," said Dr Schwab censoriously. "To think that one of my own students should show such disrespect! What, sir! do you think this is *funny?*"

The grinning Kappelmann cast an eloquent glance about the room—pointedly taking in the hoods and gowns, the banner, the throne, the scowling von Entzen.

"Yes," he said, "extremely."

"Throw him out!" said Brother Otto, and when the door closed behind him, added, "I knew him for an imposter the moment I saw his hand. That's the third time this month! Brother Theodore always wears a signet ring on his little finger, and furthermore he informed me that he would not be attending tonight. Well; that is the end of the roll."

"Then call in Herr Dunkel," said Dr Schwab. Nijam sent me a look as though to say *I told you so* and I realised, with astonishment, that we had come through the first peril, at least, unscathed. Had we, like the enterprising Kappelmann, attempted to impersonate any particular member of the society, we must have been found out. But because we did not answer to any of the names on the roll, and because no one bothered to compare the number of enrolled members with the number of bodies actually present in the room, we were left quite to our own devices.

That the brethren should be content to neglect such an obvious precaution suggested how much of their secrecy was for show, and to incite envy, rather than for any real purpose.

The Templars returned from the eviction of Herr Kappelmann. With them came Vasily, who was desired to stand before the throne, place his hand upon a volume of Pythagoras, and call down upon himself unspecified penalties should he fail either in loyalty or secrecy. Given that the imposter himself had been punished by being firmly shown out into the street, I could not help wondering what they would do to Vasily, should he betray the trust being placed in him. Snip off his buttons, no doubt!

The oath having been sworn, we were then made to endure an interminable lecture. I will not repeat it here, because even I could tell that it was pure nonsense. I am quite sure that the medieval Templars were *not* condemned by the king of France because they were thought to possess the secret to eternal life as recorded in certain ancient Syriac books of lore. Indeed, my private opinion has always been that there could not possibly have been half as many Templars who escaped the fourteenth-century purges to flourish in secret among the Jacobins of Paris, or the universities of Germany, or the empire-builders of Great Britain, as is commonly claimed. I suppose it goes to show that a professor of one subject, such as chemistry, is often as ignorant as anyone else when it comes to another—only, without the necessary humility to know when he is speaking nonsense.

On and on went the lecture. I was sidling towards the door, thinking it a good moment at which to slip away and doff the robes of the initiate in favour of the guise of the English governess, when I heard a stir in the hall and the crisp tones of a voice that seemed disturbingly familiar.

"It is our guest," Dr Schwab cried, abandoning his lecture at once. "Quickly, open the door!"

Some of the Black Templars obliged at once; and before I could draw back, I found myself confronted by the man who had twice attempted to force me to the altar, and whom I had but just now congratulated myself upon escaping—Warren Vandergriff!

I ask you! The man was *supposed* to be in America! Was I never to be free of him?

Griff advanced into the room; but since my face was shadowed by my hood, he did not recognise me. Additionally, he was somewhat encumbered by the body which he carried slung carelessly over one shoulder.

My attention fixed upon the man who was currently serving Griff as a scarf. Another grim premonition seized me at the sight of that dangling golden head—those limp, muscular arms!

The doctor rose to his feet. "Herr Vandergriff! You cannot bring an outsider into the meeting of the Black Temple!"

"Never mind about that, Dr Schwab! I'm delighted to say that I have got the ideal test-subject for your experiments."

With these words Griff bent over and deposited his burden upon the rug as tenderly as if it had been his own child. At the sight of that dazed and bleeding face, a cold hand fastened about my heart. Even over the murmur of surprise that filled the room, my transmitter conveyed Nijam's stifled gasp quite clearly to my ears.

"Gentlemen," Griff said, straightening with an air of modest satisfaction, "I give you none other than Alphonse Schmidt."

Chapter IV.

Nijam being congealed with astonishment, it now fell to Mimi to take the lead. One of the ballerina's hands fastened upon my arm, and the other went into her hood to touch her ear. Numbly, I followed Mimi's example. A moment later, so did the others.

Griff did not know—yet—that we were here with him in the room; and the sooner we switched off our transmitters, the better our chances of remaining hidden.

Really, I thought, it was too much! Not only did Griff know us for the thieves we were, but he was also able to detect and listen in upon our transmissions. When last our paths had crossed, I had been forced to go for days upon end without any communication from my crew. Indeed I was not sure I had yet recovered from the strain.

Moreover, what did Griff think he was about, dragging in our Schmidt and laying him on the rug, like a cat with a mouse? Alphonse had better not be irreparably damaged, I thought, or Nijam's already fragile calm would break altogether.

As for the others in the room, they were perhaps scarcely less astonished than ourselves.

"But Alphonse Schmidt is *dead!*" Dr Schwab protested in English.

"The evidence," said Griff, straightening his cuffs, "would suggest otherwise. Shall we begin?"

Schmidt let out a faint groan, and this seemed to persuade the company. A current of whispers began to flow through the room, and the doctor himself adjusted his spectacles with a trembling hand.

"Begin?" the doctor repeated, blankly. "The consciousness-transference experiment? But I have yet to gather information from the elder Schmidt. So far I have merely secured the assistance of a sensitive."

(By this, I presumed that he meant myself.)

"I haven't time to waste on gathering information," Griff said, in businesslike tones. "Here's the subject. You have the book. Let us begin at once."

"But how did you *find* him?" Dr Schwab demanded. "Who told you that he was alive?"

"No one told me," Griff said, with a wave of his hand. "I paid a visit to Dr Schmidt's old laboratory and happened to find this man there. That's when the truth dawned on me. He's changed his profession lately and taken up thieving. But he is without a doubt the bionic chemist, Alphonse Schmidt. Look here."

Poor Alphonse had pushed himself to a sitting position; now Griff seized him by the shirt-front and opened that garment with a rending sound. A breathless hush fell upon the company as the doctor rose from his throne and peered through his spectacles at the livid scars that had been scored upon Schmidt's skin.

Nijam made a gesture of despair. "I *told* him not to go to the old lab. on his own!"

"It *is* Alphonse Schmidt," the doctor exclaimed, and then let

43

out a long, almost avaricious sigh. "Quickly, someone—fetch a glass of brandy. My dear Herr Schmidt—what a stroke of luck this is! We all believed that you were dead! Here, drink this. Consider yourself an honoured guest."

Alphonse accepted the brandy hesitantly. As he sipped, he sent a furtive glance around the room. I ached for my transmitter, but there was no safe way to make ourselves known to him. Mimi stood beside me with tension in every line of her body; she put me in mind of a tiger about to spring. As for Nijam, she seemed almost tranquil; she stood very still, but when I peered into the shadows of her hood I could see that her brows were drawn down deep over her eyes, and there was a look of murder in them.

As for Vasily, he waited near the centre of the room, his fists clenched as though he was ready to rush to Alphonse's assistance. I could neither see his face nor guess what he might be thinking. But I remembered that previous occasion on which Griff's presence had deprived us of our communications. We had been best served then by proceeding in every regard according to plan. So, I held my peace and went back to thinking about my escape.

Dr Schwab remained firmly attentive to Schmidt, who had now drunk a little brandy and regained a little colour. "Now, my dear colleague," the doctor said, almost genially, "you really must tell me everything you know about your late brother's discoveries, and those of Dr Auberlen."

Alphonse drew out a handkerchief and dabbed at the trickle of blood running from his lip. "What about Auberlen's papers?" he asked, in a voice only a little unsteady. "They weren't at the laboratory or the Library. Do *you* have them, Dr Schwab?"

"If only I did!" the doctor replied with affable laughter. "But no. All the Schmidt and Auberlen papers are kept under lock and key at the University Library, on authority of the Imperial Government."

(It is always the way. You insinuate your way into a man's house in the guise of a governess, contemplating every scheme in the way of burgling and rifling, and in the end all it takes to uncover the truth is a direct question from the right sort of person!)

"I'm afraid *you* are our best repository of information, young Schmidt," the doctor added. "Tell me—is it true that Auberlen adapted his procedure from the *Codex Actorum Atrocium?*"

Schmidt blinked. "I afraid I don't know what that is," he said politely. "I recall nothing from my days in the Auberlen laboratory, as my memories were removed by the authorities. Now, will you call me a cab? I was in the midst of some business of great personal import when I was rudely interrupted by *this*...gentleman."

Doubtless he hoped that his lack of knowledge would persuade them to let him go. If so, we were all to be disappointed. During the long silence that followed, Dr Schwab stood pensively gazing upon the prisoner's scarred flesh. Griff glanced at his watch, evidently impatient.

Nijam reached out and grasped Vasily's arm. Despite the hush, I barely heard her whisper.

"Tell me now. That sigil—what did it mean?"

Vasily lowered his head. "The elder Schmidt had discovered how to turn living men into revenants," he murmured. "He first tried the experiment on his brother, and successfully. On the night I first met him, Alphonse was a revenant."

I saw Nijam's hand whiten on his arm. "Impossible," she

breathed. "Revenants are, by definition, animated corpses. A living revenant—that would not be reanimation. It would be—"

"Possession," Mimi supplied, under her breath. Furtively, she crossed herself. I felt a chill run all the way from my scalp to my spine.

"Consciousness-transference," Vasily corrected. "They want to transfer themselves into other bodies, as the Perrot-revenant did with the raven."

"It's impossible. It isn't *science*," Nijam repeated, although I did not think that she was arguing with *us*.

Still, the pattern had begun to make sense to me. "This is why Dr Schwab wants a medium," said I. "He knows that Peter and I can sense the fading memories, or the stray consciousness of another person."

"But who ever heard of a mind operating independently of the brain?" Nijam muttered. I was not sure what offended her most—Alphonse's predicament, or the doctor's suppositions. "Do these people think the mind is only an information process, to be replicated and run on different hardware? There is a reason we do not make prosthetic *heads!*"

"Argue about it later," Mimi said, gruffly. "First we get our Schmidt back."

"No," Nijam breathed. "First we find out what they think they're up to."

During all this time, Griff and the doctor had been muttering together.

"I tell you we must first question the elder Schmidt," the doctor said.

"But he's *dead*," said Griff.

"There is a possibility that his consciousness may be retrieved from his body," Dr Schwab insisted. "What do you say, young Schmidt? Do you wish to assist in the experiment?"

He turned towards Alphonse, who had risen to his feet and was now looking at his surroundings—the throne, the banner, the gilt-edged copy of Pythagoras, the cloaked and hooded conspirators—with an expression of distinct wariness. Upon being addressed, he turned back to the doctor with an air of confusion. "What experiment?"

"Transferring your brother's consciousness into another body," the doctor explained. "Your own, for instance, would be the likeliest platform on which to run the emulation. It ought to be quite painless, and it would give your brother a new lease on life."

"His *consciousness?*" Alphonse repeated, blinking in confusion. "You mean, his memory-imprint?"

"That precisely," said Dr Schwab, with a confidence I considered to be ill-founded. "Dr Schmidt was taken from us too soon; you must see that. You would be doing the world a great service."

By my side, Mimi muttered, "No, Alphonse! Don't do it!"

With a gentle cough, Vasily now entered the conversation. "One moment, Dr Schwab. Pardon the question, but—are we certain that this experiment would be safe for young Schmidt, here? A bird in the hand, you know! It would be a shame to sacrifice a perfectly good, living Schmidt in a premature attempt to contact the dead one!"

The sound of a friendly voice seemed to have a galvanising effect upon our Alphonse, who at once stood a little straighter. Perhaps this renewed courage was partly to blame for what happened next.

"But he isn't a perfectly good Schmidt," Griff was saying with a laugh that I can only describe as callous. (Really! How could I *ever* have contemplated marrying this man?) "He hasn't got his memories, and he can't tell us anything about his brother's work."

"I'll do it," Alphonse said, before the words were quite out of Griff's mouth. "If there's a chance of accessing my brother's memories, I'll do it."

Vasily stepped forwards, but Nijam's hand fastened again upon his sleeve. "Wait," she muttered. She always was possessed of a super-human *sang-froid*, and perhaps she believed that Schmidt, like herself, was only stringing the Black Temple along until he could discover their sinister purpose.

The doctor arose from his throne. "Come, gentlemen— follow me to the laboratory." He turned to Vasily. "Brother Basileus, if you'll be good enough to fetch the governess, we can begin."

At a signal from the doctor, Brother Otto bent down and threw back the rug that covered the floor. This revealed a trap set into the floor, which was now opened to reveal narrow stairs leading down into a dark cellar.

The faux Templars filed down into the shadows. I lingered with Vasily just long enough to throw off my hood and cloak and stuff them into one of the two large decorative urns that flanked the quasi-throne, where I would be able to retrieve them later. Then we hastened towards that dark stair.

"More cellars!" Mimi muttered. "They ought to be abolished!"

But our Schmidt was down there, and we had no choice but to follow.

* * *

I was compelled to agree with Mimi. The laboratory in the cellar was distinctly unwelcoming. It might have been the big steel table, with its leathern restraints dangling from each corner; it might have been the dark, smoke-blackened stone vaults that supported the roof above; the dusty, cobwebbed shelves of glass jars holding powders and liquids of various colours and consistencies; or the overwhelming stench in which I could detect notes of acid, blood, and burning. Perhaps, I thought, this explained how the doctor spent his time behind the locked study door.

But then I saw the great glass display-case and the thing inside it. I stifled a shriek. One expects to run across mummified corpses in the British Museum, of course; one would be positively disappointed to find none on a trip to Egypt. But in my opinion they are altogether out of place in the laboratory of a Heidelberg professor. They ought *certainly* not to be dressed up in sober tweeds and perched awkwardly on a little wooden chair, as though ready to ask you for a cup of tea.

Curiously, I could not detect the slightest hint of a memory-imprint about the body. In one sense this was relieving, as it meant that I would not be besieged by the mummy's dying sensations. In another sense it merely added to the horrible expectancy that pressed in upon me, as though this dreadful place was too dreadful even for a memory-imprint to linger. Suddenly I felt almost suffocated by the tall, black-cloaked figures that surrounded me. I knew in my rational mind that they were each of them fine, upstanding, learned men who only liked to amuse themselves playing silly games of

49

children's make-believe. But what had seemed so ridiculous in the study upstairs took on a more sinister aspect in the gloomy crypt below. I felt as though we had walked into a nest of Renaissance witches.

Vasily paused before the glass case, inspecting the mummified occupant as though he were a stuffed bear in a museum. "I must say," he drawled—insofar as it is possible to drawl in German— *"this* is a cheerful decoration!"

"Oh, that?" Dr Schwab waved a dismissive hand. "That is Dr Auberlen, an early patron of our Order and my predecessor as Chair of Chemistry. Here, young Schmidt—I must ask you to remove your shirt and lie down on this table."

Our Alphonse sent this article of furniture a doubtful look. Scrubbing had but imperfectly removed from its surface the faint, rusty stains of blood. A second table was covered with a white sheet, but this was not enough to obscure the outline of the large, perfectly still body which occupied it.

The sight of the shrouded corpse made me think of poor little Clara, who had been called downstairs by her father and never returned alive. I shuddered.

"Auberlen planned to have his body preserved for posterity," Schwab went on; while, under Griff's gimlet eye, our Alphonse began reluctantly to remove his shirt. "He died in the faith that his followers might one day be able to retrieve his consciousness. I think you'd be very interested in the mummification process, Brother Basileus! It has cleverly preserved the brain as well as the skin and bones."

"How very remarkable," Vasily said, gravely. "Dr Auberlen hoped to be restored to his own body, then?"

"Good heavens, no," said Schwab, as though this was the most preposterous notion in the world. "That old thing is used up. It doesn't pay to be sentimentally attached to something so badly designed, you know. The main thing is to preserve the brain for future transference to something better. In the meanwhile the rest, as you say, is decoration."

"I take it, then, that the revenants were not the only subject of Dr Auberlen's interest," said Vasily.

"Merely a happy accident, and incidental to his main goals," Dr Schwab responded. "No; Auberlen's great work was always the consciousness-transference. Of course, as I was telling Herr Vandergriff just yesterday—if we can solve the riddle of consciousness, then we can solve the problem of the revenants, too."

"Which will make me a big man in Washington," Griff said. "Imagine it—free, efficient, universal policing. Crime will be a thing of the past!"

He and Brother Otto had begun tethering Alphonse to the steel table. This task completed, Otto removed the white sheet from the other table with a flourish. The body that lay there had, like Auberlen's, been mummified for preservation. Its skin had darkened, and what little remained of its hair had turned a sere and sickly ginger. I knew at once, however, that this was the body of Stefan Schmidt—for unlike Auberlen's mummified corpse, this one came with a faint imprint attached. I beheld a big, burly young man with Alphonse's blue eyes and golden hair. The family resemblance was striking, and yet I could never have mistaken the one for the other. It was their expressions. Where Alphonse's face was habitually open, kindly, and very gentle, his elder brother's face was congealed into a stubborn and almost sulky expression.

"He looks like the most frightful bore," I murmured.

Nijam was not listening. Pitching her voice low and gruff, she called out, "What, precisely, do you mean to do, Doctor?"

"Aha! *Excellent* question," Schwab replied. Taking a key that hung about his neck, he opened a glass-fronted bookcase and withdrew an ancient, tattered, leather-bound book. While the volume of Pythagoras upstairs had been large and impressive, bound in gold-foiled leather, it had also been raw and new. *This* book was both larger and, I felt sure, immeasurably older.

You will say that I am an imaginative and suggestible person, and doubtless you would be correct. I have begun to think, however, that it is these very qualities that give me the capacity to see things that are really there. So, when I say that I felt an immediate sense of oppression, as though a cloud of darkness was emanating from that book and weighing upon all our eyes and minds—I hope the reader will be charitable, and will credit my gift for warning me.

"This," said Dr Schwab, carrying the book into the cone of light that glared down upon a rather nervous-looking Schmidt, "this, my friends, is an ancient text discovered in a Syrian monastery and handed down to us by the last Grand Master of the Temple, Jacques de Molay himself: the *Codex Actorum Atrocium*. The *Codex* itself actually contains two texts: an original, of unknown provenance, written in unknown hieroglyphs; and a translation into ancient Syriac. This is the only copy known to exist."

There was that name again—the book which Schwab claimed had given Dr Auberlen the basic procedure of revenant-making! Of Latin I had learned only the bare rudiments at St Alphege's, my old school; and yet I was pretty sure that what Dr Auberlen had said was *The Book of Atrocious Deeds*. I did not like the sound of *that*.

"Who can say where it originated, before it came into the possession of those monks, and thence into the hands of the Master himself?" Schwab asked dreamily. Personally, I doubted the gentleman in question had ever been in contact with the book. From the way some people speak of them, one might think the Templars had nothing better to do with their time than amass collections of dubious artefacts. But the doctor went on: "Did some sect of ancient mathematical visionaries uncover the secrets of consciousness and immortal life? Of course, the scientific processes have been almost completely overwhelmed by the occult rigmarole, which was the only manner in which these primitive folk could record the knowledge they had discovered. But I have mastered this uncouth tongue; I have, with great labour, deciphered the book, in defiance of the dreadful warnings inscribed upon the opening pages. I have, like Auberlen before me, discovered that memory-transference is not only possible—*it has been done before.*"

At my side, Mimi stirred restlessly. I could tell that she was already conceiving plans for the theft of this ghastly book. But Schwab turned towards Vasily—and me.

"Fräulein Dark," he called.

I did not much like to go forward; I now felt much less sure of my powers as a good fairy. Besides which, I was anxious to avoid my erstwhile fiancé. Well; it could not be helped. I stepped forward and managed to say in a tolerably steady tone, "Hello, Griff."

That gentleman smiled, not at all as though he was surprised.

"Miss Molly! I might have known that where one of you was, the others could not be far away. —Yes, doctor, I *do* know her; but don't worry. When we've finished our experiments

I'll tell you a tale that will open your eyes."

With that he began fiddling with the sub-cutaneous controls behind his ear, evidently hoping to catch our transmissions as they flew to and fro.

How I *did* wish Griff would not put his nose where it was not wanted!

Dr Schwab did not seem alarmed by Griff's insinuations; he was single-mindedly bent upon his inquiries. "Fräulein, can you perceive the consciousness of Stefan Schmidt?"

"I can," I said, not without a shiver of anticipation. The last time I had let on to Griff and one of his friends about my abilities, I had come within an ace of being locked up in a mad-house.

"No, she can't," Griff said. "That's all eye-wash."

I kept my eyes upon the imprint. "He's a big man, bigger than his brother," I said patiently. "There's a large black mole on the back of his neck, and he's writing in a note-book which he keeps in his pocket. His lips move as he writes."

"That's Stefan Schmidt, to the life!" someone in the crowd hissed, and I don't even think it was one of my fellow conspirators.

"She is telling the truth," Dr Schwab said, with a cold smile. "Fräulein, ask Herr Doctor Schmidt whether he consents to the ritual."

Ritual!—there was another word I didn't like! Dutifully, however, I relayed the question. The Stefan-imprint, naturally, made no response. Imprints never do. A memory cannot act, cannot think, cannot create. Therefore, when Schwab snapped, "Well?" I did a thing that had begun to come naturally to me in recent years: I told a fib.

"Yes," I said, "he consents."

"And Alphonse Schmidt," the doctor said, peering over the top of that horrible book, "do *you* consent to the ritual?"

"Don't," I heard Nijam say, very softly, in English. By my side, Griff stiffened like a dog at point.

There was perspiration standing out on poor Alphonse's brow. He looked nervously from the doctor to Griff, to the scarred Brother Otto and then to me. I felt a momentary panic. Had we gone too far to withdraw? I saw then for the first time that Otto was carried a steel tray, upon which were displayed an array of bone-saws, borers, and scalpels. My throat went dry; I recalled that Dr Schwab had not yet answered Nijam's question, as to what precisely they were about to do.

How bitterly I regretted that fib! Now poor Alphonse was about to be turned into a cautionary tale for bad children. *How Molly Dark told a lie, and had to watch her friend be chopped into little pieces by a secret society of sinister scientists.*

"I already said I'd do it," said Alphonse, while I was still wondering how we were to gracefully extract ourselves from this *very* awkward situation. He swallowed hard and looked up at me. "It's only a memory-imprint, isn't it?"

I could sympathise with Schmidt's motivation. At one time I would have given my right hand to know the secrets locked within my father's imprint. All the same, what did they mean to *do* to him? I bit my lip and looked helplessly towards our confederates. Nijam was only a shadowy figure at Vasily's side. She did not either move or speak.

"That's settled, then," Dr Schwab said, breezily. "Let us begin."

There was, on the wall behind the doctor, another banner that closely resembled the one hanging in the study upstairs. He now reached up and turned it, so that its reverse now faced the room. The moment I saw it I put a hand to my mouth to stifle an involuntary sound of horror. A crude drawing in black ink stained the reverse of the banner. The creature depicted thereon might have resembled a demon in an illuminated manuscript, were it not distinctly aquatic in its appearance—an upright, two-legged man-shape covered in crocodile-skin. But its face—how shall I even begin to describe its face? It was something like a jelly-fish, and something like a sea-urchin, and something like a head of cauli-flower—if any of those things had ever been fitted out with a long, grinning mouth full of sharp teeth. I was scarcely recovered from the shock of this hideous image when I saw that it brandished in its right hand, before the wolfish gape of its mouth, the tiny image of a struggling human figure!

By a curious chance, the sight awoke a long-forgotten memory. You will say, again, that I am credulous and suggestible—but I had seen this creature once before, in the worst nightmare of my life. I shuddered, recalling the gibbering fear that had come upon me in the face of the monster; the size of its massive frame as it trampled people and houses alike underfoot, and the shrieks of those swept up in its claws as they thrown into its gulping maw.

I felt now that I was caught once more in that nightmare; that once more I writhed in the blast of this creature's malevolence.

Even Griff looked uneasy. "Come, now, doctor!" he said. "Is this really necessary?"

"Oh, probably not all of it," the doctor said, with a dismissive wave. "But it would be a mistake to overlook the slightest detail when the mathematics is so *very* complicated. We can refine the process later, as Auberlen did. Light the candles,

Brother Otto."

With that he opened the *Codex* and commenced intoning words in a language I found remarkably unpleasant to listen to. Von Entzen immediately brought out a great many fat candles and began to set them on the floor in a large circle, surrounding not only the doctor, but also both the living and the dead Schmidts. As Griff and I retreated to give them room, I thought of rejoining my confederates; but the prosthete's brazen hand shot out and closed painfully about my wrist.

Still that chant went on, harsh and guttural—a tongue that I had never heard, unless it might be in my nightmares. What a mess we had blundered into! At last the doctor ceased his chant and said, "Shave his head. –This is necessary," he added, to Griff, "in order to locate the relevant parts of the brain."

Behind me, someone—probably Vasily—made a strangled noise of protest.

Brother Otto took up a wicked-looking razor from the sinister tray. Alphonse's eyes rolled back to watch him as the young acolyte approached, took a fistful of that cherubically golden hair, and commenced to hack it off. It was a rough job, poorly done—I cannot believe that Otto was the sort of man to wield his own razor. Poor Schmidt!

In a very little time the job was done, and now the doctor hesitated. "For best results," he said, "we should mark the sigil in the subject's own blood. But carving the skin takes time and might involve unnecessary suffering. We don't want to have to postpone the experiment because the subject has fainted."

"A *sigil?*" Alphonse asked, as though he was beginning to have second thoughts about the whole affair.

"The man's all over blood from that shaving job," Griff drawled. "Use that."

"That's an idea!" Schwab said. Schmidt pulled at his restraints in vain; the doctor advanced and began to draw upon his denuded scalp that same evil sigil which had adorned the Paris Opera revenant. Nijam must have taken a step forward; she was at my side now, no longer paying any heed to Griff. She plucked distractedly at her false beard.

"I suppose you have a scientific explanation for this business, too," Griff said, mockingly.

"I believe the Dunwich Signature marks out certain essential features of the brain beneath," Schwab replied. "Now, let me see...ah! Yes! The bone-saw, Brother Otto!"

The thing glinted in the light as it was handed over. The doctor leaned over Alphonse, who looked increasingly alarmed.

"It says here," said the doctor, indicating a place in that awful book, "that the subject ought to be a virgin. Are you?"

"What does that have to do with consciousness-transference?" Alphonse burst out, in a voice high-pitched with terror. I thought it rather a silly question, myself. One does not like to be indelicate, but I would have been shocked to hear Alphonse Schmidt reply in anything but the affirmative. Of course, the doctor did not know him as well as I did.

"Calm yourself," said Dr Schwab. "The bone-saw is for use on Stefan Schmidt. You will need to eat a morsel of his brain, as marked out by the sigil."

I saw, then, as Otto wheeled the other table a little nearer Alphonse's, that the elder Schmidt did indeed have a sigil marked beneath the scanty locks that still adhered to his scalp. This the doctor now began to attack with the bone-saw. In that moment I learned too late that I had had a happiness now lost to me: I had *not* known what a human head sounds like when it is being sawn open.

I no longer wondered at this being a *secret* society. This was the sort of thing likely to make ordinary people quite uncomfortable. Indeed, it was too much for Nijam.

"That's enough," she said, tearing off her whiskers like the villain in a pantomime. "This is *not* science, and Alphonse Schmidt will not be made to endure another moment of it. Release him at once."

She stepped forward, no doubt ready to execute her own orders, if none could be found to do so for her. But she had reckoned without Griff, who released me and seized upon Nijam.

"Aha!" he cried. "I know you! The Begum of Bihar, I presume."

"Don't be an idiot," Nijam told him. "Alphonse Schmidt has priceless information inside his head. You can't let them do this to him. Don't you know that it's dangerous to consume another person's brain? Release him, I say!!"

Vasily and Mimi stepped forward at once to obey her. As they approached, Griff lunged at the closest of them—it was, to my distress, Vasily—and tore the hood from his head.

"You! I know you!" he crowed. I wrung my hands in despair. They say that at moments of great distress one's whole life flashes before one's eyes. In this case it was *Vasily's* whole life that flashed before my eyes. Surely Griff was about to expose my lover as the late Grand Duke Vasily Nikolaevich Romanov, bringing down upon us once again the Russian secret police, their master the tsar, and all of Vasily's horrible cousins and uncles, who were intent upon his destruction.

But as it happened, disaster was averted.

"I know you!" Griff repeated. "You are that lawyer from Hong Kong! Nicks, I presume! The whole gang within my hand!"

"Oh, for heaven's sake," Nijam said, and she and Mimi made a dash to loosen Schmidt's restraints. But it was useless; Griff grabbed at Nijam once more, and Vasily and Mimi were caught and held fast by the Black Templars.

Dr Schwab and his assistant had been hard at work in the meantime, and had just extracted a shrivelled, rubbery slice of stuff from Stefan Schmidt's open skull, which I am very much afraid must have been brain.

"Hold his head," Schwab ordered. Brother Otto seized Alphonse's jaw, forcing his mouth open. Dr Schwab leaned over the struggling body of our poor friend, the *Codex* in one hand, the slice of brain poised delicately between the jaws of a pair of long-handled tweezers in the other.

"Yammu hag sithmugsk," Schwab intoned, perusing the book. The darkness that had been half imagination a moment ago, now thickened and pressed down upon me; for a moment I could scarcely see. *"Yammu hag sithmugsk!"*

The ghastly morsel had barely touched his lips, when Alphonse ceased to struggle and went into convulsions. His shoulders and heels ground into the table; and between them, his body rose like the arch of a bridge. I heard Mimi cry his name. Then something happened to Griff. There was a little blue spark and a crackling sound and he fell to the ground, twitching. Freeing herself from his clutches, Nijam shoved Otto aside and put her hands to either side of Alphonse's bloodied head.

"What have you *done* to him?" she demanded, in a voice like thunder.

"Nothing!" Dr Schwab protested, seeming hardly less distracted himself. He gestured with the slice of mummified brain. "He hasn't even tasted it!"

The gaslight was flickering hard, although there was no wind in the room. One by one all the lights went out, save for the ring of candles. In the gloom the candle-flames roared suddenly high. Out of the shadows and smoke the demon-banner loomed, grinning horribly. I caught a glimpse of Nijam's face turned up to behold it; I saw the moment at which she came close to despairing.

"We must destroy the sigil," she said, pulling a handkerchief from her pocket.

I think she meant to dab away the rapidly-drying blood on Schmidt's head—but before she could do so there was a soft leathery *snap,* and then another.

Alphonse's hand came up and seized Nijam's wrist before she could touch the sigil. Slowly, fluidly, he rose from the table. There was something wrong with him—something wrong with his eyes. His mouth opened.

"Yammu hag sithmugsk", he intoned in a hoarse voice. And then, with iron finality: *"Yammu sheegh."*

It struck me that I knew what was wrong with Alphonse's eyes—they called to mind the revenants I had seen in the streets of Paris, blank and dead.

"A revenant," I choked, although no one could have heard it save the Templar holding me. "They've made him a revenant!"

"We've done it!" the man holding me exulted. "We've achieved consciousness-transference!"

Dr Schwab seemed to be of the same opinion. "Dr Stefan Schmidt, I presume?" he cried.

Alphonse, who still held Nijam in a grip of iron, bared his teeth at the doctor.

"Keep back!" I cried, more by instinct than anything else.

"Keep back! Can't you see that he isn't himself?"

Dr Schwab paid no attention; he advanced nearer, and Alphonse lashed out at him. At the same moment Nijam came out with a strange little device, a rectangular battery with two steel prongs at the business end of it. She pressed it to Alphonse's side and there came another of those blue flashes.

Alphonse did not respond as Griff had done. Rather than collapse, he roared with pain and outrage. In a trice he had broken what restraints remained, leaped to his feet, tossed Nijam over his shoulder, and with rolling eyes and snuffing nose, marked the entrance to the cellar.

"Don't let him leave!" Dr Schwab bellowed.

Griff, having now dragged himself to his feet, pounced at Alphonse. He had but short shrift. Alphonse Schmidt had always been a fine, muscular specimen of a man; but now with a blow of his arm he scooped Griff bodily from his feet and hurled him clear across the room. The prosthete collided with Dr Schwab; they landed against the glass-fronted bookshelf in a shower of broken glass and falling books.

With another howl Alphonse lashed out again at the nearest of the Black Templars. The man fell, as dead as a stone. After that no one got in his way. I had one last horrible glimpse of Nijam's terrified face, and a supplicating outstretched hand. Then Alphonse—or what had until a moment ago *been* our Alphonse—bounded up the stair and vanished into the house.

Mimi was the first of us to react.

"After them," she gasped, and rushed off in their wake.

Vasily sent me a conflicted look.

"Go, go!" I begged him, and he followed Mimi.

I had no illusions about my own abilities. I was not cut out for a chase through the streets of Heidelberg in December, but neither did I like my chances of escaping that cellar without having to answer some awkward questions. It was Griff, of course, who forestalled me. Rising from the wreckage of the table, he thrust aside several Black Templars with his long, segmented steel arm and seized me fast.

"It worked," Griff panted, hardly seeming to pay attention to me, his prisoner. "It worked! The secret of consciousness-transference will be mine! After them, you laggards!" he added, turning upon the remaining Templars. Those who were still alive were in a state of disarray, but they obeyed him at once, rushing for the stairs and out into the night.

Griff and I were left alone in that accursed cellar between three crumpled bodies—the motionless Black Templar, the mummified Stefan Schmidt, whose imprint still fidgeted aimlessly with his notebook, and the prone Dr Schwab, who seemed to be moaning with pain.

"That man is hurt," I told Griff.

"He'll keep," said Griff. "Eternal life *and* revenants! Why, I'm about to be Uncle Sam's favourite son! And Molly Dark to boot, along with her gang! I haven't had a day like this since I shot that buffalo outside Kansas City!"

"I'll have you know I'm here as a perfectly ordinary governess!" I proclaimed, which was the truth, but not the whole of it. "Release me at once!"

Reluctantly, Griff turned his attention back to me.

"Release you? Oh no, Miss Molly! Not for the world! *You* have too much value to me now—you and your higher consciousness!"

How absolutely typical, thought I. Griff always persisted in seeing only what he wanted to see. In me, as ever, a tool to be used; in that unholy ritual, with its grisly ending, a path to peace and eternal life.

I did not think he was correct—not about me, and certainly not about the ritual.

Chapter V.

Nijam, meanwhile, was being carried swiftly and inexorably through the streets of Heidelberg in the falling snow. She told me later that her emotions, once the initial shock had worn off, were those of extreme annoyance. Her posture was undignified, her progress involuntary, and the entire situation—with Alphonse Schmidt's muscular shoulder bisecting her person and cold, wet flakes of snow falling down the back of her neck—was extremely uncomfortable.

How was she to calm him down enough to begin an attempt at understanding what had happened tonight? Nijam, as I have mentioned once or twice before in the course of these memoirs, was a prosaic soul, with a scientific explanation for everything and a great faith in her own ability to surmount all obstacles with a little scientific application of willpower. She had never believed that the sigils which Auberlen and the elder Schmidt used to create the revenants had ever made the slightest difference to what, in her opinion, was a purely scientific process.

Yet, before her eyes, Alphonse had apparently been transformed once more into a revenant—without the help of any scientific or physical processes at all. He was marked on the head with the sigil, a few nonsense words were read out of a very old book, and the man she loved had lost his mind.

She was not *frightened*, Nijam insisted, upon telling me the tale after. She was something far worse: she was utterly baffled to account for what had happened. Knowledge was the breath of Nijam's nostrils, and here she had come to the end of it. Something far beyond her understanding was at work in the man she loved, and the knot of nausea in her stomach, to say nothing of her present undignified situation, made it impossible to formulate a remedy.

There was nothing to do but surrender herself—to regain a little breath and composure, if she could, until Alphonse tired or calmed sufficiently to let her down.

He must have been travelling at a frightfully quick pace, for Nijam says she saw no sign of pursuit. It was about midnight, and the dark streets to which the Alphonse-revenant kept were mostly deserted. Heidelberg is a pretty town, full of picturesque white, cream, and grey houses, with red rooves and lintels; but this sort of romantic scenery makes no impression upon Nijam at the best of times. At that moment, it merely made her feel queasy. Once or twice she caught glimpses down narrow streets of the bright lights and merriment of the Christmas Night Market in the Universitätsplatz, but this soon fell behind them and they were alone in the darkness of the streets.

Nijam became aware that the Alphonse-revenant, or whatever he had become, was also in some distress. His breath came and went hurriedly, like a bellows. He seemed terrified of the snow; once or twice he flinched and yelped at a gust of wind. Even light seemed to daunt him. Little wonder, then, that he carried her always upwards, away from the bright centre of the town towards the high and desolate hills that bordered the Neckar valley. They came out of the narrow streets soon enough into a sort of wilderness—a wilderness of the German sort, which is to say one that has been tamed and tended until it nearly resembles a garden. It was darker here, but less sheltered. The ground rose steeply; and the Alphonse-revenant began to climb.

Nijam gasped as the ground fell away beneath her. It was only then that she began to get an idea of the creature's terrible strength, for he never released his grip upon her; he scaled that steep precipice with only one hand, in a series of fluid leaps. The lights of the city fell below her, and she saw the pale expanse of the river that flowed through the centre of the town; she saw too the old bridge lying athwart it like a diamond necklace, its lamps glowing bright against the gilded waters.

(This description is my own. I am afraid that bridges remind Nijam of bridges, and not of diamond necklaces.)

Up they climbed, and up, until the ground became less steep, and green turf appeared. Then the Alphonse-revenant was baffled, for he came to a towering wall of solid stone which presented not a toe-hold. He pushed at the wall and then beat upon it with his fist. The blow must have injured him, for he roared out in wrath and pain, cradling his bruised hand.

Nijam thumped upon his back. "Alphonse! Alphonse!" she cried. "Stop that! Look, here is a path that circles the wall!"

She did not know whether he heard or understood, but a moment later he turned to the right and set off at a hurried stride down the path she indicated. The path took them over rough ground. Sometimes the wall bent abruptly out and then back in again; twice it took a sharp turn left. Then the Alphonse-revenant must have found an opening, for he passed through what seemed to be a ruined gate. Beyond was another set of walls, and—dark against a dark sky—the outline of battlements and towers. Nijam's suspicions were confirmed: they stood in the grounds of the old ruined schloss, or castle, that occupied a spur of the hills above the town.

The wind, meanwhile, had strengthened. Snow whipped into their faces and forced itself into every fold of clothing. Both Nijam and Alphonse had been shivering uncontrollably for some time. In the courtyard which they had now entered, there was less shelter than there had been a moment before, since the wall no longer protected them from the blast of the north wind. The Alphonse-revenant gave that weird, wordless bellow once more and swiped at the flurries with a clawed hand.

"Let me down!" Nijam shouted, although the wind snatched the words from her mouth. "Let me down and I'll find us shelter!"

But the creature paid her no heed. Instead he rushed across the courtyard. The clock-tower that defended the inner gate of the keep was shut against them; the revenant turned to the right and continued following the wall, forcing his way through thick undergrowth and across dangerous, steeply sloping ground. Next came a great round tower, but this had suffered in some long-ago cataclysm. A wedge of it had collapsed, leaving a great slide of grey rubble and tangled undergrowth beneath. Up this loose scree the Alphonse-revenant carried her. A huge, open, cavernous room yawned before them; and Nijam was practically tossed to the pavement.

The revenant crouched beside her, panting with terror. It was her poor Alphonse in such torments. Nijam felt the sudden and inefficient urge to burst into tears.

All about the tower the wind moaned and howled, and the snow swept by in flurries. It was sheltered here, yet still the cold pierced to the bone.

After a moment Nijam put out a hand in the darkness and touched Alphonse's shoulder. He snarled and struck her hand away. Nijam scrambled backwards, out of reach. Trying to comfort him was foolish, she reproached herself. What they needed was fire. They would die if they could not get warm.

She reached into her pocket and drew out the box of matches which travelled with her everywhere. "I'm going to make a sound, Alphonse," she said into the darkness, "and a light."

So saying, she struck the match, and the tiny yellow flame flared up, shaky in the breezes that eddied through the gap in the tower wall. Nijam shielded the flame with her hand. In the darkness Alphonse gave a gasp and a convulsive start; she saw the flame reflected in dark, cold eyes.

Carefully, Nijam rose to her feet and searched the crumbling room. Almost at once she found a bundle of firewood in the corner near a blackened ring of stones, in which some old sandwich-papers lay half-consumed. Her hopes were confirmed: some of the students must be in the habit of visiting the tower in summer for picnics.

There was enough dry wood to save their lives, if they huddled close. The match burned out and Nijam looked over her shoulder.

"I will make more fire," she told the heavily-breathing silence. "It will keep us warm and alive."

There was no answer but a low growl. Nijam built the fire scientifically, beginning with the sandwich-wrappers and adding bark and smaller pieces of wood. One match sufficed to light the whole pile; and with a little careful feeding of bark, the fire was soon a streaming blaze.

Nijam worked in silence, always keeping half an eye on Alphonse's crouched figure. What had happened to him? How could he possibly have become a *revenant?*

Nijam hated to feel baffled, and now she felt so utterly baffled that she was sick in the pit of her stomach, and her hands had gone clammy with sweat. She sat back on her heels, despite her best efforts thinking of the raven in the Paris Opera and the impossible thunderclap in which that raven had disappeared. She had been trying not to think of that moment all week. Alphonse had insisted that it proved the existence of some benevolent intelligence beyond the merely physical. Nijam had not argued with that. She supposed that she believed in—God, if that's what you wanted to call Him. He was certainly a convenient explanation for certain things science was unable to explain—things like love, and morality, and the human soul, the existence of which had been proved to her by a lengthy acquaintance with myself.

But Nijam did not know what to make of a God who *interfered.* The natural world she understood; it was familiar, and comforting, and she could make it do nearly anything she wanted. She did not interfere in the supernatural; it wasn't her place to do so. All she asked in return was that the supernatural should not intrude upon *herself.*

She would accept a supernatural explanation only if she had no other choice.

There came a whisk of movement at her elbow, and Nijam recoiled. While she was staring into the fire, Alphonse had suddenly and silently appeared beside her. He reached out to the flames as though he had never beheld fire before. Nijam caught his hand before he could touch the glowing wood; and then a moment later she was on her back on the ground. Alphonse's hand—no, it could not be Alphonse controlling that hand; the *revenant's* hand had her by the throat, pinning her down.

The eyes that gazed into her own were alive with eternal malice, and his lips were drawn back from his teeth in a snarl. They moved, clumsily, and for a moment uttered only a wordless, grotesque series of growls. Then the growls resolved into a form of speech, one that Nijam felt quite certain had never before been uttered in this world—except, possibly, half an hour previously in the cellar of Dr Schwab's house. She could not recall any of the words after they had been spoken; but they filled her with insensate terror.

"I don't understand you," she rasped, averting her gaze from his face. What had they done to Alphonse? How could she have stood by and allowed it?

And then a cool part of her mind, with absolute certainty, observed: *This is no ordinary revenant. It is intelligent.*

Whatever it was spoke again in that abominable tongue. The hand seized her chin and forced her to look up at him. This time, when her shrinking gaze met his eyes, something horrible happened to her. She told me later that it was rather like being in a delirium, except a thousand times worse. She saw and heard impossible things; nightmarish, incomprehensible things. Shapes that obeyed no law of geometry; colours that had never been seen on the earth; sounds that were beyond hearing. Nijam convulsed. Had she bothered to eat her dinner, it would then have made an unfortunate reappearance.

The creature which was not Alphonse Schmidt gazed down

at her with dispassionate interest. It bellowed again in its ghastly tongue—and then changed, suddenly, to German.

"What...What is this place?"

Never before had she experienced such a nightmare. The creature wore the form of her beloved Alphonse like a mask. But it was not Alphonse; it was a desecration.

"It is—the castle at Heidelberg," she stammered.

The only answer was a roar of irritation. "What is this—this *form?*"

"I don't know what you mean!" Nijam protested. Ordinarily she loved questions, because either she could answer them, or she could find a book that *would* answer them. Now she was plagued by questions to which she had no answer at all. In a way that was worse than the once-beloved hand about her neck.

Unseen by the creature, Nijam drew the little shock-mechanism from her pocket with which she had attacked Griff not long ago. She suspected that it would only enrage the creature further, as it had done in the laboratory. But it was her only defence.

The terrible hand tightened about her throat. "Answer," growled the revenant, "before I tear this off!"

Nijam raised the Stunner (as she had named it); but in that moment something else happened. The hand tore away from her throat and she heard Alphonse cry out in his own beloved voice—

"*No!* Run, Patty, run! Get away from us! O God!"

And then in that angry howl: "What are *you?*"

"Alphonse!" she croaked, scrambling to her knees. "Alphonse!"

"What *are* you?" the alien Voice demanded, baring its teeth and striking at Alphonse's head.

Nijam shuffled away with a sobbing breath. Perhaps she *could* get away from the Voice in the dark; perhaps she might avoid breaking her neck on the fallen stones at the tower's foot. But Alphonse, her own Alphonse, had peered out of those eyes just for a moment. And if she abandoned him—the thought made her convulse again.

"Answer me!"

The furious bellow beat at her like a blow. Nijam raised a trembling hand. "Calm yourself. I—I am trying to help you."

"Lies!" The Voice reached for the fire; then drew his hand back with a hiss of pain. *"Stop shouting!"* he yelled, and Nijam did not know whether it was the creature or Alphonse.

"What are *you?"* she murmured, beginning to gather a little calm now that she knew Alphonse was still somewhere within that creature. "You are not Stefan Schmidt, I think."

"Someone did this to me!" the Voice roared, raking at Alphonse's chest with clawed fingers. "I will devour them in little pieces, limb by limb! And I will begin with *you,* if you stand in my way!—*No!"* it added, in Alphonse's own despairing yell. Then at once it slammed his fist against the stone floor, and uttered a wail of pain, and fell panting to the ground.

Nijam swallowed hard. "I am not one of the people who did this to you," she said, warily. "Whatever you are, whatever has trapped you within that body, I will get you free of it."

Alphonse's eye rolled up to glare at her. "Why should I believe you?" the Voice asked, as though it had never heard a more foolish suggestion.

Nijam stared at him for a long moment. "Ask Alphonse," she said.

There was another silence. Then the poor misused body

began to twitch and mutter in different voices. Nijam went down on her knees and took the head between her hands. They were trembling, but that hardly mattered. "Alphonse," she murmured. "Listen to me! Come back to me!"

A shudder ran through Alphonse's frame; and a moment later Alphonse himself was looking at her with wide, horrified eyes. "I thought he'd kill you," he hiccoughed. "Oh, Miss Nijam!" Then he wound his arms around her and sobbed.

Nijam held him close, although she kept her Stunner ready in one hand. "Is it gone?" she asked, when he seemed a little calmer.

He raised his head. "I—I think so—I don't know!"

Thinking that it might calm him, and knowing no other way to relieve her own feelings, Nijam kissed him. For a moment Alphonse responded, and Nijam found that her own trembling was also subsiding. And then Alphonse recoiled from her with an exclamation of horror.

He moved so quickly that Nijam was, happily, unable to employ her Stunner. One moment he was kissing her; the next he was backed against the wall of the tower, one hand pressed to his heaving chest.

"It's still here," Alphonse gasped. "In my mind. Speaking to me!"

Nijam's heart sank into a cold despair.

"What *are* you?" Alphonse panted, his eyes unfocused. Then he beat a fist against his chest. "You're lying! You are not my brother! Be silent!"

Nijam moved nearer, but Alphonse held up a trembling hand to stop her. "Don't."

There was a long silence. At length, Nijam said, "Well?"

Alphonse allowed his hand to fall. "It's gone silent," he said.

His face had gone white, and he was trembling again. "We ought to go back."

"Absolutely not," Nijam said. "Not at the dead of night, in this snowfall. We might break our necks."

"*I* might break your neck!" Alphonse cried. But with those words he fell back against the wall in a posture of resignation. Nijam laid a little more wood on the fire, and then she seated herself beside him, meaning to cover both of them with her scholarly robe. Alphonse tried to move away.

"Don't," he said again. "I'm dangerous. I oughtn't to be anywhere near you..."

Nijam said firmly: "We can worry about that once we have survived the night. Here, let me try to clean some of this blood from your head."

"The sigil," Alphonse hiccoughed, half laughing, half weeping.

Nijam fetched her handkerchief and began to rub at the crust of dried blood. "Vasily said you were turned into a revenant, and it was in that state that he first met you. Heaven knows how Stefan managed it. A living revenant? Who has heard of such a thing?"

Alphonse was silent a moment, his eyes dull. "We know precisely how," he said, at length. "We saw it happen tonight."

Nijam clenched her teeth. After a moment she said, "Vasily ought to have told me sooner. Then, at least, I would have known why you never—"

She caught herself before going on.

"What?" Schmidt asked, anxiously. "What did I do wrong, in that life I have forgotten?"

Perhaps, had he not asked *that* question, she might have answered.

"Go to sleep," Nijam said, testily. "I have already told you that you did nothing wrong."

"I made myself into a *revenant*," he pointed out. "Does that not trouble you?"

Nijam turned to look into his eyes. "I know the worst of you, Alphonse Schmidt, and I love you regardless. Does that mean *nothing* to you?"

He swallowed. "I'm sorry."

Nijam snorted. "Thank you. Now try to sleep, if you can. I am going to risk a transmission."

She tapped at the transmitter implanted in her temple. "We are safe," she told the humming ether, not knowing whether any of her friends—or her enemy, Griff—were listening. "Until tomorrow."

Vasily's voice crackled in her ear, muffled by the snow in the air. "Until tomorrow," he repeated—evidently he had kept his transmitter open, in case. Without another word, Nijam severed the connection, content that the rest of the crew had received her message.

The wind howled; she and Alphonse shivered before the fire. Neither of them slept.

Chapter VI.

Left in Griff's unwelcome clutches, I was compelled to trust Schmidt and Nijam's safety to my friends. Instead, I spent a rather trying evening. Dr Schwab had to be gathered up by his devoted acolytes and taken off to the University Hospital. Griff had to be pacified and assured that I was indeed present at the doctor's house as a genuine governess. I could tell that he did not believe me, any more than he liked the thought of leaving me at large; but in the end I persuaded him, perhaps even correctly, that Dr Schwab would be offended if his children's governess and principal caregiver was removed from his house without his consent. In the end he went away and left me in peace; but not before warning the housekeeper, with soft threats, that I must not be permitted to leave the house without his leave.

What he thought Fräulein Angermeyer could do to prevent me doing as I liked is, I confess, a mystery to me.

Nor was the morning much better than the night had been. It took me long to fall asleep, and my window was still dark when I became gradually aware of little scufflings and whisperings going on outside the door. I groaned and opened my eyes, and that was a mistake. Little Clara was hovering in the air at the foot of my bed, gazing down at me in perfect silence. I defy anyone to keep their countenance upon waking to such an apparition. At least I had the presence of mind to clap my hand over my own mouth before I could let out a scream to wake all of Heidelberg.

Clara startled when I did so; then she fled silently through the closed door. A moment later, while I was still catching my breath, the doorknob turned very softly and two tousled heads peered in.

"Oh, you're awake!" said Heidi, as though pleasantly surprised. "Do you want to come outside with us? We want to find a nice grub for Aunt Dete's dinner."

They were wearing boots, but no jackets. A glance at my watch showed what time it was.

"No one needs any dinner at ten to six in the morning," I said firmly. "Take yourselves back to bed!"

It is for this reason that I was still asleep an hour later when a sharp sound brought me out of my slumber. For a moment I lay wondering what had awoken me. Then there came a second sharp *crack!* against the window and I peered out into the half-light between dawn and sunrise to see Mimi in the next-door garden wearing a thick ulster and a terrible scowl. The whole world was white with snow, but Mimi did not seem to care. She beckoned imperiously.

I made signs promising that I should be with her shortly; then I hurried the children through breakfast and dressing and took them out to play in the snow in the back garden. Once they were thoroughly occupied in grubbing through the flower-beds in search of Aunt Dete's supper, I let myself out into the mews and hurried to the house next door.

"Have you found them?" were my first words, when Mimi opened the door to my knock.

"Not yet," she said, "but we heard from Nijam by transmitter last night. They are both safe."

"And where's Vasily?"

"Asleep." She sniffed. "After everything that has happened! We ought to be making plans!"

"I'm inclined to agree," said I. The children's voices were still audible from the garden next door; I thought they would be happy there for half an hour at least. "Take me to him."

Vasily was in the best front bedroom, fast asleep. He looked so unusually peaceful that it seemed a shame to wake him; but I sat beside him and placed my dripping, icy hand lovingly against his neck. He awoke with a little gasp.

"Am I dreaming?" he murmured. "Is this an angel?"

"No, it's a thief," Mimi said. "Get up, lazybones!"

Vasily sighed. "You see what I have to put up with," he said. "Molly-my-dear, won't you marry me and take me away from all this?"

"I can't," I told him, with mock sadness. "I left my wedding-ring in Paris."

He sat up and lifted my hand to his mouth with a wistful look. "But you would *like* to marry me, wouldn't you? You *do* love me. You sewed up my pyjamas!"

"Oh," I said happily. "You noticed!"

"Of course I noticed! You would never have done that if you didn't love me!"

In the past week or so, Vasily had taken to proposing to me in fun, as though he thought it the most tremendous joke. It crossed my mind now, for the first time, that perhaps he was really in earnest!

Marry Vasily! It was a very great change, when I had scarcely accustomed myself to thinking of him as my lover. In a flash, it all unfolded before me. Marry Vasily—give up my last chance of escaping him unscathed—abandon my comfortable, independent spinster existence for a life with a man who, while no longer quite as bad as he once had been, was still untidy, feckless, histrionic, and not at all what a proper young lady from Brixton ought to wish for!

I might have come to the conclusion that Vasily suited me better than any other person I had yet met—but that was not the same as making up my mind to marry him.

"Of course I love you," I said. "Still, we have barely been courting for six months!"

"Then perhaps when we return to Paris?"

I did not know how to answer that, and I sighed. "Not now, Vasily! We must make plans. Everything went wrong last night, and now heaven only knows where Nijam and Alphonse have got to. Come to the drawing-room when you're presentable, and we shall hold a council of war."

War could not be counselled, of course, in the absence of tea. Mimi had the tray and all the things hot, and Vasily did not keep us waiting, for his notion of presentability meant bare feet and a dressing-gown of figured silk.

He laid a fire in the grate while Mimi, striding up and down the length of the rug, made a report on her own doings.

She had managed to follow Schmidt's trail eastward through the town before the snow-storm became too thick and obscured his tracks. It seemed to her that he was aiming either towards the castle, or the forest that surrounded it. She, like Vasily, having heard Nijam's message of reassurance, had called off the search and taken herself home.

"We should try searching the castle," Mimi now declared. "It is the most likely place of shelter, and what if Griff finds them first?"

"Trust Nijam to take care of Griff," said Vasily. "Didn't you see the effective little gadget she used on him last night? She was telling me about it yesterday. It delivers a measured electrical shock, which is exactly what that man needs."

"No matter how effective it is, I'm afraid that Griff is going to be a problem nonetheless," I said. "He wants to bring back the revenants, *and* he believes that they hold the secret to consciousness-transference. More to the point, he has got it into his head that *I* can help him. Why, Vasily! What on earth has happened to your pyjama-trousers?"

In the position he had adopted, kneeling before the hearth as he coaxed the fire into life, I now saw that the lower six inches of the pyjama-legs had been cut away, leaving behind only trailing threads and a pair of pale, chilly ankles.

He looked at me adoringly. *"You* happened to them, Molly-my-dear."

"I sewed them up," I corrected him. "I didn't cut them off entirely!"

"No, I did that. Wasn't it clever of me?"

"Clever?" I sent Mimi a despairing look. We would have to add rank improvidence to the list of Vasily's failings. "You could simply have undone the stitching, you know!"

"I didn't know how! And I couldn't ask Schmidt to show me, because even if he *had* been here and in his right mind, he isn't my valet anymore, and I'm not supposed to ask him to do my menial tasks." Abashed, he glanced down at the trailing threads. "I was rather proud of myself for managing it on my own…"

"Oh, Vasily," I said, mollified despite my internal terror at the thought of actually tying my lot to his forevermore. He meant so well! and he was trying so hard!

"You must sew up the rest of his trousers, Molly," said Mimi, "and then he will learn to snip the thread rather than the flannel. What's that?"

That was the sound of a key in the front-door. Mimi dashed for the hall, and a moment later Nijam and she came in, supporting a limping Alphonse Schmidt between them. The reader can imagine what a state the two wanderers were in—cold, wet through, hungry and tired. Schmidt had lost a shoe.

We got them into dry clothes and set them in front of the fire with hot cups of tea and thickly-buttered slices of *stollen.*

"What happened to you, Schmidt?" Mimi demanded. "Why did you let those people run their foolish experiments on you? And what were you doing, letting *Griff* get hold of you in the first place?"

"Let him eat," Vasily protested.

"I'm not hungry," said Schmidt, who indeed merely picked at his food. "I went to visit the old lab., as I think you heard. I thought that it would stir up old memories—but all it brought back were feelings." He shuddered. "And then Griff came in and got the better of me. I'm sorry about that."

"You don't have to apologise for that," Nijam said, with a glare in Mimi's direction. "But what were you thinking, offering yourself up for that ridiculous rigmarole last night?"

Schmidt sent me a pleading look. "They said I would only be concerned with my brother's imprint. I never imagined something like *this.*"

I patted his shoulder. "I know. But at least you have cleaned most of the sigil from your head. It's over now."

The look on Schmidt's face made my heart sink. "No," he said. "I can still hear its voice in my head. It says that I gave it my consent, and now the sigil does not matter."

Nijam threw up her hands. "The fact that the thing was titled *The Book of Atrocious Deeds* didn't give you pause?" she demanded. I think the strain of the previous evening had begun to tell upon her, now that she was reunited with safety and clean socks. "I was willing to play along with those clowns *so* far, but not *that* far!"

"I…" Schmidt hung his head, biting his lip with shame. "Don't you understand? Once, I must have been neck deep in all of this. I did not think that a little more would hurt—and if it could have given my brother life…"

"Let us not point fingers," I said, hurriedly. "Tell us what happened after the ritual."

A pale sheen of perspiration stood on his forehead, despite his shivering. "It was like a nightmare," he said, hesitantly. "I was a prisoner in my own body. I saw—heard—felt everything. But I was not in command of my own actions. I knew only that a vast and seething malice had seized upon me and was using me as its tool." He reached out hesitantly and took Nijam's hand. "I cannot imagine what would have become of me, had Miss Nijam not recalled me to myself."

"Oh, no!" Nijam cried, rising to her feet like a wrathful goddess. I do not know that I have ever seen her so angry. "I am *not* your conscience, Alphonse Schmidt, and I refuse to save you from your own weakness!"

Poor Schmidt blinked at her. *"Weakness?"*

"What else would you call it?" she demanded. *"You* gave your consent to the thing. *You* can tell it to leave."

"Do you think I didn't *try?"*

Nijam pressed her lips together until they paled. For a moment there was no answer but the light of wrath in her glittering eyes. At last she said, almost grudgingly: "Very *well.* We don't yet understand precisely what caused the phenomenon. We must study it first. But I warn you—" and she stabbed at him with an accusing finger— "I cannot save someone who has no wish to save himself."

Schmidt seemed to shrink in upon himself. Vasily, who had been busying himself in the kitchen, chose this moment to enter with a large jug and a handful of pewter mugs.

"Who wants mulled wine?" he sang out. "We can heat it on the hearth."

Nijam whirled upon him. "Do you ever think of *anything* but pleasure, Vasily Nikolaevich?"

Vasily blinked at her. "But it's Christmas," he said, plaintively. "The one time of year when thinking of pleasure is a religious duty!"

The mention of Christmas reminded me of the children, and it struck me that it had been a little while since we had heard their shouts from the garden next door. I went into the passage and peered through the back-door towards the Schwab residence. At once I found myself nose-to-nose with little Clara, who gave me a sweet smile. Evidently the child had been shamelessly sneaking up to the house, and her two more substantial siblings could be seen clinging to the top of the fence beyond, watching our garden with avid interest.

I shook my head at Clara, signalling the child to return to her garden. Behind me, Vasily put his head out into the passage, "Who are you signalling, Molly-my-dear?"

"It's only the children," I said with a sigh. "They've climbed the fence and are staring in at us."

"How exceedingly unmannerly of them," Vasily said. "My father would have had me whipped."

I elected not to dignify this with a reply. "I won't be able to stay much longer," I said, returning to the drawing-room. "We must find out what happened to poor Alphonse before we can have a hope of reversing it. Nijam, you must have a working theory."

"I have nothing," Nijam said, bitterly. "Only a guess. After moments of great stress, it has occasionally happened that a person manifests a new personality—sometimes a quite different one to their own native personality. I suppose that this might be what has happened to Schmidt. Although if so, it is not like the case with which I was familiar, some time ago. *She* could not remember her actions while under the influence of her alter ego; but Schmidt can."

Mimi muttered under her breath, "It still sounds like possession to *me*."

I coughed gently. "I'm afraid I'm inclined to agree with Mimi. Not because I know anything of the condition you describe—for I don't—but because I was there last night, and there was something very wrong with that horrible book, and that ghastly image. Couldn't you feel it? You said yourself, Nijam, that what those people did was not science."

Nijam scowled. "Very well, then—you may try your way of addressing the problem, and I will try mine."

Schmidt had been looking from one to the other of us with a rather pained expression on his face. "If either of you are interested in what *I* think," he said, "there is something horribly familiar about the Voice. I think that it is what I have always been afraid of reawakening."

Nijam sent him a sharp look. "I beg your pardon! Is this *not* the first time you have experienced such a thing?"

"I don't remember," he said, with a shudder. "But I don't

think so."

We all considered this a moment. Vasily said, "I don't suppose there's any chance at all that it's actually Stefan Schmidt."

"No," I said, at the same moment that Nijam said, "None whatever."

"Stefan Schmidt's memory-imprint was there last night," I added, "but it was incapable of doing anything but jotting things into a note-book. It could not converse with us, as this thing could."

"That," Nijam put in, "and besides, it's as I was saying last night: there is no reason to believe that human minds can simply be transferred from one brain to another. These people think that the mind is nothing more than a sort of complicated long-division sum, and that the brain is nothing more than a sort of abacus. They think that it is simply a matter of creating a new kind of abacus on which to do the same old sums, only better and faster, and without having to wear out and die. There's only one problem with such a hypothesis: there's no proof for it! We don't know how the mind works; we don't know how the brain works. We cannot even *begin* to reduce the mind to equations, and even if we could—even if we did run an emulation of these equations on another brain, whether man-made or natural—how could such a thing be truly alive? Would it have free will?" She turned to Schmidt. "It is as you yourself said in Paris—that a person is *not predictable.* There is not a single machine in the world with the capacity to run on any tracks but the ones laid down for it by humanity. There is not a single equation that can think for itself. And that is why I can make a prosthesis of any limb in the body, and a great many other things beside—but I cannot make a prosthetic *brain."*

Schmidt gazed down at his hands. "I never thought it was my brother," he said, softly. "The thing could not even speak at first. It had to rummage through my memories for words."

In the silence that followed, Nijam paled, touching a tongue to her lips. Likely *that* did not seem to her like a stress-induced alter ego, either.

"Clara!" I exclaimed suddenly. Everyone started. "I beg your pardon," I added, for the apparition had now once again withdrawn through the wall. I hoped that the shade-child had not overheard too much. She was a quiet little thing and indeed I had not yet heard her speak, but for their own sake, I did not like to risk the children learning too much about our doings.

When I looked out the back-door again, there was no sign of the children, whether living or dead. Something told me, however, that they had not yet lost interest in my doings.

"The children again?" Vasily drawled as I returned to the drawing-room. "Ah! I would have been whipped within an inch of my life!"

I sent him a look of daggers. Just because his father had been a monster did not mean that he must be!

"All this is theory," Mimi said, doggedly returning to the main subject. "What are we going to *do* about it? Griff wants the revenants, Dr Schwab and his secret society have done something to Alphonse which we cannot undo, and we still have not found the Auberlen papers—let alone destroyed them!"

Schmidt, who had been sitting as silently as ever, now rose to his feet and turned towards the door.

"Where are you going?" Nijam asked. If she had been

unusually testy all morning, I thought, it was mainly that she worried for him.

"Away," Schmidt said in a hollow voice. "Down to the kitchen. Somewhere neither I nor *It* can overhear what you are planning."

There was a momentary silence at this. It had not occurred to any of us, I think, that we might need to keep our plans a secret, not only from Griff, but also from our Alphonse.

"Stay," Nijam said, more gently. "Didn't the Voice tell you that it was only by your own consent that it was able to control you? And you seized back control before it could hurt me. We trust you, Alphonse."

"But you *shouldn't*," Schmidt said, with a sudden passion of feeling. "I gave it my consent once, and now it is always with me! Don't you understand? I might break out at any moment into more violence. I'm dangerous—I've always been dangerous—now more than ever. If you had any sense you would keep me locked up!"

There was a moment's silence. Then Nijam said, frostily, "Remember that you are speaking of the man I love."

Schmidt's throat worked, and he dropped his gaze once more to his feet. "I'll go and wash up," he muttered, and then opened the drawing-room door.

There in the hallway, hand in hand, were the Schwab triplets, looking extremely guilty.

"Children!" I cried, despairingly.

Peter looked up at me under bent brows, which made him appear rather threatening in aspect, and whispered, "We're hungry."

"Children!" I repeated. "You can't follow me about like this!"

"But you've been for *ever*," Heidi said, with a stamp of her foot.

Vasily must have followed me to the door, for he now remarked, "My father would have whipped me like a *peasant.*"

The joke, never amusing to begin with, had worn thin. I turned to him.

"Very well, then. Do as you think fit."

Vasily blinked at me, evidently startled. "I beg your pardon? Do what?"

"Take them off and give them a whipping, since I am not doing the job as you wish!"

I have rarely been so gratified in my life. Not only the children, but also Vasily, turned as white as paper.

"I couldn't possibly!" Vasily gasped. "I was joking!"

"We'll be good—we'll be good!" Heidi and Peter protested.

"Don't prevaricate!" I told him.

"I can't beat children! I don't know how! You can't make me!"

"Then don't make threats," I said. With Vasily routed, I turned to the children. "This is why you must not follow me about," I told them, firmly. "I might be meeting with any kind of scoundrel. Now, run along with Mr Schmidt, there, and let him find you something to eat in the kitchen."

"Miss Dark!" It was Alphonse's turn to pale. "I don't think—"

"You can trust him," I said, firmly, and I had absolutely no doubt of it. Alphonse might perhaps have continued to refuse, except that the triplets seized hold of his hands and tugged him into the hallway. Nor did Clara shrink from him, but followed without the slightest appearance of worry.

"Are you *quite* sure, Dark?" Mimi asked, when I had shut the door again.

I glanced at Nijam, and she nodded. "I don't think that he

will lose control of himself again," I said. "Not where anyone might be hurt. But in the meanwhile, *what should we do?*"

"Good question," Nijam said in a softly menacing voice. "Where is Dr Schwab, Dark?"

"They took him to the hospital."

"What, already?"

"Why, did you mean to send him there yourself?" I asked. "If you remember, last Schmidt threw Griff at him, and he seems to have broken at least a few ribs."

"Which leaves the coast clear for *us*," said Vasily, now visibly chastened. "It may not be the Auberlen papers, but we ought certainly to take care of that *Atrocious Deeds* book."

"*And* the Black Templars at large," I agreed, "before they find out how to bring back the revenants—or run any more experiments on Schmidt—or on the children."

The other three sent me startled looks. "On *whom?*" Vasily breathed.

"On the children," I repeated. "He has already killed one of them. They're triplets, you know."

"My God," said Vasily. He tugged at his pointed beard. "And I said—Molly! If I had known, I would never have said such a thing!"

Nijam had gone very still and there was a hard glitter in her eyes. "He ought to die," she said softly.

"We can't *do* that, Nijam," I said.

"Why not?" she answered. "I would get away with it."

"I have no doubt of *that*," I assured her. "But we are *thieves*—not executioners, and certainly not a jury."

"I'm afraid I agree with Molly," Vasily said, with a sigh. "What a shame! But I've given up killing people; it isn't good for me. Leave the doctor and the Black Templars to me, Nijam.

You must work on finding Auberlen and the elder Schmidt's papers. Didn't Schwab say they were kept under lock and key at the University Library?"

Nijam bit her lip, but spoke no more of killing people. "That explains why we were unable to find them on the shelves. We need those papers urgently—they might contain the information I need to help Alphonse."

"And in the meanwhile?" Mimi demanded. "What if you're mistaken about that Voice? What if it takes him over again?"

"Then we will need to take precautions," Vasily said. "I don't suppose that the old salt-circle trick would work on him?"

"Salt?" Nijam inquired.

"Back in Coburg—with Lupei and Miss Sharp—they used to keep me shut up all day in a circle of salt, for fear of my tearing out their throats." A look of nostalgia crossed Vasily's face. "Those were the days! I had nothing to do but read Anthony Trollope and plot my revenge. But of course salt never worked on the revenants."

Salt-water had been our weapon against the monstrous royalties before we had managed to win Vasily free of them; and I wished I had known that there were other ways to use that useful substance. Nijam, however, seemed distinctly unimpressed.

"I can fit up his room with locks and bars," she snapped. "But there's no reason why Alphonse should lose command of the creature. I shall want his help at the Library. And it's absolutely necessary to recover his memories; only he can explain what happened in the time between my leaving Heidelberg and Vasily's retrieving him from British custody."

"I agree," I reassured her. "We have a bigger threat to worry about. Griff is in Heidelberg, and he suspects we're up to something. What are we going to do about it?"

"Can't you distract him, as you did last time?" Nijam asked.

I sent her a censorious look. "No doubt I can," said I, "given how *very* excited he seems to be to enlist my help in bringing back the revenants!"

"Then the main trouble is our communications," Nijam said, so calmly that I wished to beat her over the head with a sofa-cushion. "We ought to have *some* method of securing our transmissions. What a shame we cannot achieve some sort of instantaneous encryption!"

"Like speaking a language he cannot understand, for instance?" Mimi suggested.

"Exactly like that," Nijam said. "A non-European language such as Chinese, or Swahili, would be ideal."

"The only problem is that none of us *knows* any non-European languages," Vasily put in.

"I personally have all but mastered Gilchrist's *East Indian Guide to the Hindoostanee*," Nijam said, with quiet dignity. "But something else might work in a pinch. It's a shame that Mimi is the only one of us with any Finnish."

"He certainly would not know Finnish," Mimi said, with a grin. "I will teach you all, if you like."

"I would like to learn," I said, quite honestly, for I thought Finnish quite the prettiest language I had ever heard. "But come to think of it, I don't believe Griff has any German."

"Everyone has German," Mimi said, scornfully. "Even Nijam has German!"

"But Dr Schwab made sure to speak to Griff in English all yesterday evening," I pointed out. There was a silence as we all remembered this.

"Heaven help us if we could have been speaking German in

his presence all this time!" Vasily exclaimed in disgust.

"It will do for the present," Nijam said, "although it is too common a language to keep us safe for very long. That's settled, then!"

I did not know whether it was settled entirely to my own satisfaction. I did not at all like the thought of having to go on distracting Griff, apparently until the end of my days, given what was beginning to feel like persecution. He did not like me; he did not even particularly desire me. It merely seemed to please him to annoy me.

But what else could we do? Griff knew that we were here, and I was the one of us who was best suited to distract him.

I made no further objections, therefore; merely comforted myself with the thought that this time I would not be wholly cut off from communications with my crew.

Chapter VII.

It was doubtless time to return myself and the children to the Schwab house, and so I went out to the kitchen. Alphonse was sitting at the table looking a little thunderstruck. The surface of the table was coated in *stollen* crumbs, amidst which Heidi and Peter were happily employed in taking apart his pocket-watch. Clara, unseen, knelt on the table in front of Alphonse and appeared to be poking at his eye with an insubstantial finger. I focused my attention very closely upon that finger and began to see a shadowy mass which rippled and seethed in discontent as she prodded at it. Each time she did so, a faint shudder ran through Alphonse's whole body. Otherwise he seemed quite unaware of what was going on.

"Climb down, Clara," I said, very gently. "Some things are not safe to play with."

Peter looked up from the watch. "There's something wrong with Herr Schmidt," said he, with ghoulish relish. "He's got *tentacles* growing out of his head!"

"Yes, dear, I know."

Alphonse looked at me with horror. "What do you see, Miss Dark? Do *you* know what's wrong with me?"

"I could not venture to say," said I. "Only when I look very carefully, there's a sort of—mass—inside you; like a cancer of the mind or the spirit. But we already knew that."

Alphonse shuddered. I patted him on the shoulder, not knowing how else to reassure him. Having taken the children out into the street, I hesitated.

"Children," I told them, "I'm afraid we are all going to have to tell some fibs about where we have been this morning."

Heidi's eyes gleamed. "Ooh, *really?* Can we tell Fräulein Angermeyer that we've been on a trip to the moon with a good fairy?"

"I'm afraid that we shall have to tell her something she is likely to believe," I said, trying not to laugh. "Say that I promised you *kugelhopf* and a walk by the river because yesterday you went to bed like good children."

"But we didn't," Peter said, anxiously. "We stayed up *ever* so late."

"Ah, but Fräulein Angermeyer doesn't know that," I pointed out. "I would not ask you to do such a thing, except that it's like the things that Peter can see, which no one else can. You know that you must keep those a secret, mustn't you?"

They had now become very solemn, and all three of them nodded their heads.

"All right," Heidi said cheerfully. "But if we tell the *good* fibs, then can we have a tree for Christmas this year? We didn't have one last year."

Heidi could teach Mimi a thing or two about driving bargains, I reflected ruefully. All the same, the thought of whisking the children away from their horrible father, and showering them with Christmas-trees, was tremendously appealing. After all, I was a thief, wasn't I? I took money, and jewels, and paintings, from people who did not merit them. Why not children, too? Dr Schwab, I suspected, would be in no kind of position to care for them once I and my crew had finished with him. He was not caring for them at present; they were neglected, and ill-used for the sake of his horrible experiments.

I had always wished for children of my own; only I had thought that in order to find any, I should need to get decently married first. But I was now independently wealthy. I might adopt as many children as I liked. I would not need Vasily for *that.* We might remain cordial as friends. Wouldn't that be easy? Wouldn't it be ever so much *safer?*

Then I remembered the aunt in Nuremberg, and the poor Frau Schwab in gaol, and I heaved a wistful sigh. There were, after all, others who had a nearer claim upon the children than myself.

The children watched me expectantly, as though they expected me to produce a Christmas-tree at once from my pocket. Still, there were not very many days left until Christmas, and it was anyone's guess how much longer the job would take.

"I'll do my best," I said. "Where's Clara run off to?"

The house which Vasily had taken was one of a long row of semi-detached buildings that jostled shoulders up and down the street. Clara had run ahead of us and was now looking up at a lady who stood outside the doctor's house, staring fixedly at the windows. She was a thin, poor-looking woman in a thick black veil and a respectable dress that was a little too large for her.

Taking Peter and Heidi by the hand, I went up to the bystander and asked, "Excuse me, Frau. Can I help you?"

The woman turned with a start. She did not look at me; rather, her gaze seemed to fix upon the two living children.

For a long time she said nothing, and the children, feeling her scrutiny, drew a little closer to me.

"Frau?" I asked again.

The woman hurried away without speaking.

"Did you know that woman, Clara?" I asked, watching the retreating figure with great curiosity.

Clara shrugged, and Heidi said, "She was in the street yesterday, too. But we don't know who she is."

After that I took them into the house and sent them upstairs to change their wet, snowy things. While they were racketing about in the nursery, I risked another peep through the hall window and was rewarded with a view of the mysterious veiled woman hurrying back again. This time she went to knock on the door of our own headquarters.

Curiouser still! No doubt the fair stranger had seen us emerge from the house next door. Was she now investigating who lived there?

Internally, I made a note to ask Vasily later; but in the meanwhile, I had a task to do. The house was quiet today. Fräulein Angermeyer was the sole servant, apart from the cook and myself; and she must be busy somewhere upstairs, cleaning or tidying. *One* room she must have been forbidden to touch. I went to the study, rolled back the carpet, and opened the trap-door which led to the laboratory in the cellar.

It was dark down here, and horribly quiet. With trembling fingers I lit the gas and stood for a moment looking about. The horrible banner was still reversed, showing the hideous figure of the jellyfish monster. The floor was still all over broken glass and overturned tables from the previous night's fracas; and there was one ghastly splash of blood upon the floor, where poor Schmidt had brained a Templar. The body itself had been removed, but its imprint remained, still bleeding upon the stone floor. As for the mummified Stefan Schmidt, he still lay motionless beneath a sheet; but his own imprint had vanished entirely.

Neither of them was quite as unsettling as the sunken sockets of Dr Auberlen, which seemed to follow me across the room.

At the back of the room, I found the *Codex Actorum Atrocium* on the bench where Schwab must have left it once the Voice took possession of poor Alphonse.

It was not the first time I had had something to do with artefacts of this nature. You will recall the business of the Noor-Jahan diamond, and how upon touching it with bare hands I had been overwhelmed with the most ghastly visions. Now, therefore, I took my handkerchief from my pocket and wrapped it about my fingers, meaning to get a hold of it in this way.

Even as my hands approached the book I felt suddenly faint and nauseous. I had again the feeling that a great seething darkness emanated from it; but nevertheless I set my teeth and took the thing in my protected hand.

I do not like to say exactly what happened after that. Suffice it to say that I became aware, very suddenly, that the book was bound in human skin; and that the skin had been acquired— but no! I cannot write it.

I came to myself a moment later to hear Heidi saying, "Fräulein Dark! Fräulein Dark! What are you doing? Why are you taking a nap down *here?*"

I opened my eyes with a sob and folded the child into my arms. Clara and Peter, more sensitive than Heidi, were watching me from across the room, evidently unwilling to venture any further into the laboratory.

"Children!" I gasped. But whether it was a reproach or not I could not tell you.

"You shouldn't come down here, Fräulein Dark," Heidi said, in a muffled voice, from my neck. I could feel her shivering. "It's a bad place; Peter says so."

"That it is," I said, getting shakily up. The book lay where I had dropped it upon the floor. I touched my transmitter and said in German, "I have found the *Codex,* but I cannot touch it or move it, even with gloves."

"Never fear," Vasily answered. "Don't try to touch it again. I'll collect it after I've been to the hospital." He had arranged to visit Dr Schwab, and to pay his respects.

"I don't know if I want *you* to touch it, either," said I, shakily; but I switched off my transmitter to find Heidi staring in fascination at the horrible banner.

"What's that?" Heidi asked, pointing at the hideous form depicted.

"I don't know," said I, with great feeling, "and I don't want to know." But I had a nasty feeling that I was going to learn a great deal more than I wished.

We hurried up the stairs and got the trap-door covered just in time, for the doorbell jangled and summoned Fräulein Angermeyer from her work in the drawing-room. While she answered the door, the children and I tried to beat a hasty retreat up the stairs. But it was not to be.

"I want to see Miss Molly Dark," announced a familiar, rather bloodless voice in English—which was useless, for Fräulein Angermeyer did not speak that language. "Tell her to come down. No, never mind. There she is."

I congealed with one foot upon the stair. Griff pushed past

the housekeeper and strode up to me. Without so much as a *good-day* or a *by-your-leave* he plucked my transmitter right out of my ear.

"I beg your pardon!" I exclaimed.

"You're up to something, Miss Molly," Griff declared, shaking the transmitter in my direction. "*I* heard you jabbering away with your confederates just now!"

"It's rude to eavesdrop on people," I said, with dignity. "Do all Americans have such bad manners?"

His face darkened. "You'll get good manners when you've earned them, Miss Molly. Now, come clean with me: what are you planning?"

I clicked my tongue. "No manners, and no German! What *do* they teach you in that country?"

Griff reddened. The triplets giggled.

"Clear out, kids," he ordered, speaking in very loud English, as though they were more likely to understand if he shouted at them. "Miss Molly and I have business to discuss."

"You had better go upstairs," I told the children, in German. "I'm afraid that this man is not only very wicked—he's also terribly dull."

They giggled again as they ran off—not that I had any great confidence in their ability to stay away for very long. Griff sent me a resentful look, no doubt wondering what I had said to make them giggle like that.

"Well?" I asked him.

"There's a parlour, isn't there?" Griff asked me. "And a cup of tea?"

Sighing, I explained to Fräulein Angermeyer that the visitor required tea in the drawing-room. Griff followed me into the room thus indicated and wrinkled his nose with distaste. The air was indeed, as I have said, horribly musty. I do not think the doctor used the room often.

"All right, Miss Molly; time to come clean," Griff said, hitching up the legs of his grey trousers to seat himself in an armchair. My former fiancé had not changed much since the day I first met him on the train from Constantinople to Paris. He was as grey and old-maidish as ever, in that peculiarly American way; but I thought that he did not look well. He had lost flesh. The lines in his smooth grey skin had deepened, and there were deep pouches beneath his eyes.

"Have you been in poor health?" I asked, with curiosity and a little pity.

But Griff only scowled.

"Don't avoid the question," he said, placing the tips of his fingers together. "Explain what you are doing in Heidelberg."

"I'm not avoiding it," I said, giving him my most charming smile as I seated myself on the sofa across from him. "I'm *considering* the question. But since you evidently mean to hector me until I confess, why not begin?"

Griff frowned, evidently caught off-guard by this defiance. The door opened and Fräulein Angermeyer brought in the tea-tray. Griff beheld it with discontent.

"There's no cream," he said. "Send her for cream."

I beheld him with grave alarm. "Are you—are you *quite* sure?"

"Why wouldn't I be?" he snapped, so I sent for cream. When I turned back to him, Griff had leaned forward in the chair and begun spooning tea into the steaming pot. One—two—*three* spoons-full. I could not help myself. I reached out involuntarily.

"Let me," I said, but it was a lost cause. In went a fourth

101

spoonful.

"I know how to make tea, thanks," Griff said. The lid went back onto the pot, and I put down tea-making and truthfulness as other things that were poorly understood in America. Griff leaned back in his arm-chair. "I warn you, Miss Molly. I want the secret to consciousness-transference, and I mean to get it."

"Really?" I asked, pretending surprise. "Well, I'm sure you will manage it. You usually do get what you want."

"May the best man win, you mean?" Griff laughed. "Don't be in any doubt of *that,* Miss Molly. I certainly mean to."

I opened my eyes very wide. "I'm sure *I* won't stand in your way, Griff! If that's what you are afraid of, then let me assure you that I have no desire for consciousness-transference whatsoever."

"Don't give me that," he said, contemptuously. "Here is Molly Dark, an heiress worth thousands of pounds, governessing a pair of kids in Germany merely out of the goodness of her heart? Do you think I'm a fool? Of course you have got your eye on the prize."

"What prize?" I objected. "Last night I saw a man driven mad. How is that a prize?"

Griff's eyes burned with fervour. "We live in a world where science is breaking down every barrier that once held us back as a race."

"Do you really believe that was *science,* last night?"

He snorted. "What do *you* believe that it was? Magic?"

I shrugged.

"We could have unlimited power. We could have eternal life. If you and your friends think you'll be able to keep that knowledge for yourselves, you'll have to think again. This could benefit all of humanity. I, Warren Vandergriff, mean to make sure of it."

"Eternal life!" There were those words again. "Doesn't that seem a little—I don't know! A little far-fetched?"

"We can summon light to our homes by moving a finger," Griff declared. "What's so incredible about abolishing death?"

I did not quite know how to answer. I could not very well ask him whether he thought himself greater than God. Instead, I reached for the tea-pot, thinking that I might be able to rescue some decent tea if I caught it quickly enough.

"Leave it," Griff said. "It hasn't finished steeping."

I pursed my lips to hold back the indignant words upon them. Meanwhile, I was thinking furiously. It struck me that it might be worth Griff thinking that we wanted the secret to consciousness-transference, for we might in this way be able to distract his attention from the assault upon the Library.

"I will admit nothing to you," I said, with dignity. "As to why I am playing the governess, it is a feminine instinct which a man could not possibly understand. I am very fond of children. They—they bring out something maternal. They make me feel young."

Griff gave a snort. "Feel young all you like, Miss Molly. It won't make you *truly* immortal. But we can make a deal, you know. I came here to propose an alliance."

Griff did love to make deals, I recalled. It was only a shame that he was not as good at them as he believed himself to be.

"An alliance," I said, wearily. "I believe that in Hong Kong, I made my views on *that* subject quite clear."

"So did I. I meant to have you then, and I still do now. More than ever, now that I know you really can perceive other consciousnesses. Imagine what we could achieve together—

with my gadgetry, and your perception, and our combined fortune. We might rebuild the world."

"There is one obstacle," I said primly, "and that is, that I wouldn't marry you if you were the last man in the world."

"Miss Molly, you wouldn't wish to stand in the way of human immortality, would you?"

"Not at all," said I. "Only I think it ought to be achieved in the old-fashioned way, by repenting of one's sins."

Griff snorted. "Pshaw! Don't try to be holier-than-thou with *me*. I know that you stole the Noor-Jahan. The only reason I haven't prosecuted you for it is out of respect for the Russian Emperor, whose cousin was involved. But don't try my patience. I'm not a particularly religious man myself, but I'm pretty sure the true sin would be to deny humanity eternal life on a paltry religious scruple."

That was Griff all over—if he didn't get what he wanted, he simply bullied you until you gave in. And he would do it all with the most touching belief in his own rectitude.

"Surely we needn't get *married* in order to join forces," I said, wearily but without much hope. So far, every rejection had only made Griff more determined. "Beyond that, I am not sure that my gift would be very helpful to you. Memory-imprints cannot speak or communicate; they are only meaningless repetitions of things that were done in life—and no," I added, at his look of puzzlement. "I was *not* quite truthful last night, when I said that Stefan Schmidt's memory-imprint consented to the consciousness-transference ritual. It was incapable of doing anything but scribbling in a notebook, and now it has faded away altogether. I was simply curious to know what would happen next."

Griff beheld me with narrowed eyes. "Hmmm," he said,

thoughtfully. Then he lifted the lid on the tea-pot, and, being satisfied with what he saw, began to concoct—no. I cannot call it tea. Into each cup he poured a foul, inky liquid that smelled of brutalised tea-leaves. He followed this with a slosh of pure cream and two lumps of sugar each.

Having offered this witches' brew to me, Griff sat back in his own chair, sipped, and gave a sigh indicative of pleasure. I did not follow suit. The smell of the tea had told me all I needed to know, and I am ashamed to say that although I had once been sufficiently desperate to try my tea with cream rather than milk, that once was enough. The burned hand teaches best. As for sugar, no properly brewed tea needs it, let alone that *much* of it.

"What about this?" Griff offered, setting down his cup. "I want Alphonse Schmidt, and I want Padma Nijam. The first actually worked with Auberlen and Schmidt, and the second is one of the foremost prostheticists of her generation. If they are willing to come to New York and work in my laboratory, I'll reconsider my matrimonial plans."

It was the most bare-faced extortion imaginable. No—in a way it was worse. Most people were content with extorting money; Griff wished to extort my friends.

"I will ask them," I said, concealing my revulsion, "but what if they refuse?"

Griff leaned forwards, and under his eye I began to feel like a rabbit marked down by an eagle. "Every life in the world depends upon it," he said. "Theirs—yours—*mine*. And the law, Miss Dark, gives a man special latitude to defend his own life."

"I will ask them," I repeated. As usual when speaking to Griff, I felt rather dizzied; not so much because of the towering naïveté of his selfishness, as at the thought that I might once have intended to marry him, only because he was rich and respectable, as Vasily was not.

Griff reached into his pocket and cast my transmitter onto the table. "Here," he said. "Ask them now."

This was a step forward, at any rate. Retrieving the transmitter, I connected it to the battery which I wore concealed in my hair.

"Are you there, Nijam?" I asked in German—looking Griff in the eye as I did so, as though daring him to bid me use English. "Griff is over here and making all sorts of demands, as usual. But I think his game isn't me this time—it's you and Alphonse."

In a few words, I summarised what Griff had told me.

"Giving him Alphonse is out of the question," Nijam declared at once. "But if it's a matter of prosthetics, I'll build him whatever he wants so long as he lets us alone."

"I don't want to give him *anything*," I grumbled.

"It's no use," said Nijam. "Tell him to meet me tonight at the old lab."

She was manifestly in the right of it. Griff now knew all our names and faces, except perhaps for Mimi; and only a stroke of luck had prevented his recognising Vasily as the Russian Emperor's cousin, who was supposed to be dead. We did, indeed, need to bargain.

"Not tonight," Vasily put in, through his own transmitter. "I have been to visit Dr Schwab, and there is to be a meeting of the Black Templars tonight. I shall want you all there. Don't forget your robes."

"Then tell Griff I'll be in communication with him shortly," Nijam said, before severing the connection.

I closed my own transmitter. "Miss Nijam is at your service,"

I told Griff, "but not Alphonse Schmidt. He doesn't have his memories, and he isn't to be bothered."

Griff sipped his—beverage. "Really?" he said mildly. "I expect you to double-cross me, of course, Miss Molly, but if so, wouldn't it be reasonable to sweeten the deal a little more?"

"I believe that in this instance, Miss Nijam means to keep her word," said I. I was telling the strict truth, but for the sake of distraction, I let myself look just a *little* too innocent to be believed. "She will be in communication with you shortly."

"Very well," Griff said, rather smug and self-satisfied. "Your tea is going cold."

It had been a most unpleasant morning, and this was the final straw. I rose from my chair, drew myself up to all my considerable height, and fixed him with a scornful gaze.

"*That,*" I said, "is not tea. *That* is a crime against the noble *camellia sinensis,* and the angels will lay it to your account on the Last Day. Good day to you, Mr Vandergriff."

After that I went up to the nursery, and then out into the garden, and then down into the laboratory, where at last I found the children. This explained why they had not intruded upon my *tête-à-tête* with Griff—because they had found some other mischief to get up to. Heidi had got hold of the *Actorum Atrocium* and the three of them were looking at the pictures, which were not at all pleasant. I was, however, pleased to see that Heidi could handle the book without ill effects; and so I had her conceal it under old Dr Auberlen's viewing-case, where there was a dark cobwebby gap only a few inches wide. After that I took them all upstairs for a grammar lesson, and it was verbs and subjects and prepositions until lunch-time.

Chapter VIII.

Meanwhile, Nijam and Alphonse were on their way to the old laboratory in which the two of them had once worked as assistants to Stefan and Dr Auberlen. It had at first been Nijam's plan to take Mimi for a renewed assault upon the University Library; but Alphonse had forestalled her.

"There is something you ought to see at the old lab," he told her. "I came upon it last night before Griff interrupted me."

Nijam saw that he was very much in earnest, and so, despite her anxiety to retrieve the Auberlen papers, she agreed to put off the Library expedition in favour of a search of the laboratory. Off they went to the Plöck.

I do not know if you have ever been to Heidelberg, but in case you have not, I might as well describe it. Heidelberg is a perfectly charming old German town situated at the mouth of the Neckar river gorge, where the green forested hills open out into the broad valley of the Rhine. Much of the town sits upon the south bank of the Neckar. The old castle, which is a very well-preserved and picturesque ruin, stands upon an eminence at the easternmost end of the settlement. The town itself is in the best German tradition: pinny-neat with smooth and tidy cobbled streets. The houses are no more than two or three storeys high, with steep tiled rooves and plenty of red brick and plaster. The Plöck is one of these streets, very long and narrow, which runs from west to east through the town in parallel to the river. Near the east end of the Plöck, practically beneath the shadow of the castle and not far from the charming, red-brick Peterskirche, there stood a cream-coloured building belonging to the University, distinguished by a large oriel window at one corner. In the basement level of this building was the old Auberlen-Schmidt laboratory.

The room was all more or less as Nijam remembered: all the old equipment was there. The tables and shelves, beakers and tanks, chemicals and instruments were all present, and even one or two old projects of her own, which she had been obliged to leave behind in the haste of her departure. Only the books and papers were missing.

"Old Auberlen must have kept the place locked up after the rest of us were gone," Nijam mused. She tried to light the gas, but the supply must have been cut off. The lab. was now lit only by small, high, semi-circular windows at the level of the street; in the dim December light the place looked even more forlorn and gloomy than she remembered in the days when it had been full of corpses. Now it looked itself rather like the corpse of a room. "What did you find, Alphonse?"

"This," he said. A large black-board covered one wall at the end of the laboratory. It had hung there for as long as Nijam remembered, crusted with chalk-dust and rarely washed. Now, carefully, Schmidt unhooked the board from the wall and lowered it to the ground.

On the wall behind—traced onto the whitewashed bricks of the wall with thick, crudely painted lines—was the same hideous image that had presided over the Schwab laboratory on the previous evening. There was the jellyfish head; there the grinning mouth gaping to receive its prey; there the trampling feet, the crumbling houses, the terrified human figures.

Nijam stood transfixed. There was something inexpressibly ominous about that image; but there was something more sinister yet about its presence here in the laboratory where *she* had worked. The image was crusted with old, brown cobwebs which had collected behind the blackboard. There was no room for doubt. It had quite clearly been there for years.

"I never saw this before," she said, turning to Alphonse. "Why? We were doing *science.* Why was *this* here?"

"I don't know," he said, in a bleak voice. "But I dreamed about this thing last night. I was in a dark city, and this thing was trampling the city underfoot, crushing people, snatching them up to feed into its mouth." He shivered, turning his head away. "No—that wasn't the worst of it. Miss Nijam, *you* were there—*you* were with me. And I was afraid, so afraid, that I—I threw you to the thing to save myself."

"It was only a dream," Nijam told him, scornfully. "What, do you seriously believe yourself capable of betraying me, Alphonse Schmidt?"

"But it *wasn't* only a dream," Alphonse insisted. "That *thing*—that laughter. That *Voice.* It's always been in my head, I think. It's laughing now. Oh, heaven! What were we doing here, all along, without knowing it? Or what if I *did* know about it? What if I kept it a secret from you?"

"What if you did?" Nijam demanded, feeling as though the silence was like a scream. "Speak plainly! What are you afraid of?"

"I don't know." Alphonse glanced up at the image with a shudder. "I think it's trying to get back into the world. I think it wants to be worshipped again. It wants to crush and devour until nothing is left—nothing."

Nijam shuddered, too. If Mimi was correct, if the dreadful Voice was some ghastly demon that held him in thrall, then what could she do? She was ignorant. She was helpless. Everything she had believed about the revenants—and her own part in them—was false. She had, with her own two hands, assisted in abominable rites.

"You don't *know* that," she whispered.

Alphonse said, "It's in my mind, you know. I know everything it plans."

"And that's the *only* place it is," Nijam retorted. "Whatever this Voice is, it has no power but what you give it."

"And I've already given it so much," he said. "Why? Is this a punishment? Am I the one who led my brother into this evil?"

This, mercifully, was something of which Nijam could be quite certain. "That's nonsense. If you remembered the first thing about Stefan Schmidt you'd know it was nonsense. I'll restore your memories, and you'll see!"

"No," he said, pleadingly. "Don't torment me any longer— tell me what you know. *Tell* me what we did here, and how it happened that we parted."

Nijam pursed her lips; but in truth, none of the things she had attempted to jog Alphonse's memories free had worked. At this moment, memory-restoration seemed scarcely more likely than consciousness-transference itself.

"Dr Schwab is correct, at least to my knowledge," she said wearily. "Auberlen told me himself that he used the *Codex Actorum Atrocium* to develop the revenant-making process. You had no hand in *that*. Auberlen and Stefan were already working as partners in this laboratory, making revenants, for at least a year before you and I came to Heidelberg. Stefan was seven years your senior, for heaven's sake! After they took you on as an assistant, you put my name forward; which I took as a kindness, because there was no other laboratory in Heidelberg willing to accept me. But apart from the sigils, there was never a whiff of anything unscientific until this very hour. You and I only preserved the bodies. It was Auberlen and Stefan who reanimated them."

A little hope came back to Alphonse's eyes, but was as quickly quenched. "I might have concealed something from you."

"I would have known," Nijam insisted. "Do you think I don't know you? We worked together every day. After two years, I knew that one day I would marry you. There were no secrets between you and me, and no rift. The rift was between me and Stefan. Auberlen had retired and Stefan wanted to build a factory creating revenants to sell to the Great Powers—not just as policemen, but as soldiers, too. For Stefan, science was not a way to help others—it was only ever a way to money, and thence to power. He never wanted to share his knowledge. He never told either of us exactly how the revenants were made, or why. Perhaps even he did not rightly know! But how could I be content with that? I had come to Heidelberg for the sake of *knowledge!*"

"And then?"

Nijam smoothed down her hair, lest it had become ruffled in her vehemence. "Then Stefan began talking about creating revenants from *living* people," she whispered. "Revenants which would not decay and fall apart after only a few months; revenants with the life-span of any ordinary human being, but without will or conscience of their own. At first I could not believe that he was in earnest. It was an outrage against science and humanity... When it became clear that he was resolved to do it, I determined to leave. I begged you to come with me."

"Go on," Alphonse whispered, as Nijam hesitated. She had come now to the darkest days of her life, but she did not mean to let Alphonse see how much they had affected her.

"At first you were reluctant," she said. "You begged me not to make you choose between me and your brother. You said that you would go to Vienna with me and work on prosthetics; but first, you wanted to appeal to Stefan, to convince him to abandon the living-revenant project. The next morning, we would have met at the train station. You never appeared. My ticket to Vienna was all that I had of any value; I had no choice but to take the train. That was the last I heard from you. No letters—no telegrams." Nijam took a deep breath, trying to steady her voice. "I was glad, a few months later, when I heard that Stefan was dead and saw the revenants lying lifeless in the streets. Until the day we met at the Schloss Frohsdorf, I never knew what had become of you. For all I knew, Stefan might have done away with you in secret. The truth had never occurred to me: that *you* were his first, successful attempt to make a living revenant."

Alphonse let out a long, unsteady sigh. "So that is the truth of it," he said. "A revenant. I feared something of the sort."

"Vasily said that his friends freed you, that night in Coburg when the revenants were all unmade," Nijam added. "I don't know why he didn't tell me before. It would have explained everything. But that's the truth of it: you went to your brother, and he made you into a revenant, and after that you were stripped of your memories. You never...you never abandoned me."

* * *

On those words Nijam's voice trembled a little, and Schmidt, as he told me later, was struck to the heart.

"I was a fool," he cried. "I ought to have listened to you. Now I will never be free."

"Don't say that. You *were* free—for years you were free."

"Was I?" Schmidt passed a hand over his poor shorn head, which was nicked and scraped from the previous night's adventures. "I could always feel this thing hanging over me like a shadow. I always had a sense that one day it would seize me again. And now how shall I get rid of it? I gave it my *consent.* Now the sigil has gone, and it remains."

"Perhaps there is something more that ought to be done," Nijam said, scowling. "Some additional step, beyond merely defacing the sigil. I have questioned Vasily, but he was no help. Those who actually witnessed the undoing of the revenants are in Australia now. But I'll get to the bottom of it. If the Auberlen papers do not give us answers, then I'm sure Elizabeth Sharp will."

Schmidt gnawed upon his nether lip. "There is another source, nearer at hand," he said.

It took Nijam a moment to understand what he meant. Then she choked. "You cannot mean that Voice inside you!"

"What harm could it do?" he protested. "Either it is only a figment of my own mind, as you say, and it will tell us nonsense. Or it is something *Else,* and it may lie to us. But for that we will be prepared, and even its lies may tell us something."

He had anticipated and answered her arguments even before she had made them. Nijam said in a dull voice, "You don't think that it's a figment, do you? You think that Miss Dark is correct."

"And that is why we *must* question it," he agreed.

There was a stained and dented steel table at the centre of the room, with little gutters down either side of it, which Schmidt knew without quite knowing how had seen a great many dead bodies. Perhaps he and Nijam had worked at this table together, draining blood and extracting organs from the bodies of the dead unfortunates who were to be changed into revenants!

"Here," he said. "There are restraints. You must fasten me down. This way I will not hurt you if I am unable to control the Voice."

As he laid himself on the table, Nijam seemed unable to tear her eyes away from the thick leathern straps at each corner, so reminiscent of the ones in Dr Schwab's laboratory. "They must have put those there after I left," she muttered. "For the living revenants they made. For *you.*"

Schmidt shuddered as the thick, heavy straps fastened about his limbs and body. For a moment the feeling of impending darkness was stronger than ever. It was a feeling like the one when you have forgotten a word, but can feel it on the tip of your tongue. Then, just as suddenly, it was gone.

"You should have some chloral on hand, just in case," he said, half without thinking. "See if there's some in that cupboard in the corner."

Nijam sent him an astonished look. "You remembered! That's where we used to keep the chloral!"

"Was it? I didn't know," he said. "It was a hunch, nothing

more."

"It's working," Nijam declared, as she went over the cupboard and fetched out a dusty bottle, together with a syringe with which to administer the drug. "Your mind is repairing itself."

But Schmidt felt only despair. He must remember far more than this, if he was to save himself from the Voice.

Nijam drew a strong dose of the drug into the syringe and then placed it carefully on a low trolley beyond Schmidt's reach. "Ready?" she asked.

"Ready," he answered, and drew a deep, quivering breath. He felt as he had on that bridge in Vienna the evening sir's brother had nearly caught them, in the moment before he had leaped into the dark and distant water of the river. With the difference that at that moment he could not have imagined how cold the water would be, and today he recalled with ghastly clarity what it was like to be under the Voice's mastery.

He could still feel the Voice lodged deep inside, nibbling at the edge of his awareness like a black tide at a crumbling shore.

"You," he muttered, looking inward to the darkness. "Who *are* you?"

The thing pushed against his awareness as it did from time to time, attempting to test the barrier of his will. Schmidt opened his eyes. Nijam bent over him, her lips parted slightly in expectation. There was a faint crease between her black brows; for a moment he simply beheld her in a kind of desperation. The lovely smooth warmth of her skin went to his heart like an arrow; the sleek darkness of her hair; the thickness of her lashes, and the delicate symmetry of lips and eyes...

"You are so beautiful," he whispered, because he did not know whether he would ever have the chance to say it again. Then with a sigh, because he would lose his nerve if he waited any longer, he let down his guard. And the Voice came roaring in.

* * *

One moment it was her own loving Alphonse gazing at her out of those gentle blue eyes; and then Nijam gasped as all the warmth and life went out of them, like a candle that has been snuffed. At the same moment Alphonse's face distorted in a snarl; he lunged against his restraints, teeth snapping, as though he wished to bite the nose from her face.

Nijam started back with a gasp. The Voice roared at her without words. For a moment she could say or do nothing, such was the shock of seeing so much rage and frenzy on a face that had always been so kind and gentle. The thought occurred to her that perhaps Alphonse was right; that this was perhaps what he had always been, deep down, just as the laboratory had always been an unholy temple; that nothing she had thought she had known was true.

The thought lasted only a moment before Nijam recoiled with a sound of horror. She fell back to the trolley where the syringe lay and raised it with a shaking hand, lest the creature break free.

But the straps held; and after a moment the Voice relinquished its struggle and allowed Alphonse to lie panting for a moment. Then Nijam approached the table. The cold light of his eyes, so like those of a revenant, fixed upon her. The Voice snarled again.

"Lie still," Nijam said, still feeling sick and a little faint. There were already purple welts upon Alphonse's wrists, but the Voice paid no heed to her, only snapping and growling at her.

It was taken quite by surprise when Nijam hitched up her skirts, put a boot on a nearby stool, and scrambled up onto the table. She knew she was neither particularly heavy nor strong, but she thought that all her weight on his chest might make the Voice think again, if the sight of the needle did not.

"Behave yourself and answer my questions, or I'll put you back to sleep," she told the Voice firmly.

Alphonse's body ceased to struggle, although she could feel it quivering like a harp-string beneath her.

"Good," Nijam said. Dimly she felt aware that she had frozen a thin crust of anger over a deep, swift-flowing river of terror that would sweep her away if she allowed that ice to crack. "You heard the question. What are you, and what do you want?"

"I am Yammu," the Voice growled, hurling the name like a weapon. "There is none like me!"

"There is none like Alphonse Schmidt, either," Nijam said, but once again she felt a little sick. *Yammu*—that was one of the words Dr Schwab had intoned last night before the change came over Alphonse. "What are you doing in his mind?"

"Let me out," snarled the Voice—Yammu. "Let me free, and you shall see what I do when I am in it no longer!"

"So long as you're trying to bite my head off, I've no reason to let you free," Nijam said. "But if you'll listen nicely and answer his questions, I'll reconsider injecting you with this chloral."

There was a moment's silence. "And how am I certain that you will keep your word?"

"You'll have to trust me," she replied.

The Voice tried to throw her off; Nijam set the needle against his neck, letting a drop of blood well, and he stilled again. For a moment the man gasped and sobbed; and then his eyes cleared. He was Alphonse again.

Tenderly, Nijam touched his cheek. Tears sprang to his eyes at her touch, but he did not speak to her.

"Yammu," said Alphonse Schmidt in a hoarse voice. "What, precisely, *are* you?"

"A god!" The Voice that now spoke was a roar. "Long ago my brethren and I roamed the earth, and all feared and loved us! For years beyond count you have believed us dead. We do but sleep! The time is near now when we shall awaken—when we shall feed!"

"Then we have little incentive to release you, have we?" Nijam asked.

Yammu replied with a stream of syllables in his own hideous speech. "Do not be foolish! To those who serve me I shall give the right to continue living, and to rule over their fellows! That is worth much!"

"We'll consider it," Alphonse said, taking back the command of his own lips with an apparent effort. "How do you propose we should separate?"

Yammu laughed, low and malevolent. "What is the word you mortals use for it these days? *Consciousness-transference*—yes, that is it."

"Transference to *what?*" Nijam demanded.

"A body!—Find me another body."

"How did you get this one?"

"He offered it to me, the fool!" Yammu snarled: a horrible and unaccustomed expression on Alphonse's face. "He *invited* me!"

Nijam gave a snarl of her own. "And I am to—what—feed a slice of Schmidt's brain to someone else? How will he survive that?"

Yammu only laughed.

"Out of the question," Nijam said, through numb lips. "I'll find another way." And she went to inject the chloral.

Yammu snarled again and tore at Alphonse's restraints. A loud snap echoed through the laboratory—then another. One crushing hand fastened about Nijam's throat just as she slid the needle into Schmidt's vein and depressed the plunger. The other grasped at the table and heaved. The whole world up-ended. Nijam landed on her back on the flagstoned floor; the next moment Yammu threw off the table and made a tigerish leap upon her.

Already the drug was impeding Alphonse's movements. Yammu made another grab, but his hand missed her throat. Leaning forward onto Alphonse's bruised knuckles, he spoke in a slurred, almost drunken voice.

"You cannot keep us caged forever," Yammu said. "Your world *belongs* to us. You mortals will have what you want— and what you want is power and terror and worship. We will return, and bring with us the ancient reign of blood. You shall revel; you shall feast; you shall become vessels for me and my kindred. And all the world shall—shall—worship."

As the last of those unholy words slurred from the lips of Alphonse Schmidt, his eyes drooped and closed. All the strength went out of him; and his slack body fell upon hers.

For a long, terrifying moment, Nijam did not breathe at all. Then she did. It sounded to her ears uncomfortably like a sob.

Chapter IX.

Mimi found Nijam some minutes later still fruitlessly trying to extract herself from beneath the weight of Alphonse's body.

"You appear to be stuck," Mimi said, bending gracefully down to peer at the flattened inventor. She put a finger on Schmidt's pulse to satisfy herself that he was alive, if unconscious. "What *happened?*"

"Aren't you going to help?" Nijam gasped. "I can't get any leverage with him like this."

Nijam subsisted mostly on peppermints and did not believe in leaving her laboratory if she could help it. Alphonse was a muscular young man who amused himself with Swedish dumb-bell exercises four times a week. Mimi was not much over five feet and commensurately dainty, but years of dancing had strengthened her: in heaving Schmidt aside she did not even lose her breath. Thus liberated, Nijam sat up reflecting that she had been caught at a disadvantage; it was a peculiar and undignified sensation, and she did not like it.

"Vasily sent me," Mimi said, darting a glance towards the capsized table and broken restraints. "The Black Templars will meet tonight at our house, and he says we must be there. Have you been crying?"

Nijam, who had been rubbing at her eyes, now hastily put

121

her damp sleeve behind her. "He crushed the air out of me," she said, brusquely.

"You *have* been crying," Mimi insisted. "What happened?"

Nijam stared at the unconscious Alphonse. "I don't know how to fix him," she muttered. "I could have warned him to refuse that ghastly ritual. Now he has a creature living inside his head, which says that it is an ancient deity, and that there's no way to extract it without killing Alphonse."

"I see," Mimi said. "Why not invent a gadget? It's worked every other time. And now: how are we going to get him home? Should we call Vasily?"

Nijam blinked. "No," she said. "I might in fact *have* a gadget for that. Let me see—it ought to be in this cupboard."

The gadget was indeed where she had left it. Mimi whistled as she opened the cupboard door and whisked off the dust-sheet which had protected the contraption within.

"Is that—"

"Yes, it is," Nijam said with pride. "One of my first inventions. Crude, but promising. Let us see whether it still works."

Ten minutes later the three of them were home again—not without some odd looks from the students and lecturers who, at regular intervals throughout the day, could be found rushing from one lecture to another through the narrow streets. "Look after Schmidt, will you?" Nijam asked, once she and Mimi had settled him into his bed. "Yes, Vasily, I know there's no room in the house for this contraption; will you take it back to the laboratory? I have something else to see to."

With that, she made her escape.

At the Schwab house, I happened to be snooping in the study when I heard the knock at the door, and in the same moment, my transmitter crackled.

"Dark, it's me," Nijam told me, a little breathless. "I want to have a look at the *Codex.*"

"You know that it's not in English," I said, as I answered the door. "It might not even be in Hindoostanee."

She sailed past me, evidently undaunted. "All I need is an Ancient Syriac grammar, and I'm sure Schwab has one of those."

"Nijam," Mimi cut in from her own transmitter. "Schmidt is awake. He's asking for you."

Nijam's resolute look faltered. "I can't, Mimi," she said. "Not until I have some answers. Molly will go instead."

"He doesn't want *me,*" I objected. But I could not ignore the pleading look Nijam sent me. "Oh, very well—I hid the book beneath Dr Auberlen. Try not to let the children run amok."

With that I let myself out the door, and Nijam was left alone in the house. My last remark struck her as somewhat ominous, but there was no sign of any children, running amok or otherwise. She hurried down the trap-door in the study and quickly found the *Codex* where I had left it. The book, of course, made no impression upon Nijam's insensitive soul. She placed it on a bench, quickly located the *Grammar of Ancient Syriac* in the ruins of the glass-fronted shelf beside Dr Auberlen, and drew up a seat to commence her study.

That was when she saw the two children watching her from the stair. For a moment they beheld each other in silence.

"Did Fräulein Dark send you?" whispered the little girl.

"Yes," said Nijam.

"Do you want to help us catch flies for Aunt Dete?" asked the little girl. The little boy raised a small glass jar with a perforated lid, in which reposed an unusually large house spider.

"No," said Nijam. "Do you know any other games?"

Their faces lit up. "Yes, lots!" the girl said. "Our favourite is called Murder in the Dark!"

"Good," Nijam said, putting on her pince-nez. "Go and play it. If you disturb my study, I'll dose you with cod-liver oil, and you shall go to bed without any supper."

This had a dampening effect upon them; they took themselves off, and their spider. I do not think they did play Murder in the Dark, which is raucous and requires more than two participants, but they did play very nicely by themselves for the rest of the afternoon. Say what you like about Nijam, she certainly has a way with children.

Nijam, however, sat looking at the *Codex* in black despair. She could not get the image out of her head of Alphonse thrashing upon the table, shouting imprecations. An old god—that was what the Voice claimed to be. She thought of the raven in the cellars of the Paris Opera. It was possible, she acknowledged, for a spirit to subdue and inhabit another body. And it seemed possible—perhaps even likely—that this was what had happened to Alphonse.

At this thought a deep blackness fell upon her.

This was a trouble beyond her ability to understand—still less, to cure. Likely Alphonse was right, and Nijam was too late to find the solution. He had given his consent and could no longer retract it. Against such a creature he was too weak to save himself.

But then, *she* was too weak to save him, either.

It was her fault. All those years ago, she should have acted differently. She should have looked behind the blackboard. She should have taken and read Auberlen's journals when he used to leave them unattended in the lab. She should have *known,* and then she might have warned Alphonse.

But she had closed her eyes. She was allowed the use of the lab. so long as she asked no questions, and that had been enough for her.

Nijam sat in a welter of shame, regretting everything she had ever done.

I, meanwhile, went to sit at Schmidt's bedside. He had awoken in his right mind, which was a mercy.

"You should go," he whispered, clinging to my hand like a drowning man. "It isn't safe. I can feel it all the time, trying to—trying to get *in.*"

"You seem well in command of yourself *now,*" I told him gently. "How did you manage it? Did you tell the Voice it had to let you back in?"

"No. Nijam injected me with chloral, and when I awoke I was myself again."

"There," I said. "That proves it! The thing isn't able to use you without your consent. If so it would have been back in control when you awoke. You have the upper hand!"

"It doesn't *feel* like it," he muttered.

Alphonse looked very pitiful and almost childish, huddled into his bed like a frightened child. It was all wrong, I thought, that this big, steady, gentle man should suffer so much, when he had always been so ready with a smile or a word of comfort or an application of fists whenever any of us needed it.

And that was the trouble with him, wasn't it? I could understand that; I had had something of the same trouble myself.

"Sometimes in order to do justice, we must learn to fight for ourselves," I told him gently. "I know it's hard when we've been told all our lives that it's selfish to do so. But there comes a time when we may be the properest ones to do it. That was something I had to learn, too."

Poor Schmidt! He made only a faint murmur in response, and I did not know whether I had been as comforting as I wished to be. So I did not speak again. Because it was Christmas, and because he looked so very tired, I began to sing.

> *Stille Nacht, heilige Nacht,*
> *Alles schläft; einsam wacht*
> *Nur das traute hochheilige Paar.*
> *Holder Knabe im lockigen Haar,*
> *Schlaf in himmlischer Ruh!*
> *Schlaf in himmlischer Ruh!*

Before the end of the song Alphonse had slipped away into sleep—real, healing, comforting sleep, such as he had been too frightened to take all that long, chill night in the old castle. "Indeed," said I, as I rose to leave him, "sleep in heavenly peace, Alphonse Schmidt!"

* * *

"May God forgive me for the nonsense I am about to speak," Vasily murmured under his breath.

Evening had come, and with it the meeting of the Black Templars. Vasily had prepared the house for this event by helping himself to the throne, and the banner, which had hung in the Schwab house on the previous night. These had been moved to the drawing-room of our own headquarters, where they clashed violently with the mood set by the chintz sofa-lounge. Vasily had further accessorised the setting by positioning Nijam and myself, in robes and hoods with the latter drawn down low to conceal our faces, to either side of himself. We looked, I flatter myself, extremely impressive. As for Vasily, he himself lolled with magnificent abandon upon the throne, looking thoroughly bad and wicked.

"Nonsense it may be, but mind you speak it convincingly," Nijam said. The first knock at the door had come, and Mimi, got up as a maid, had gone to answer it. Schmidt was upstairs awaiting his own cue. "We can't have these people getting in our way."

"Don't be *too* convincing," I put in, feeling a little anxious. Vasily might find the notion of being the leader of a secret society a little too enjoyable.

Nijam sent me a severe look, but was too late to scold me as no doubt she would have liked to do. Instead the drawing-room door opened, and Mimi ushered in the Black Templars.

It seemed that nearly all of them had arrived in a body, with Griff and Brother Otto at the head of them. Advancing into the room, Otto folded his arms and sent Vasily a resentful look.

"What's the meaning of this?" he demanded. "We were summoned by the Master's signet. Where is he? Why are *you,* an initiate of the lowest rank, in the Master's chair?"

"That's an excellent question, Brother Otto," said Vasily, very smoothly. "In fact, the Master gave me his signet and appointed me his deputy for the evening. He is in hospital—a very sad business. Broken ribs, you know."

"What did he say?" Griff asked Otto. "Why can't he speak English?"

Vasily cleared his throat. "I am familiar with the English

language," he said, mildly. "Brother Otto here wishes to know why *I* am the Master's deputy, and not himself."

Some of the other Templars gave Otto suspicious looks. I resisted the urge to laugh. Vasily had identified the doctor's favourite, and marked him out to the others.

"I think that if the doctor is going to be out of commission, we ought to vote on his replacement," Griff said, becoming at once the hopeful American politician. "And I trust you'll vote for me, gentlemen. We achieved something remarkable last night. We can put that success to work and make more success from it. It's true that the test subject escaped us, but I'm confident I can lay my hands on him at any moment. I've got the money, and I've got the grit, to carry this thing through. We're going to spread immortality around the world, gentlemen."

Griff had manifestly not completed his speech; but he paused for effect, and this was his downfall. Vasily cleared his throat gently and interrupted.

"Oh, no," he said. *"That* would never do. Immortality is a secret of this order, and that lays a great responsibility upon us, doesn't it? We don't want *everyone* living forever. Imagine what would happen if the Jews had eternal life—or the anarchists!"

Mutterings from among the ranks, some of them dubious, some of them approving. A shout of "Hear, hear!"

Griff reddened—the most colour I had ever seen in his lifeless grey face. "Well, naturally we don't want *everyone* getting immortality," he said. "Certainly not the criminal elements, or the Negroes. But a *little* Jewish blood has got to be all right."

"Why?" Vasily asked. *"You* don't happen to have Jewish

blood, do you, Vandergriff?"

"So what if I do?" Griff replied, turning redder still.

Vasily said nothing; but he sat back magisterially in his chair, with an expression that seemed to ask, *What more could be said?*

The Black Templars muttered among themselves. I heard those who understood English explaining to their fellows in German whispers. The mood in the room became chilly; they drew themselves back from Griff as though his presence might contaminate them. I felt a little chilly myself, and sorry for our stratagem, which had worked so well. Jews had been treated with disdain and suspicion in Vienna, too, when I worked there.

"This is ridiculous," Griff blustered. "I can provide this society with far more resources than Dunkel can! I can't help who my grandmother was!"

Brother Otto cleared his throat. "Really, Vandergriff, you should have known to disclose something like *this.*"

"I'm afraid we must ask you to leave," Vasily said, in his lordliest tones. "The future must be German." And he rang the bell for Mimi.

Griff ground his teeth together. "Don't be duped," he announced loudly. "This man, who calls himself Herr Dunkel, is an imposter and a thief! When I met him in Hong Kong he was calling himself Basil Nicks!"

"Really!" Vasily retorted at once, laughing. "I might say that when I met you in Odesa you were calling yourself Judas Maccabeus! Good *day,* Herr Vandergriff!"

Some of the Black Templars laughed, and not in a very nice way. Griff ground his teeth. For a moment I was afraid that he might actually seize upon Vasily and throttle him the way he had once seized upon and throttled me in a London tenement. But he must have seen that the current of opinion was against him. He went away, therefore, with a great flounce, leaving one of his little transmitting-bugs in a vase as he went. Apparently he found it easier to bully a woman than he did a room full of men. I took great pleasure in extracting the bug from the vase and grinding it beneath my heel until it was quite useless.

Vasily was now left in undisputed possession of the field. He directed a bland smile at the others in the room and asked, "Has anyone else any undesirable ancestry to disclose?"

There was an uncomfortable silence, and the Black Templars gave each other dubious looks. But no one spoke, and Vasily straightened with a smile. "Very good," he said. "It appears that the secret of immortality is safe. Now I must tell you that there is good news. I have recovered the test subject, Alphonse Schmidt; he is at this moment resting upstairs. The consciousness-transference experiment was a success. Schmidt's body now plays host to two personalities."

The Black Templars raised a cheer, and Vasily paused to allow a flood of excited chatter.

"When we're immortal, we shall have no trouble putting down the anarchists, and the communists, and the suffragettes!" I heard one of them declare.

"England and Russia must look to their colonies," said another. "We shall be the masters of Africa and India!"

Glancing at Nijam, I saw that her gloved hands were clasped very tightly before her. I did not think that she liked this talk, so far as it concerned the continued subjugation of both her sex and her people. I did not like it myself. I was not entirely sure that I wanted the vote; but I was absolutely certain that I did not like the gloating way these men spoke of maintaining their privileges over my sex. And I felt more than ever that we have made a mistake. Vasily had not *given* these men their disdain for anyone dissimilar to themselves; but he had, in a few words, made it possible for them to voice their opinions, and thus to act upon them.

Well! it was only a few dozen German intellectuals, I reassured myself. What harm could they do?

One of the Black Templars stood unmoved by the general enthusiasm, his arms folded. "You found Alphonse Schmidt, did you?" sneered Brother Otto. "How busy you have been! But where is he? Prove that you really have him!"

"Of course," Vasily declared, arising from his throne. "Follow me!"

Nijam and I attended him upstairs with the rest of the group following. I wished fervently that my sisters had been there to enjoy the spectacle, for it was as much as I could do not to laugh aloud. Here were Vasily, Nijam, and I pacing solemnly at the head of a procession of sinister black-robed figures through a charming little German town-house all done up in gay chintz and sentimental water-colours.

"Here we are," Vasily declared, pausing before Schmidt's door. "I will ask, gentlemen, that you allow *me* to converse with the patient; we don't want to overwhelm him with questions."

With that, he opened the door.

Nijam had, as promised, affixed a gate of iron bars to the inside of Schmidt's door. This remained locked in place despite the opening of the door. Beyond this screen Alphonse was visible. He was not in bed, where I had left him; nor was he pacing about and roaring like a lion, as he had been instructed to do for the edification of the Black Templars. Instead he stood upon the bed with a shard of glass in his hand from the tumbler which lay smashed upon the floor. He was frantically scratching marks into the paint and plaster of the wall—a peculiar mixture of German and hieroglyphics, numbers and nonsensical diagrams, daubed here and there with smears of blood from where the glass had cut his hand. All the time he muttered, feverishly, in a low growl.

Whatever Vasily had been about to say died on his lips. Nijam stepped forward. "Alphonse!" she growled; in her place I should not have had the presence of mind to disguise my voice. Poor Alphonse turned with a snarl and we all saw that once again the ghastly Voice—Yammu—had the upper hand of him. His eyes gleamed with cold malice, and there was something almost bestial in the bared teeth and hunched shoulders with which he watched us.

"It's true!" Brother Otto breathed. "Success at last!"

"Yammu hag sithmugsk," intoned one of the Black Templars, reverently.

Vasily looked rather green, but he forced a smile. "The—er—the other personality is uppermost at present," he said, "and already working on future experiments, as you can see! I may say, a very remarkable…success."

And then, as though he could no longer bear the sight of poor Alphonse in the possession of that hideous Voice, he slammed the door again. At that, a murmur of disappointment ran through the assembled scholars. But Vasily seemed better able to perform his part with Alphonse no longer in view.

"Gentlemen," he said, "although Schmidt there is busy working on new hypotheses, there are still gaps in our knowledge—problems which Auberlen and Stefan Schmidt resolved in their own researches. For this reason, and to keep our secret from falling into the wrong hands. I propose that we should retrieve the Auberlen papers from Imperial custody." I sent him a startled glance, but he went on: "In fact, gentlemen, I propose to rob the Heidelberg University Library."

I expected this to meet with a decidedly chilly response. Instead, the Black Templars absolutely cheered. "It's about time!" said one old gentleman with a snort of indignation. "It must have been some anarchist, or some suffragist, who ordered those papers locked up, lest the revenants be brought back! To think that the Imperial Government should have been infiltrated by such traitors!"

To this startlingly unproven theory, the others gave enthusiastic approval. "Let us go at once," said another of them. "Should I bring my revolver?"

"No! No!" Vasily said, half laughing, over the eager chorus that now filled the hallway. "No weapons, and no rushing off without a plan. This is not the *Charge of the Light Brigade*, gentlemen! Go home and await my orders, and anyone who takes a single step without my—or without the Master's—personal direction shall be drummed out of the Order."

He held out the heavy, glimmering silver thing which he had got from Dr Schwab at the hospital—the signet-ring of the Order. One by one each of them kissed it, even a scowling Brother Otto. Then Nijam and I herded them out the front door; shot the bolt behind them, and took a deep breath—not precisely with relief. There was, after all, Alphonse to think of.

As Nijam bolted up the stairs, Mimi emerged from the kitchen.

"What's wrong?" she asked me.

"It's poor Alphonse," I said, already hard on Nijam's heels.

"I think he's fallen to the Voice again."

"What! How?" Mimi demanded. I could not tell her that. A moment later we reached the top of the stairs and found Vasily at Alphonse's door, which once again he had opened.

Our poor friend was still hard at work adding a rather disturbing set of occult symbols to the wallpaper.

"Chloral!" Nijam hissed, digging into her pockets. "I knew I would need it!"

Even as she fumbled for her vial of the drug, Vasily spoke in a voice like a bugle.

"Schmidt, you lazy fellow! Why are you loitering in bed? Why haven't you blacked my shoes? Why haven't you tidied my room? Socks littered about everywhere—it's a disgrace!"

Alphonse turned with a start. There was a clatter as the shard of glass fell from his bloodied hand. "Yes, sir! At once, sir!"

I cannot deny that a sob rose to my throat as I saw the madness in a moment dissipate from his honest blue eyes.

"Sir!" Alphonse cried again, as his situation dawned upon him. He looked at the writing on the wall. Then his knees gave way, and he fell to the bed, burying his face in his hands.

Nijam turned upon Vasily with flashing eyes. She looked magnificent—and so murderous that Vasily quailed a step backwards.

"How *dare* you?" she cried. "Black your shoes? I'll black your eye!"

"Don't," Alphonse gasped. "He saved me. Oh, I was lost!"

Nijam turned her fury upon her lover. "Didn't I tell you to save yourself?" she demanded. "What did you do to give it your consent, *this* time?"

"Nothing!" he protested. "It's as I told you—I gave my

consent once, and now there is nothing I can do!"

Perhaps no other words would have as effectively silenced Nijam. She stared at him, the fury slowly giving way to terror. "He took charge of you against your *will?*"

"He's getting stronger," Alphonse said. Rising from the bed, he approached the door. "Soon I won't be able to hold him back at all. If I'm lost—"

"No," Nijam said. She gripped the bars and held them until her knuckles went white.

Alphonse's enormous hand closed upon hers. "If I am lost," he repeated, "promise me that you will destroy this body. Better that I should perish, and not the world."

Nijam trembled. "No," she repeated. "No, never."

"My love." He reached through the bars as though to caress her cheek. But Nijam turned her back to him. In the dim gaslight of the corridor, she fixed each of us in turn—Vasily, Mimi, and myself—with a ferocious scowl.

Her voice was little more than a whisper.

"I am better able to destroy the world with my own hands than I am to stand by and let one hair of his head be harmed," she declared. "I warn you now. Raise a hand against Alphonse Schmidt, and I will *break* it."

I do not think that any one of us was able to draw breath, so masterful was her warning gaze. Not until she turned her attention again upon Alphonse.

"You will find a way," she told him. "You *must.*"

And then, without another look at the three of us, she went down the stairs.

Chapter X.

It took us a moment to recover our breath. Then Mimi called after Nijam, "Wait! We must make plans!"

"Downstairs," Nijam proclaimed. Mimi hurried after her, and Vasily and I were left with a rather horrified-looking Alphonse.

"Sir," he began, but Vasily put a comforting hand on his.

"She's right," Vasily said. "You'll get the better of this thing, old fellow. I have every faith in you."

We left him shaking his head and went downstairs to the drawing-room. Here we found Nijam sitting in a softly-upholstered armchair with her fingertips pressed together, scowling into the grate. Either she or Mimi had torn down the sinister banner and left it in a heap upon the wooden throne, which now stood empty. Impressive though it appeared, it was not at all comfortable.

"First of all," Nijam said almost before we had closed the door behind us, "what did you mean, Vasily, by dragging the Jews into it?"

"It's no use crying over a dead horse," I put in, "but I'm not looking forward to explaining it to Herr Haber." I put in. Franz Haber, the gentleman who financed our activities, had asked me to provide him with reports of all our doings. He also happened to be Jewish himself.

"Oh, that!" Vasily shrugged. "My dear, I don't suppose you thought I *meant* it? Only we *did* agree that we ought to gain command of the Black Templars, if we could, during the doctor's absence."

"Was there not some other way of doing it?" I asked. Of course such talk was quite common, and not merely in Germany. Most people thought nothing of such remarks, but I had been in the Jewish cemetery in Vienna, and had seen in the unquiet imprints of the dead the ghastly results of such talk.

"I don't think there was," said Vasily. "I know how to handle these people, you know. The only way to do it is to make yourself more extreme than they are; and then you become someone they look up to. They won't listen if they think you've gone soft."

"It isn't wise," Nijam said, with a scowl. "Or safe. The problem with starting a train is that sooner or later, it ends up arriving at the next station."

"If there is a train on the track at all, then someone is bound to start it—whether Vasily or someone else," Mimi put in. "What *I* want to know is this. Why are they helping us to rob the library? Don't you think that I am capable?"

"My dear Mimi, I have every confidence in you," Vasily said. "But you know what they say about many hands! Stealing from a library is a risky business, because the take is so unwieldy. We may need to move a great number of books very quickly; and then we shall be glad of help."

Mimi pouted, but Nijam shrugged. "I will allow it," she said. "We want all of Auberlen's journals, and he left fifty years' worth behind him when he died. And we want Stefan's, too.

Mimi, you and I must go to the library tomorrow; it's high time we located those papers."

With that the meeting broke up. Mimi went upstairs to let Schmidt out of his cage for a bite of supper, and I reluctantly turned down Vasily's offer of mulled wine and *lebkuchen,* as it was high time I returned to the Schwab house. Vasily satisfied himself by escorting me to the hallway and wrapping me up tenderly in my old woollen coat.

"There!" he said, buttoning the coat high beneath my chin. "Now you will not freeze in the street!"

"Don't be silly," I said, but my thoughts were not on Vasily. "What do *you* think of Schmidt's request?"

The laughter in his eyes dimmed. "To kill him, you mean?"

"Hush—yes! I noticed you said nothing at all."

"How could I, with Nijam vowing blood and vengeance if I so much as tweaked his nose?" Vasily shrugged. "It's as I said before, Molly-my-love. I can't kill people any more. It isn't good for me."

"But if he's right—if that thing inside him can hurt all of us?"

"He is right, of course," said Vasily, with a heavy sigh. "In his place I should do no differently. But I would sooner cut my own throat than his."

He looked so unhappy that I kissed him good-night to cheer him up, and the next minute passed so agreeably that I feared he might disarrange my hair.

"That's enough," I said at length, attempting to disentangle myself.

"But it's Christmas," he said, plaintively.

"It may be Christmas, but I still draw the line at going out into the street with my hair down," I said. "People don't stop peering out their windows and gossiping just because it's

Christmas, you know!"

Vasily made a thoughtful face. "I suppose not," he said. "Still, do you think we ought to deprive them of their fun? It *is* Christmas, after all!"

I sighed. "What am I going to do with you?" I asked, peering into the mirror to make sure that I was presentable.

"I might make some suggestions," he said, wickedly. "You *did* say you were not averse to marrying me."

I stilled, watching him in the glass. There it was again—that flippancy with which he cloaked his feelings. Did he not trust me enough to be plain and honest? We had shown each other the worst of ourselves, after all.

But then, I should have to be plain and honest with *him.* If he asked me honestly, would I be able to say yes? Or would I have to admit that I was plainly terrified of how real and earnest this had become?

My stillness caught his eye, and I forced myself to smile. Perhaps we were both a little terrified. Perhaps it was only natural to fear such a momentous decision.

Perhaps, for now, I need not say anything at all.

So I only said lightly: "You'll have to take your place in line—for Griff wants me to marry him, too."

In the glass, I saw Vasily wrinkle his nose. "You wouldn't marry Griff if he was the last man on earth."

"That is precisely what I told him."

With my hat pinned on, the state of my hair was not too bad. I stared at the flyaway strands and imagined with a shudder what it might be like to marry Griff, who had chosen to cut off his own hands. Now one of them was made of metal; it could be extended or retracted at will. The other seemed still clothed in flesh, but a blade was hidden within the forearm; it took only a certain flick of the wrist, and the weapon would spring from its hiding-place.

As marvellous as those hands were, I wondered whether they could still feel anything—the warmth of another person's skin, or the silk of her hair. Such hands would not marvel, as Vasily's did, at the softness of hair or the smoothness of a cheek. They had been turned into weapons, and one could only fear them.

Vasily's arm—warm, living, and human—stole about my waist. "What a serious look! Are you thinking of your ne'er-do-well lover?"

"No, indeed!" I smiled up at him. "I was imagining how horrible it might be, to be touched by a man who has cut off the feeling in his own hands."

Vasily understood at once what I meant.

"Griff has cut off the feeling in his own heart," he said, "and that is a greater sin."

That made me laugh despite myself. "What mush!"

Vasily muttered something about the pot calling the kettle black.

"By the way," I added, remembering something that I had forgotten. "What about the veiled lady who called on you this morning? What did she want?"

"Nothing that you ought to worry yourself about, my sweet. My heart will always be yours."

"Worry about *you*? Don't flatter yourself," I said. "Only she was loitering outside the Schwab house when I passed with the children, and I thought she took some interest in them."

"She did. Schmidt opened the door to her; he said that she asked who the children were, and who *you* were, and whether I was a friend of the doctor's. And he, like the cautious fellow he is, asked who *she* was. Whereupon she hurried away without answering."

"H'm," I said, thoughtfully.

"H'm," he agreed.

"We must look into her more closely," I said. "Tell me if you catch a glimpse of her again."

With that I managed to tear myself away, but my evening was not yet over. I had climbed the steps to the doctor's door when something moved in the deep shadows beside the stoop.

I let out a gasp. Then the figure moved again and I saw that it was Alphonse, which on some other occasion might have been a comfort. Tonight, my first thought was that that creature—Yammu, or the Voice, whichever one liked to call him—had gained the ascendancy. I recoiled and might have toppled from the step altogether, had a steadying hand not arrested my fall.

"Miss Dark," he whispered hoarsely. "It's me—Alphonse!"

"What are you doing here?" I demanded, regaining my equilibrium.

"I know I ought not to be," he said, which was not quite what I meant. "Only I wanted to speak to you. Listen, Miss Dark: there's something inside me that means to tear the world apart, and I've given it charge of me, and no one knows how to get it out. I know that Miss Nijam means well, but I am in earnest. Promise me—if there's no hope, if this thing can be stopped in no other way—promise me that you will kill me."

His hand, still tight on my arm, increased its crushing grip. I smothered another gasp—this time, of pain.

"Please, Alphonse," I whispered. "You're not yourself."

He released me abruptly. "I'm sorry," he said, full of remorse. "Now I've hurt you—but, God in heaven! Can't you understand? I am myself *now,* and *now* I am begging you to help me. Don't let me become this creature's instrument of destruction!"

I thought of Vasily, saying that he had shed too much blood to make himself Schmidt's executioner, and I could have cried with vexation.

"I cannot kill you! I cannot even kill a sick kitten! Why do you ask *me?*"

"I ask you because you are the only one I can trust," he said, heavily. "You are the only one who will do what is right, regardless of the cost. Please, Miss Dark."

I let out a laugh. The cost! Yes—the cost was likely to be high indeed, for if I did anything to hurt the man she loved, Nijam would have her revenge on me, I was sure of it!

But, like Vasily, I understood his request. In his place, I, too, would sacrifice myself for the fate of the world. Alphonse only asked me to do what he might not be capable of doing of his own volition.

Yet Nijam's objection, too, I could understand. With his mind set on self-immolation, would Schmidt forget to fight for himself, as he was entitled to do?

"If there is *truly* no other way," I began, but Alphonse raised a hand, cutting off my words.

"On second thought, don't," he said. "Promise yourself, but not me. I don't want *him* to know."

Slowly, I nodded. Alphonse took my hand and pressed a kiss to it; a moment later he was gone.

I stood a while shivering on the doorstep, my heart heavy with what I had said, and what I must leave unsaid. I could confide in no one about this—not Vasily, upon whom it would lay too great a burden, and certainly not Nijam. There was

Mimi—but what was the point? We would never agree to destroy him, and failing that our only hope remained what it had always been: the lost Auberlen papers.

We had no other plan to fall back upon; and that was not enough for our poor friend. With the liveliest misgivings I took my key and let myself into the house.

* * *

Nijam, Schmidt, and Mimi set out the following afternoon for the University Library, whose main collection was then housed on the Augustinergasse. The morning was grey and cold, as was the slush that lay heaped in the gutters; yet the streets were alive with people. There were young ladies out for walks with their dogs—the people of Heidelberg had a great fondness for dogs, I found—young students in the coloured caps and scarred countenances of the corps lounging about in the cafes and beer-gardens, and every so often a great crowd of the more hard-working students, robes flapping as they pelted from one lecture-hall to the next.

Nijam was surprised, therefore, when Mimi pushed between herself and Alphonse, who had been walking side by side in a glum silence.

"We're being followed," Mimi breathed. "Four men have stuck to our heels ever since the Ziegelgasse. —Don't *look*, Alphonse!"

Alphonse restrained himself with an effort. "The Black Templars?" he asked, in a low, despairing voice.

"No—policemen," Mimi said, "probably English, since they're wearing yachting caps."

"In *Heidelberg?*" Alphonse asked, bewildered.

"That's policemen for you," Mimi said, with a shrug.

"Let's shake them off," Nijam said.

They had approached the Universitatsplatz from the north—a broad, paved square lined by cream-coloured buildings and bare, leafless trees. At present, a few days before Christmas, the square was full of stalls and booths and tall evergreen trees all hung with tinsel and lamps; there were merry-go-rounds and puppet-shows and lucky dips and toy-stalls and other attractions to delight the souls of children. Of course, during the day, the place was all fenced in, and the booths and stalls were emptied out and covered over. Not until late in the afternoon would it come to life—and then the lamps would be lit, and the merry-go-rounds and hurdy-gurdys would begin to play, and the place would be filled with the aroma of every kind of hot, sweet, spiced food.

Nijam spotted a gap in the fence and immediately slipped through. Mimi followed, lithe as a cat; and then they had to help Alphonse, who was neither so slender, nor so agile. The four men behind them pretended not to notice; but once our friends had taken shelter within a mulled-wine booth, the policemen broke into a run and assailed the fence themselves.

One appeared to be a stolid, bowler-hatted English bourgeois; the others included a man in a yachting-cap, another in lederhosen, and a third in a flat cloth cap and neckerchief that would have marked him out as a factory-worker had he not been a little too well-nourished. Evidently Mimi had exaggerated. Only one of them was a yachtsman, but all of them looked distinctly out of place in this land-locked university town.

"Well," said Nijam, when the "yachtsmen" had wormed their way through the fence and gone stealthily past their hiding-place. "You were right, Mimi; they are certainly looking for us. Stay hidden, Alphonse, and let them tire themselves out. They'll never find us among all these stalls."

But Alphonse was not watching the pursuit; he was gazing up at a great neoclassical facade on the far side of the square. It was done in cream and pink, with a tiled roof the shape of a candle-snuffer and reddish pilasters with gilded capitals. "The University of Heidelberg!" he breathed, in a kind of awe. "To think that this has been here for more than six hundred years!"

"As a matter of fact, that's the student prison," Nijam said. "The University Hall is behind us."

"They wrote the Heidelberg Catechism in this city," Alphonse added, overlooking this interjection. *"What is your only comfort in life and death? —That I am not my own, but belong with body and soul, both in life and in death, to my faithful Saviour Jesus Christ. He has fully paid for all my sins with his precious blood, and has set me free from all the power of the devil."*

Nijam could not resist raising her eyes to the heavens. "There's your problem, Alphonse Schmidt," she said. "You don't believe you belong to yourself, and you keep giving charge of yourself to other people."

Poor Alphonse seemed to be utterly quashed by this. "Well," he murmured, *"I* found it comforting."

Nijam felt the bite of conscience, but she did not apologise; she felt quite certain that she was in the right. "I think we have lost the policemen," she observed. "Let us continue."

"They are looking for me," Alphonse said, as they emerged from the mulled-wine stall and slipped through the fence again. "I should not have come. I am only a burden."

"If that were so, I should have left you at home," Nijam said.

145

"As it is, you're absolutely necessary to the library job; you're our best hope of getting Mimi in to map the place. Come along—and do keep an eye out for those policemen, Mimi."

She set off at a brisk pace, touching her transmitter to inform Vasily and myself that they were being followed, and by whom.

"Let us know if you need help," Vasily told them. We had, of course, laid plans for the inevitable appearance of the gendarmerie. "We can come to collect you at any moment."

"Don't bother," Nijam said. "We've shaken them off for the present and I'm far more worried about Alphonse's Voice than a few masquerading policemen."

She shut off her transmitter, but Mimi was not so confident. "We don't know for certain," she muttered, "that what we want is here in the Augustinergasse at all! And that Yammu creature has been making itself a very great nuisance."

Nijam sighed. She was satisfied with her own assessment of the risk; she did not need Mimi checking her figures, so to speak. "The library's collections are so great that they are spread out across a number of buildings in the town, just as the University itself is. I think we can get the Head Librarian, old Karl Zangemeister, to tell us which building we want; but he's more likely to tell Schmidt than either you or me."

Mimi shrugged. "If it's trousers we need, *I* could try wearing some."

"She's right," Alphonse added, sombrely. "Yammu is getting stronger."

"Then mind *you* are stronger still," Nijam growled. Alphonse simply needed to employ a little willpower, she thought; why couldn't he get that into his head? "I told you that you were necessary. Now pay attention. The library is open only two hours a day, every day but Sunday and public holidays. The borrowing limit is one book. There are a great many rare manuscripts, because each faculty has its own collection of books donated from the libraries of dead and gone doctors. To prevent theft, therefore, bags and coats must be left in the cloak-room."

"What a puzzle!" Mimi observed happily. "Is the cloak-room watched, then?"

"The door to the library is watched," Nijam corrected. "Old Karl has eyes like a hawk. He once caught me trying to smuggle out Mertz's five-volume *Molybdenum* in my pockets."

"He knew you when you were a student?" Alphonse asked, paling.

"He knew you too, and it wasn't reasonable," Nijam said. "A book in five volumes is still one book!"

"But then he'll recognise me as Alphonse Schmidt."

"Oh, yes, he will," Nijam said. "In fact, I'm counting on it."

As Nijam sketched out the further particulars of her plan, they circumnavigated the Universitätplatz and entered the little Augustinergasse that ran between the white University Hall and the Library. This latter was a less ostentatious building, three stories tall and painted white save for red-brick quoins and lintels. Within they entered a dim entrance-hallway, with a door opening into a cloakroom lined with lockers. Here they divested themselves of their coats before continuing to the librarian's alcove which watched the great double door giving onto the Library itself.

A young man sat there scratching with his pen at a great ledger. "Herr Zangemeister?" he repeated, when Nijam questioned him. "He's in Modern Philosophy."

"Busy time of year?" Mimi inquired, levelling an enchanting

smile at the youth.

"Not very," said the assistant librarian. "Some of the students have already gone home for Christmas."

"Excellent," Mimi replied. "I suppose you close shop for the holiday?"

"Christmas Eve and Christmas Day," Nijam put in, impatiently. Now that they were about to find the Auberlen papers in earnest, she could not bear a moment's delay. "Stop chattering, Mimi, and come along!"

Mimi and Schmidt trailed behind as she led the way to Modern Philosophy through dark, towering rows of bookshelves that blocked out what little light straggled in by the windows or glowed through the green-shaded lamps at either end of the great shelves. This was a part of the library Nijam knew only in passing; she did not often concern herself with philosophical questions. But she knew the place well enough to lead the others unerringly to where old Herr Zangemeister stood lifting a great heavy volume of Schopenhauer onto its shelf.

Schmidt hurried ahead and took the book from the old man's shaking hands. Herr Zangemeister peered up at him through his spectacles. The old librarian, Nijam thought, had barely altered with the passage of years—his silvery hair had grown a little more scanty, and his spectacles had grown even thicker, but his manner was as owlishly earnest as ever.

"Bless my soul!" he exclaimed. "It can't be young Alphonse!"

Schmidt had already paid a visit to the library a day or two since, of course; but Nijam had been careful to keep him away from Zangemeister's sharp eyes, signalling him to enter the building only when a younger assistant was watching the door.

"It's true, Herr Zangemeister," she said. "Alphonse Schmidt

has come back to us."

"My dear boy!" the old librarian quavered—for despite his unreasonable adherence to the letter, rather than what Nijam felt to be the spirit, of University law, he had always been a kindly old fellow who knew all the students by name. "My dear boy! They told me you were dead!"

And he threw his arms about the startled Alphonse.

"He is not dead," Nijam said. "Only, well, he has been unfortunate enough to lose his memories. He recalls none of what he learned here."

"Ah! That is a tragedy nearly as bad!" Zangemeister said, dolefully. He held Alphonse out for inspection, tutting. "Ah, Fräulein Nijam, he was one of the most gifted students I have ever seen, and might have been a titan in his field, as you are in yours! But what brings you back, Herr Schmidt? Have you returned to repair what has been lost?"

"In a manner of speaking," Alphonse admitted. "I hoped that returning to my old haunts might help jog some memories free. But I am here to ask a favour for my cousin Wilhelmina."

Mimi, looking frightfully scholarly in Nijam's pince-nez, reached out gravely and shook Zangemeister's hand.

"My cousin is a keen amateur chemist herself," Schmidt added, "and she would dearly love to see the Chemistry collection."

"Indeed," Mimi said, very earnestly. "I have a terrible need to see Mertz's five-volume *Molybdenum*."

"Ha! Well, you wouldn't be the only one," said Zangemeister, with a sharp look at Nijam. "You will find Chemistry upstairs, on the third floor."

"Wilhelmina is even *more* anxious to see the journals of Dr Auberlen," Nijam put in, feeling that Mimi's joke about

Molybdenum was in danger of distracting them from their true goal.

"Ah, yes," Alphonse put in. "I believe his research, and my brother Stefan's, would have been left to the Library?"

"Yes, yes, of course," Zangemeister said, "but I must disappoint you; those records have been sealed. Imperial orders, I'm afraid."

"Why so?" Alphonse asked. "Surely, if there is absolutely no hope of creating more revenants—"

"Hush!" Zangemeister sent a glance to either end of the long shelves; then he lowered his voice. "We don't know for certain that there can be no more revenants, do we? God knows it was tried after the great collapse, but only for a short month or two. Then, as I said, the orders came from Berlin to seal everything up. If this knowledge was spread about, perhaps one of our enemies—France or Russia or Britain—would send spies to the University, and then they might bring back the revenants before we can. And then how shall we fare in the great war?"

Nijam knew that it was rather an article of faith among the Great Powers that each of them was bound to go on growing and becoming more powerful until at last there was nothing left for them to do, but to fight and devour each other in a great war which would prove once and for all which of them was the fittest to survive—and to rule.

It struck her, too, that Schmidt's Voice would rather approve of this than otherwise.

"I'd rather there wasn't a war," she said. "And speaking of that, may I ask you a favour, Herr Zangemeister? Poor Schmidt must lie low these days, for we've had trouble with the French and Russians already trying to snatch him up for what they think is locked in his mind. It's useless, of course, for he doesn't remember any of it. But they are anxious to get their hands on him nevertheless."

"You may depend on me," Zangemeister assured them. "It would be a sad day for Germany, Herr Schmidt, if our enemies got hold of you!"

"For Germany—yes," Alphonse murmured, drily. "I suppose that all *my* old journals have been sealed, too."

"All the materials produced in Auberlen's laboratory," Zangemeister confirmed. "Even your own, Fräulein Nijam."

"That is unfortunate." Alphonse cleared his throat, for the ticklish part of the conversation had now come. "Do you know where it is kept? —I would not ask, but it had occurred to me that if I could only get a look at my old journals, it might bring back some memories. Some of the knowledge I once had, for instance. Perhaps…perhaps even the secret of revenant-making."

The old librarian looked very thoughtful. "I see!" he breathed. "Yes, I see! It might just work—and then *we,* and not the French or the Russians, should have the revenants!"

"Then you'll help us?" Nijam asked, trying not to sound *too* eager.

"Indeed I will," said Herr Zangemeister. "Follow me!"

Leaving the cart with its collection of philosophers to see to its own affairs, the old librarian set off through the stacks. But instead of leading them further into the library, he took them out again into the entrance-hallway, shooed off the assistant-librarian, and began to look through the pigeon-holes behind his desk.

"Here we are," he said, brandishing a sheaf of papers.

Nijam and Schmidt found themselves looking upon a

bureaucratic form written in particularly dense German.

"Fill it out in triplicate," Zangemeister said, "and within about six months you ought to hear from Berlin."

Mimi, peering over Nijam's shoulder, let out a snort. "Did you forget what Germans are like?" she murmured in Nijam's ear.

Nijam shrugged her away, and Alphonse cleared his throat again. "Is this the only way?" he asked. "I may not have six months, Herr Zangemeister. I am sure that I am already being followed by the English police."

"Dear me," said Zangemeister. "That is unfortunate. But Germany will be happy to protect you. I am sure there is a form for that, too, only I do not have it here."

"It's all right." Nijam picked up the librarian's fountain-pen and doggedly began filling out the form. "I have a feeling that Berlin will respond to this particular request very quickly, indeed. Ah! Here they're asking which of the sealed archives we are requesting access to. Do you remember, Herr Zangemeister?"

"There's only one in Heidelberg," Zangemeister said, which was not helpful. But then he added, "Ours is right here on the third floor. Mostly rare historical manuscripts, of course."

Nijam was careful not to let her sense of triumph show on her face. "The third floor," she repeated. "Isn't that where Chemistry is located?"

Mimi gave a broad grin. "Yes, and that reminds me—I must go and look for *Molybdenum*. Enjoy yourselves!"

She went away, leaving Nijam to labour through the business of filling out the form and asking inane questions about it. Should it be sent by post? To whom would Berlin address their permission?

Then the library doors opened and a chill wind blew in from the street. Nijam threw a glance to the door; and then, like Schmidt, she stiffened. Four men entered: a bourgeois gentleman, a navvy, a mountaineer, and a yachtsman. The policemen had found them!

The bourgeois gentleman removed a bowler-hat which had almost certainly come out of Clapham, or possibly even my own Brixton. "Alphonse Schmidt, I presume?" he asked, in English.

"Mr Cakebread!" Alphonse sent Nijam a look of alarm, but she shook her head slightly. They were practically cornered, and must now rely upon their wits.

Nijam's transmitter, which happened to be open, transmitted these words very clearly to the rest of us: "Did he say *Cakebread?*" I asked. Nijam, feeling rather harried, slapped her transmitter off again.

"Do you know this man, Alphonse?" she demanded. But he did not answer—he seemed incapable of speech.

"My card," the bowler-hatted gentleman declared, proffering a square of pasteboard. Nijam accepted and read that his name was indeed Cakebread—William Cakebread—and his occupation was listed as director of the Reformatory Ship "Akbar", moored in Birkenhead.

A chill overwhelmed her at the sight of these ominous words. It was at this reformatory that Alphonse had been stripped of his memories. It was there that he had been taught to think of himself as a violent criminal, fit only to be hollowed out and employed as a servant. It was there that he had been trained to iron and mend, to cook and tidy, and with every effort of his body and mind to serve, defend, and worship his royal master, Vasily Nikolaevich.

This was all she knew of the place: Alphonse never chose to speak of it. Nijam's hand found its way into her pocket, closing about the powerful little gadget she kept there.

"Is something the matter, Mr Cakebread?" she asked coolly. "As far as I was aware, Mr Schmidt is now a free man."

"That he is, my dear! That he is!" said Mr Cakebread, with such offensive familiarity that Nijam scarcely restrained herself from drawing the Stunner and shocking him into a quivering heap. "We only wish him to come back to the old Reformatory for a day or two. A routine inspection, if you will. All our graduates are required to participate every three years."

Alphonse was as white as a sheet and trembling slightly. Nijam stepped in front of him, prepared to do battle.

"If it's a routine inspection, what brings one of the directors hurrying across Europe to summon him in person?" she demanded. Perhaps she took too combative a tone. The yachtsman, the mountaineer, and the navvy had at first hung back, but now they began to move nearer.

"Well," Mr Cakebread said, adjusting his round spectacles, "*ordinarily* we would notify Mr Schmidt's royal master, but he is unhappily deceased."

It was almost convincing. Nijam smiled thinly.

"But don't you know that Mr Schmidt is already in the service of another Empire? We are in Heidelberg on pressing business for the German government. Aren't we, Herr Zangemeister?"

The librarian had been watching their exchange in great alarm; but now he winched up his jaw and nodded vigorously. Not even a criminal record would sway Zangemeister against a loyal son of Germany who might be able to bring back the revenants.

"Yes, *mein Herr,*" he said. "Quite true. The Kaiser is deeply interested in this young man."

Mr Cakebread wavered and sent a glance over his shoulder at his motley friends. "Ah," he said. "We can wait until you have finished your business for the day, Mr Schmidt. But you will have to come, and it is better if you come willingly."

Feeling the shudder that run through Alphonse's body at these last words, Nijam smiled with clenched teeth.

"That's very kind of you," she said. "And now, if you don't mind, we'll get back to our business. Herr Zangemeister! Can you direct us to that archive you mentioned?"

"Oh! Oh yes, at once!" Zangemeister said, and ushered them quickly back into the library.

They were followed at a distance, by Mr Cakebread and his myrmidons.

"Overcoats in the library!" Herr Zangemeister murmured, evidently distressed. "But what can I do with three foreign agents?"

"You are *quite* sure they are foreign agents?" Nijam inquired.

"Oh, yes! Don't you see the peculiar way they are dressed? They are all enemy spies, I assure you!"

"We knew the French would come," Alphonse said "but they've summoned their Russian and English allies too—and Cakebread! What can we do?"

"We must shake them off before we can do anything else," Nijam declared. "Never mind about that archive, Herr Zangemeister. We must slip away, if we can. Is there a back door we can use?"

"Of course! Of course!" the old man assured them. "This way!"

He darted down the long, dark passage between the towering shelves and led them a winding course through such varied subjects as Philosophy, Ancient History, and Phrenology. As quickly and quietly as they went, however, the pursuit was never more than a turn or two behind them.

Nijam opened her transmitter. "Mimi," she gasped, "you must find your own way out. We have yachtsmen following us."

"Do you want me to distract them?" Mimi asked.

"Not at all," I put in from the Schwab house, where I was watching the triplets yawning over their nature study. "Finish your mapping work."

Of course we had known, before we set out from Paris, that we would be quickly followed to Heidelberg by French agents eager to recover the secret of revenant-making. This was a known risk, and far less sinister than the mysterious Voice which had seized upon our poor Alphonse. The library job could wait for no policemen.

Nijam and Alphonse, meanwhile, followed Zangemeister to a locked door which was tucked behind the great stair leading to the library's upper rooms. The key was ready in the old librarian's hand: he flung the door open, whisked them through, and locked it behind just as the yachtsmen flung themselves against the other side.

The door-handle rattled; the door itself jumped and shuddered beneath the impact of fists. Muffled voices could be heard—cries of *Open up!* in English, and oaths in French—and Russian.

"God in heaven! the whole lot of them are after you!" Zangemeister panted, backing away from the door. "You must leave them to me. Follow this corridor to the end—there is a door onto the Marsiliusplatz."

"How can we ever thank you?" Alphonse asked, gripping his hand.

"Do not thank me! Serve the Fatherland!" Zangemeister declared, returning the grip with enthusiasm. Nijam wasted no time on pleasantries; she seized Alphonse by the cuff of his sleeve and hurried him at a run to the end of the corridor.

Chapter XI.

"I'll be in the Marsiliusplatz to collect them within five minutes," Vasily told me via transmitter. He, too, had been listening to the events which were unfolding within the library.

A glance through the window of the Schwab nursery revealed Vasily hurrying into the mews, to the vehicle which waited there. We had, for this precise purpose, arranged for the use of a covered, horse-drawn cart which had been got up to look like a baker's van.

"Wait for me," I told him, darting towards the nursery door. "We may need a distraction. —No, children! Stay there!"

They treated this, of course, as an invitation. Two minutes later, with my coat flung over one shoulder and my hat in my hand, I was standing on the front doorstep attempting to explain to the three children why they ought not to come with me.

"It might be dangerous," I told them. "Really, children, must I call Fräulein Angermeyer to lock you into your nursery?"

"But you're supposed to be in the nursery, too!" Heidi protested. "Teaching *us* our nature lesson!"

This was an excellent point, which left me momentarily struggling to come up with an answer. As I did so, the baker's van issued from the mews and drew to a stop. Vasily leaped down, throwing open the hatch at the back.

"Into the van, my dear." Then he saw the children, and silence descended upon him as well.

"Where are you going?" Heidi asked him. "Can't we come too?"

"Of course," Vasily replied at once. "The more the merrier! Jump in!"

I opened my mouth to protest, but Vasily had already tossed a laughing Peter into the cart. There was no help for it; time was pressing, and this was the path of least resistance. I hastily closed the front-door and allowed Vasily to help me into the vehicle, praying that I would not come to regret this highly irresponsible decision.

The van had been fitted with two long, low bench-seats at either side. As Vasily fastened the hatch, I made sure the children—or at any rate, the two living ones—were seated towards the cab, lest a sudden movement topple them out the back. As we trundled off in the direction of the Library I switched on my transmitter.

"Vaska-my-pet, for the future I'll thank you not to undermine me with the children."

"Well, what else was I supposed to do?" he asked. "Thanks to your calling my bluff the other morning, they know quite well I'm a soft touch."

The transmitter crackled as another, more breathless voice joined the conversation. "Do you *mind?*" Nijam asked between gasps. It sounded as though she had been running; a pastime in which she was uniquely inexperienced. I hastily stopped transmitting.

"Were you talking to Herr Dunkel just now?" Peter asked,

regarding me with interest. "Is that something fairies can do?"

"More or less," I said. "Fräulein Nijam made us a little piece of magic that sits in our ears, do you see? It allows us to speak to each other across long distances. Maybe I can persuade her to show you how it works. Would you like that?"

To my surprise, the children shook their heads. "No," Peter said. "Fräulein Nijam is *frightening.*"

"More frightening than Brother Otto?" I asked.

Heidi pursed her lips. "No," she admitted, "but *much* more frightening than Herr Dunkel, or even Mother Flog."

Even Clara nodded her head at that. Perhaps Nijam should have been the one acting the governess!

* * *

Meanwhile, Schmidt and the frightening Miss Nijam had found their way into the Marsiliusplatz. The grey December day was so bright compared to the library that for a moment Nijam's eyes were dazzled. She was still blinking, a quiet corner of her mind contemplating the possibility of designing a prosthetic eye that would be more adaptable to sudden changes in the intensity of light, when shouts and the thud of heavy feet intruded upon her.

Nijam turned to find two or three more navvies—Okhrana men, from the thick Russian accents in which they desired her to stand and deliver herself into custody—rushing towards her from the direction of the Augustinergasse. She threw a swift glance about them. The Marsiliusplatz in which they stood was a broad, open thoroughfare surrounded by tall white University buildings. At the far end could be seen the sheer, red-brick wall and traceried Gothic windows of a church.

That way lay retreat—if only they could first repel the Russian secret police.

Beside her, Alphonse was breathing heavily. His fists were clenched, but his eyes were shut. He seemed in no shape either to run anywhere, or to repel an ambush.

Nijam reached out to steady him. "Alphonse, what's the matter?"

"Yammu," he breathed, his voice ragged with some invisible effort.

"Don't let him win," she said. Then the Okhrana men were upon them. Breathless though she was, Nijam now became terribly clear-minded and efficient. Her right hand emerged from her pocket with a Stunner. As the policemen converged upon Schmidt, she sank the fine teeth of the mechanism into the back of the nearest and administered a brisk charge of electricity, at which he crumpled to the ground. The second seized Alphonse, who at once dealt him a powerful blow to the midsection; he collapsed into a painful, wheezing huddle. The third, seeing what had happened to the first, seized Nijam's right wrist; whereupon she withdrew her left from her pocket and administered a second shock with a second Stunner.

It was all over in a moment; but Alphonse stood bent double over his fallen enemy, making soft noises of distress. "No," he murmured, "no, no, no!"

Nijam seized his head and saw from his eyes that Alphonse was yet himself—though lost in a dreadful struggle

.There was no sign of the baker's van; only the sound of me and Vasily in her transmitter, arguing about the children. Grasping Schmidt by the arm, Nijam dragged him towards the church. "Do you *mind?*" she snapped.

They stumbled together into the Schulgasse and Nijam

stared up desperately at the great red bulk of the Jesuit-enkirche. Where next? Rumour had it that a revenant could not tread on holy ground, and although Nijam did not quite believe this, neither did she wish to risk her only Alphonse bursting into flames. That ruled out the sanctuary of the church, which meant that she ought to turn north in hope of evading their pursuers and meeting the rest of her crew.

"This way," she began; but just then Alphonse made a strangled sound of surprise.

Turning, Nijam beheld Mr Vandergriff hastening up from the Marsiliusplatz. The importunate American had appeared apparently from nowhere—although in truth he must have been hot on the heels of the Okhrana men—and now seized Alphonse by the throat with his retractable arm. Long, sinuous, whiplike, and brazen in the sun, it reeled poor Schmidt inexorably towards his attacker.

"Got you!" Griff panted. "What do you think, Schmidt? Wise of me to watch the back-door!"

"Watch *this,* if you please," Nijam said, lunging at him with her Stunner. But Griff, this time, was prepared for her. With a flick of his right hand, a long gleaming blade emerged from the forearm; he lunged forward with a sweeping cut.

Had it not been for the boning of her undergarments, Nijam would have perished on the spot. As it was, the blade shore through all her layers of sensible black bombazine and drew sparks from the tight coils of steel that stiffened her waist. Though only the tip of Griff's blade scored a shallow cut at the edge of her ribs, the force of the blow was enough to knock her down. She rolled across the stones, losing her grip on both her Stunners.

Nijam did not see precisely what happened next. There

was a bellow from Schmidt. A bare moment later, Griff landed upon the cobblestones beside her as though hurled with inhuman force. Cradling her bleeding side, Nijam turned and looked up. Alphonse stood four paces away, his head lowered, his hands open at his sides like a bear squaring up to fight. And in his eyes was a cold angry light.

Once again, Yammu was in the ascendent.

"No," Nijam wheezed, still barely able to breathe after that punishing blow.

Not far away, Griff climbed shakily to his feet. His greyish hair had been disarranged, and there was a smear of dirt on his face as he wiped blood from his lip.

"You had best turn yourself in, Schmidt" he said, straightening his tie. "You cannot possibly hope to win a fight against the policemen of three great Empires, let alone myself!"

"Insolent mortal!" were the answering words. "You shall learn the might of Yammu, the unconquerable!"

"Bah," said Griff. "Who are you calling a mortal? I'll teach you to get fresh with me, my lad."

He staggered to his feet, charging at the Alphonse-revenant. Yammu did not wait for him. Instead he turned and rushed north up the narrow Schulgasse with Griff in hot pursuit.

At nearly the same moment, the Marsiliusplatz filled up with shouting men. Nijam, her head whirling, had an impression of yachting caps, lederhosen, and Mr Cakebread's Clapham bowler. They all went past in a rush, hard on Griff's heels. A moment later—Nijam was still trying to regain her wind—a hand dropped on her shoulder.

"Fräulein Nijam!" said the voice of kindly old Herr Zangemeister. "What has happened? Where is Alphonse Schmidt?"

Nijam looked up and found herself surrounded by solemn

163

Teutonic gendarmes, all looking very magnificent in brass buttons and gold braid. She sighed. Of course this was old Zangemeister's idea of *dealing with* the foreign policemen.

She gave forth no more than a puzzled wheeze or two before the German policemen caught wind of the chase towards the north. Then they rushed off. Herr Zangemeister helped Nijam to sit up and inspect her hurts. She was scraped and winded, and there was a shallow gash in her ribs; but otherwise she was unhurt. She tottered to her feet, bent like an old woman; and then there was a scuffle from above, and Mimi dropped lightly into the street beside her, apparently having exited the Library by a third-storey window.

"What has happened?" Mimi asked, making Zangemeister jump. "You look awful. Where is our Alphonse?"

"Out of his wits," Nijam gasped. "This way." She let go of Zangemeister and took a couple of tottering steps towards the Schulgasse; but just then a baker's van halted before her. Vasily leaned down from the driver's seat.

"Into the back," he called.

It took me and the children some pulling, and both Mimi and Herr Zangemeister some shoving, before Nijam could be got into the van. But her mind had recovered, even if her body had not. From an undignified position on the floor, she glared up indiscriminately at all of us.

"What are the *children* doing here?" she demanded. "And you, Mimi—you ought to be mapping the library!"

"I *did* map it," Mimi declared, "or at least, the important parts. Ow!" she added, as the van took a turn much too fast. "Vasya! What are you doing?"

"Trying to catch our fugitive before the police do," Vasily replied over the transmitter. "Hold on, all of you. He is running for the river."

After that we had a dark, bumpy, break-neck ride, which thrilled the children tremendously. "What has happened to Herr Schmidt?" Heidi asked. "Why are all those men chasing him?"

To which Nijam sniffed and said, "Grown-up business." After that Heidi subsided into a mutinous silence.

After some minutes the sound of the carriage-wheels changed, as though the narrow streets had opened into a wider place. Then the sounds of the town dropped away altogether. There came a gentle upward slope, and the van pulled to a halt.

"There they are," Vasily said, the van rocking as he leaped to the ground. "Up on the bridge. Come!"

He threw open the back flap and in a moment we were all disembarked—even the children, who of course could not be left to their own devices. We found ourselves upon the Old Bridge of the town. I am sure that this would be a perfectly lovely spot on a warm summer's day, if one had nothing to do but sights to see and picnics to eat. The bridge is built of the same reddish stone and brick as the rest of the town and spans the broad Neckar river in a series of graceful arches. The far end of the bridge lies among the thickly forested hills north of the river, while the town end of it terminates in an utterly charming gatehouse fitted out with such poetic accoutrements as an archway, a portcullis, and two round white towers with candle-snuffer spires. There is, from the bridge, also an excellent view of the town with its steeply-pitched rooves, its domed and spired steeples, and over everything the big rambling hulk of the Schloss.

On this particular cold, grey December afternoon, there

was not a great deal of traffic. The wind scoured the bridge mercilessly. Up ahead, what few passers-by there were had drawn their carriages or their steps to a halt, and had drawn aside, watching with caution the drama unfolding to the right. Here the footpath swelled out in a square bulwark atop one of the massive stone piers of the bridge; to either side of this bay was a lamp-post glowing a dull gold in the dingy winter light.

Here poor Alphonse, evidently still under the sway of his Voice, stood at bay with his back to the stone balustrade. Griff, pale and determined, had the blade of his arm extended; the tip of it rested against Alphonse's throat, letting forth a thin trickle of blood that appeared nearly black in the fading afternoon light.

There was no sign of the police, either German or otherwise. But we could not depend upon this happy situation continuing very long.

"Griff first," I said, taking in the situation at a glance. "We need a distraction."

"I could show him my ankles," Mimi suggested. "Don't laugh, Vasya! He's American. Not even the English are so bad with ankles."

I judged that the last thing we needed was Mimi getting taken up for public indecency. "Never mind, Mimi; I'll do it. Children, stay with Vasily."

"We'll distract him too!" Heidi protested, clinging to my hand with all her strength. "We're *very* distracting, Fräulein Nijam says so!"

"Take them," Nijam said, forestalling what I had been about to say. She was white to the lips, and her eyes were sparkling with murder. "They'll make you look innocent."

It was a reckless thing to suggest, and I remembered, with

some discomfort, the way Nijam had spoken on the previous evening—*I am better able to destroy the world with my own hands than to stand by and let one hair of his head be harmed.* Were the Schwab children also to be sacrificed for Alphonse?

Still, it was not as though I meant to *fight* Griff, or to interpose myself between him and the Alphonse-revenant. So, with a sigh, I led the children to the fringe of the crowd of onlookers. Here, in the silence, I could hear the little speech Griff was making to Alphonse and his Voice.

"You can see yourself that we're at an impasse," he said in that colourless, reasonable voice of his. "I'd rather cut your throat than let you escape me, and you've seen for yourself that you can't beat me in a fight when I'm prepared for you. I suggest you do the smart thing and hand yourself over. I'll make it worth your while—which is more than you'll get from the policemen yonder."

My heart sank as I saw that Mimi's "yachtsmen", together with more than a few German policemen, were beginning to join the onlookers.

Yammu snarled. "Trust you? When you threaten me with *death?*" He spat on the stones. Well! I suppose that ancient deities are not taught the best manners.

"I can help you," Griff proclaimed, as though this was quite an ordinary thing to say when menacing someone with a naked blade. "I reckon you'd rather be in control of this body, and not squabbling with Alphonse Schmidt for it. Wouldn't you?"

"Alphonse Schmidt, ha!" the creature roared. "The mortal is no match for me! Soon he will be utterly subdued!"

I judged that it was time I intervened.

"Mr Vandergriff!" I exclaimed, in tones of high-pitched

indignation. "What is the meaning of this? You and I had an *agreement,* sir! We would help you, and you would leave poor Schmidt alone!"

Griff startled, but he did not remove his gaze from Alphonse. "Miss Molly," he said, not at all as though he was glad to find me among those present. "I'll thank you to stay out of this."

"We *will* stay out of it," I said, with the best I could manage in outraged dignity. "Miss Nijam will be *delighted* not to have to help you create new prosthetics."

"Stop trying to distract me," Griff said. "It won't work. Well, Schmidt, or whatever you are? What do you say?"

Heidi tugged on my hand. When I looked down, I found that she was waving a glass jar at me.

Here I must go back a little, and fill in some of the details which the exciting nature of my narrative may have rendered momentarily superfluous. I have mentioned that I had been interrupted in the midst of the children's nature lesson. In fact, I had had them making sketches of Aunt Dete; counting her legs, and labelling her sundry parts. I had been hitherto unaware that the spider had accompanied us to the bridge; and yet, like a gift from Heaven, here she was.

"Oh," I said. "That's very clever of you, Heidi."

There are few things more distracting than a spider with a four-inch leg-span, particularly when it is dropped unexpectedly onto the bare skin of the neck. I must say that Griff was wonderfully quick on the uptake. No sooner had the spider been deposited, than he uttered a word which I hoped devoutly the children did not understand, and grabbed frantically for the creature with his retractable hand. In the same moment, Yammu, who had evidently been preparing to act, thrust aside the blade at Alphonse's neck and dealt a blow powerful enough to send Griff, spider and all, hurtling into the crowd behind.

"Now, Nijam!" I cried, the flying Griff having missed me by mere inches.

Nijam had a syringe ready, charged with chloral. But Yammu, too, was not to be caught a second time unawares. He lashed out and struck the instrument from Nijam's hand; the syringe smashed upon the cobble-stones.

Then in a trice he leaped upon the parapet of the bridge.

"Keep back," he growled, reaching out a commanding hand as the rest of us pressed forwards—my crew, and the policemen of half Europe. "Keep back! The brown woman, most of all! Or I'll throw us together into the water and drown!"

"No!" Nijam cried. She was on her knees, clutching at the broken syringe. "No! *Alphonse!*"

"It's all right," Mimi said, pushing to the front of the crowd. "Leave him to me." Then she planted her hands on her hips and squared up to the Alphonse-revenant.

"Stay back, if you don't want him dead," Yammu growled.

Mimi rolled her eyes. *"You,"* she said, "are bluffing! If it did you any good to kill our Alphonse, you would already have done it. But if you kill him, it will not set you free, will it? It will only make you bodiless. Powerless. Oh, no. I think you will take very good care of our Schmidt."

"Silence!" Yammu roared. "Do not tempt me!"

"Tempt you to do what?" Mimi demanded. "Ten to one you cannot even swim."

It must have gone through Nijam's mind in a flash what Mimi meant to do next.

"Mimi, *no!*" she cried, reaching out.

But it was too late. In one fluid, graceful moment, Mimi

darted forth—caught both of Alphonse Schmidt's ankles—and gave them a swift, decisive tug.

With a howl, our poor friend toppled from the bridge and disappeared into the deep water below.

"Mimi!" Nijam cried, horror-stricken.

"Oh," Mimi said, as though the possibility had only just occurred to her. "Can Alphonse not swim?"

Chapter XII.

Mimi need not have worried: Alphonse Schmidt was an accomplished swimmer. Moreover, her gambit was a success. On the bridge Alphonse had been a helpless prisoner within his own body; but then the icy water struck him a punishing blow that drove all the air from his lungs, and he found himself struggling in the chill, dark depths of the Neckar.

"Swim, you pathetic creature!" The Voice echoed within his head, an imperious command. "Get us out of here!"

Alphonse struggled upwards and burst into the chill evening with a gasp. Far overhead, the arched underside of the bridge blotted out the dusky sky. His body, racked with spasms of pain and cold, could scarcely draw breath. For a little while it was as much as he could do to keep his head above water. The current, slow and inexorable, drew him out from beneath the bridge. He saw dark heads silhouetted against the sky, but could not tell if any of them had seen him. Then, slowly, the bridge drifted away from him and Schmidt found that he was breathing again.

"Swim!" the Voice urged him. *"Swim!* This cold is intolerable! For this I will have the small woman flayed alive!"

Alphonse shuddered. Then it occurred to him that he might get the better of his demon, if he only ceased to struggle and let the river take him…

"Swim," the Voice commanded. "Allow yourself to drown, and I will myself drag your corpse from the waters."

"It wouldn't last very long after that," gasped Alphonse. According to sir—to Vasily, rather—this was the entire trouble with the revenants. A corpse, despite revivification, did not remain useful for very long. Flesh and sinew rotted away, bones became brittle, and in time, the animating principle could no longer hold a crumbling body together.

"Swim!" Yammu demanded, "or I'll do it myself!"

Indeed, with every moment that Alphonse used to keep himself afloat, he knew that Yammu was studying his movements. Quite likely it was already too late to try drowning the creature—and besides, although he had resigned himself to death, there was yet hope. He could not leave Nijam a second time to mourn him—not yet, at any rate.

Accordingly, Alphonse struck out. The river was wide and he was feeble from cold and weariness, but he did not fight the current, instead allowing it to carry him down the length of the town as he angled towards the nearer north bank. There were glowing lights atop the slope where the houses of Heidelberg's outlying suburbs stood; but the steep bank, dotted with trees and shrubs, was dark, and welcoming, and safe when at long last Alphonse dragged himself ashore.

He was weak and exhausted—so weak that he could only drag himself into the shadow of the trees and fall into the long, sere winter grass. He shivered violently, but could not yet face the long walk back up the river and across the bridge, not in this cutting wind. Perhaps it would be better not to try. He did not know whether he could hold Yammu at bay, should the creature attempt to seize him again.

It did not. "What is wrong with us?" Yammu demanded, instead. "Are we ailing?"

Alphonse answered only with a weak snuffle.

"Answer me! What ails us?"

"Mortality," Alphonse gasped. "Bodies tire, Yammu. They wear out, and eventually, they die."

"Ridiculous," the Voice said. "What is the point of such a limitation?"

Alphonse watched the dark branches shaking in the wind above him. "As I understand it, the point is to prevent such wicked creatures as *us* from attaining all our hearts' desire."

"Unacceptable!" Yammu proclaimed. "If I am to return to this earth I cannot be constrained. I must have a new body, a body that will never tire."

Alphonse was stuttering with cold, but he laughed anyway. "You too?"

"You mock me?"

"Everyone wants new bodies," he replied. "Everyone wants immortality. The thing is, I might have been able to help you once. But my memories were taken—locked away. And now I could not help you even if I wished."

"Oh, is that all?" Yammu asked with withering contempt. "You should have said so before. Here—"

And something deep within Alphonse Schmidt broke free.

It was like a strain of music, or a passing scent, that recalls a long-forgotten memory; except that instead of a moment—a meeting, a conversation, a song—what returned to Alphonse was a whole lifetime.

It came back to him in a wild flood. His school days at the gymnasium. The courtship in which he patiently pursued Padma Nijam, despite her repeated rebuffs. His mother's smile as she held his hand while the doctor put stitches in his knee. The choir-master who was so kind to him the day Stefan had incited all the other choir-boys to tease him. The morning when Stefan tethered him down to a table and began chanting unspeakable things from an ancient book, when Yammu first began to torment him.

Alphonse forgot how cold and tired he was: snatches of his life were flashing before his eyes, all out of order. He was dimly aware that he was making delirious noises, repeating long-forgotten words and formulae, uttering brief, strangled sounds of mirth or horror...

And he knew. He knew everything.

"You were wrong," Yammu told him, with malicious pleasure.

He *had* been wrong.

For years he had believed himself to be a desperate and dangerous man, a law unto himself, who had tempted his brother into wrong-doing. Lies, all lies. Yet not entirely lies. Alphonse Schmidt had stolen fruit from forbidden orchards; had watched, with a guilty knot in his stomach, as small animals and other children were tormented; had kissed a girl for whom he did not care; had desecrated the bodies of the dead; had turned himself over, body and soul, to an ancient evil.

None of it because he wished to do so. None of it because he was black-souled and heartless; but only because where Stefan led, Alphonse must follow.

Now he lay in darkness beneath a brooding sky, laughing like a madman until the laughter turned to tears. What a fool he had been! He was the most miserable of evildoers, because he had done none of it for himself; only for others.

He did not hear the footsteps, or the voices, until they were already upon him. When he did hear them, he did not care. He felt a darkness loom close, and a slender arm slipped beneath his head.

"Alphonse," she said—Padma Nijam, who had been so much more patient with him than he deserved. "Alphonse, can you hear me? —Bring a light!" she called to the others.

A lantern flashed in his eyes. He was aware of others crowding near—he could hear worried voices, asking whether he was himself, whether he was hurt. Alphonse made no answer to them: he had eyes only for Nijam. He reached out to grasp her hand.

"How can you forgive me?" he asked.

"Not now, Alphonse," she said, holding him close.

"You don't understand," he told her. "I could have gone with you to Vienna! Only *I chose not to.* I did as Stefan asked. I—*I let him* make me into a revenant, because I was too weak to say no."

Her face became as stiff as a mask, and Alphonse tore himself away from her. No one moved; no one said anything.

No one but the Voice. Inside him, a flickering mirth burned like a fire.

"And now it is too late," Yammu told him. "Now I am with you forever. There is no one to blame but yourself."

* * *

Luckily we had managed to find Schmidt before anyone else did: he had, after all, the police of four Great Powers after him, to say nothing of Griff himself. Vasily it was who led us unerringly to our friend, for he was nearly as good as a bloodhound. Even in the dark, the prosthetic eye which Griff had given him was able to follow Alphonse as he began to swim for the further shore. Moreover, Vasily's nose had been unusually sharp since he had been bitten in Moscow by his vampire cousins, and this led us unerringly to the stand of trees where we found our poor friend huddled shaking in the grass.

No one spoke as we made the journey home in our baker's van. Nijam was in a towering silence which it did not seem wise to disturb. Heidi and Peter huddled forlornly over their empty jar, for Aunt Dete had lost no time, once released down Griff's neck, in securing her escape. The moment we returned to the mews, I whisked the children indoors, where we found that we had returned just in time for dinner. Our absence could not be concealed from Fräulein Angermeyer, who informed me, apologetically, that I ought not to be running about with the children after dark. I explained that there had been a disturbance of the traffic on the bridge, which had prevented our returning sooner from an excursion to the forest. With that, she was content. I gave the children their dinner and sent them to bed, promising that if they remained there like good children, I would tell them in the morning whether Herr Schmidt was expected to live—a question of which they were in some doubt.

I then returned to headquarters to find the rest of the crew assembled in the drawing-room, plotting murder.

"This is all Griff's fault," Nijam declared. She was on her feet, pacing to and fro like a she-lion. "Dark was right: we had an *agreement*, and he went back on it!"

"Be reasonable, Nijam," I told her. "There isn't much we can do about it."

"Oh! *isn't* there?" she snarled.

"Think of the bright side," Mimi said. She was at work stoking the fire, no doubt in aid of warming up poor Alphonse, who was all wrapped up in blankets with his feet in a hot-mustard bath. "We have proved one thing, at least. That Voice needs Alphonse alive."

"There's a reason for that," Alphonse said, hiding behind a cup of chocolate as though it was all that shielded him from a cruel and unloving world. "I am not merely the creature's hands and feet in this world. I am also its prison."

"Explain," Nijam told him.

"I don't quite understand it myself," he said, apologetically. "But I'm not a revenant now like I used to be. I allowed Yammu to return, but I don't belong to him the way I did before—before Coburg, I mean. If Yammu loses me now, he has no others to whom he can retreat. He must go back to whence he came, until such time as new revenants may be made."

"And so he requires my help in transferring himself to a new body," Nijam said, thoughtfully.

She had not alluded once to the revelation on the river-bank: instead, she seemed single-mindedly fixed upon the problem at hand. It was left to Vasily to raise this subject.

"But, Schmidt! This means you have recovered all your memories!" he exclaimed. "What excellent news!"

Alphonse shuddered. "It makes no difference," he said, in a hollow voice, as though responding to something that had not been spoken aloud. "Yammu can do little while I am here to contest him. But let him get free of me, in a body that does not die, and nothing will stop him. He wishes to fill the earth with revenants, ghastly puppets of his own power. There is only one sure way to stop him."

"You aren't to think of it," Nijam hissed, turning upon him.

The old Alphonse would have wilted beneath her scorn, but this Alphonse turned a grave, sorrowful gaze upon her.

"Shall I be ruled by you?" he asked. "Shall I give over my conscience to you?"

Nijam looked for a moment stricken. "I'm giving you advice, not orders!"

"And I must decide for myself whether to take it," Alphonse said steadily.

"Now, now, now!" Vasily protested. "Let us consider some other alternatives before we toss poor Schmidt off a cliff. We have yet to recover the Auberlen papers, for one thing. I say, Schmidt, *do* we still need the Auberlen papers, now that you have your memories?"

"Yes, I'm afraid so," he answered. "My brother and Auberlen kept all their consciousness-transference work, and most of the revenant-making procedure, a secret from both Patty and myself. I know little more than she does."

Patty! I had never heard him refer to Nijam like this before, and I thought that even the lady herself flushed a little with pleasure.

"So we must burgle the library," Vasily said, rubbing his hands together as though the idea pleased him. "Mimi—am I to understand that you have located the archive in question?"

"I have," she said, brightening up in turn. "It is on the third floor of the library, down the south end." She produced a crumpled sheet of paper from her pocket and dragged over a tiny occasional-table to smooth it out upon. We clustered near, peering at the hieroglyphics thus displayed to our attention. "Here is the archive," she said, pointing to the southwestern corner of the building. "Here is the reading room where anyone with permission to view the archived documents may sit and look at them—of course, only in the presence of a librarian, who brings out the item and returns it to the archive once the visitor is finished. Unless, of course, the documents are sealed on imperial orders—as these are."

"And modes of egress?" Vasily inquired.

"Oh, you mean ways out," Mimi answered after a moment's confusion. "The main stair is here, at the centre of the building. And here at the south end is the back stair, leading towards the Marsiliusplatz. Both stairs end within the library, where a librarian is on duty whenever the library is open."

"Not just when the library is open," Alphonse put in, unexpectedly. "The librarians work all day, and often late into the night. We would have to go in by night, and even then…"

"Getting into the archive is one problem," Nijam said, briskly. "Getting a lot of books *out* is another. We might bypass the stairs altogether, and carry them away by the window."

"That might work if I was only stealing a pearl necklace," Mimi said, with a sniff. "But *not* all those books. The only way onto the roof is through the window, and from the roof, then where? There's no easy way onto the neighbouring rooves, and if we let the goods down into the street, someone would notice."

"I suppose that a librarian could do it," I said, forestalling what Nijam had been about to say. "He might carry the books out in his pockets, one or two at a time over the course of months, and no one be any the wiser. But we haven't the time to waste."

"It's a shame there are no Black Templars among the librarians," Vasily said thoughtfully. "But I asked, and there aren't."

"*Quiet,*" Nijam said, imperiously. "Of course I wasn't suggesting lowering the books into the street. As long as there is a window from the archive—yes?—then you can leave the rest to me. The main problem is to get *into* the archive."

There was a silence. I looked thoughtfully at Vasily.

"Well, then," I said. "If we don't have a librarian, we'll just have to *make* one."

Chapter XIII.

From there our planning progressed smoothly, and the next morning found everyone busy about their tasks. Mimi ventured out to inspect that part of the University Hall which stood across the Augustinergasse from the Library. Vasily went off with a long list of things which Nijam wanted for her own work, and Nijam herself announced via transmitter that she would be spending the day at the old Auberlen lab.

"I'll come with you," Alphonse offered. "This time I might in fact be able to help."

"Absolutely not," Nijam retorted at once. "You mustn't show your face in the streets—not with all the policemen of Europe after you."

Alphonse heaved a sigh but did not argue. Later, as I got the children ready for their morning walk, I reflected upon what Schmidt had confessed last night, by the river—that he had allowed his brother to make a revenant of him, only because he was unwilling to say no.

In my heart I had often blamed Nijam, thinking that she judged Alphonse too harshly for his gentle and yielding disposition. Now that I knew the truth, I rather wondered at her loyalty to a man who had failed to stand by her precisely when it was most important. Vasily, for all his faults, had wavered from my side only when he was in doubt of my own feelings, and only when he believed it was the only way to secure my life and freedom. I thought the world of Alphonse Schmidt, but all the goodness in the world turns to vice unless it is strengthened by courage.

"Where are we going today, Fräulein Dark?" Peter asked, hopefully, as we left the house.

"We don't have Aunt Dete this time," Heidi said sadly, "but I brought Papa's sword-stick. He keeps it sharp, you know!"

"Did you indeed!" said I, eyeing the battered old walking-stick with alarm. I knew that Vasily carried one of these, although I had rarely seen him use it. "I think you had better let me carry that, Heidi! And I'm not taking you anywhere. I have to go and see a very bad man about some very bad things that he has done, so I am handing you off to Herr Dunkel, instead."

The children's eyes lit up. "Herr Dunkel! I do like him!" Heidi declared. "He promised us *kipferl* yesterday if we were good!"

"Sorry, Clara," Peter said to his dead sister, who followed, as ever, silently on our heels. "We'll let you have a good sniff before we eat them."

Poor thing! I thought. And yet, this was the existence which Griff wanted—a life in which he would always be tantalised by things he could never truly enjoy. Such a life would never appeal to *me*.

Vasily, when I tracked him down inspecting scrap metal in a hardware-shop was not particularly happy at being left to take care of the children; but when I told him what I had determined to do, he capitulated. Perhaps he found it a good excuse to sample yet more of the apparently inexhaustible variety of festive German cakes and biscuits. Off he and the children went towards the nearest bakery; and off went I—in search of Griff.

I meant to try reasoning with my erstwhile betrothed. We could not have him chasing poor Alphonse around Heidelberg, or hounding us with various sorts of policeman. Alas! Griff was not at his lodgings, and although I loitered expectantly for an hour or two, I had no view of him. Among the passers-by and fellow-loiterers I saw Englishmen in yachting caps, Frenchmen in lederhosen, Russians in neckerchiefs, and what I am fairly sure were German policemen in academic robes—but no Griff. At the end of the long, cold, trying morning, I saw Vasily strolling past with the three children in tow. Peter's face had a smudge of powdered sugar across it, evidently from the paper bag of *kipferl* which he carried. Heidi had a hammer, with which she seemed greatly enamoured.

I crossed the road towards them.

"There you are!" Vasily said, evidently relieved. "Did you speak to Griff?"

"He hasn't so much as showed his eyebrows," I said. "Did you find everything Nijam wanted? —Good. Give the hammer back, Heidi! It's time to go home."

"It's *my* hammer!" Heidi protested. "Herr Dunkel bought it for *me!*"

I blinked at her and then looked at Vasily, who shrugged helplessly. "What else was I supposed to do?" he asked.

"Vaska," I said, "I have seen you say *no* to vampires and werewolves; you can say *no* to a small girl. The hammer, Heidi, and stop shilly-shallying!"

"Shan't!" Heidi answered at once.

Vasily beheld the child with a look of awe. "How does she

do it?" he murmured. "Molly-my-dear, I am never able to defy you when you use *that* voice!"

Quite likely Heidi was accustomed to more frightening things than the displeasure of a mere governess. I did not say so, however. "You may have it back when you have something constructive to do with it," I told her. "But there is a mischievous little imp that lives in this hammer and makes you wish to bang away at things that don't need it, only to get you into trouble with your Papa. You had best give it to me, and I will make the imp behave itself."

Heidi giggled despite herself. I waited patiently, and at length, seeing that there was no help for it, she put the hammer into my hand.

"Wonderful woman," Vasily murmured. "Now, don't look behind, Molly-my-dear, but that veiled person has been following us again most of the morning, and she is still there."

"Is she indeed?" I cried. "Then in one respect, this morning might not be wasted! You must go and ask her what she wants!"

"I'll see what I can learn," he promised; and with that, we parted.

I took the children home for their lessons—grammar and long division and English—though not before we had read the service for those lost at sea, in memory of Aunt Dete.

But what had become of Griff?

The answer, as it happens, lay with Miss Nijam.

* * *

The attentive reader will recall that our inventor had promised Mr Vandergriff a personal interview in the next day or two.

This, after recent events, she felt was now a pressing matter of business. Upon arriving at the lab., therefore, Nijam summoned a boy who was loitering nearby with a crutch to help bear the weight of a misshapen foot. A silver mark quickly persuaded him to bear her message to Griff, and within half an hour the American himself approached in the company of his limping guide.

"Miss Nijam! You honour me," Griff said. He handed the boy a second silver mark. "That's for you, my boy. And think about what I told you! Get rid of that foot and have it replaced with a good prosthetic, and then you won't inconvenience other people so much."

Nijam smiled, tight-lipped. "There are inconveniences, and there are people," she said, "and if you want my help, Vandergriff, you ought not to confuse the latter for the former."

The boy limped away, and Griff gave her a sunny smile.

"Funny opinions, for the world's finest maker of implants and prostheses," he said.

"If he believes his foot serves him well enough, then it's not my place to tell him otherwise," she said, scowling. "He may prefer a foot that half works to one that might need expensive upkeep if it is to work at all. As for implants, you know as well as I do how dangerous *those* can be. There's no saying when one of them might break down and emit something that kills you."

The smile disappeared from Griff's face as though it had been wiped away with a sponge.

"All right," he said. "I'll come directly to the point. I want to try transferring consciousness to a whole new body—an artificial one. Can you make me something suitable?"

185

"I think so," Nijam said, keeping an unblinking and possibly somewhat unsettling gaze upon her prey. "I can machine a skeleton of steel and cable, that is, and coat it in lab-grown flesh. I've already created something very like it. What I cannot promise is that I would be able to create an artificial head to emulate the foreign consciousness. To achieve this, I would recommend grafting an entire biological cranium to the whole-body prosthesis."

"The head," Griff mused. "Yes, that might be best. But you say you've already created the kind of artificial body we want?" He did not seem remotely disturbed by this talk of severing and transferring heads from one body to another.

"I'll show you," Nijam declared. A sort of steel circlet lay on the bench, which she now placed upon her head. Griff watched in fascination as she took a pair of steel cuffs and anklets, fastening them to the extremity of each limb; then attaching each by a wire to a small electrical cell in her pocket.

Nijam reached into her pocket and switched on the electrical battery. There was a low answering hum from the cupboard in the corner. She raised her hand and made a pushing motion; in the same instant, the cupboard door swung open, and then, as Nijam moved, so did a great, gaunt steel object—stepping over the threshold of the cupboard, and clanking out to stand at the centre of the room, immediately opposite a slack-jawed Griff.

"The devil!" he exclaimed in mingled awe and astonishment. "What *is* it?"

"An automaton," Nijam said. In fact, it was the very invention which she and Mimi had used two mornings previously to carry Alphonse's body home: a creature of clockwork and pistons, gaunt and now flecked with rust, but a clever bit of work nonetheless. "As you see, I designed it to respond to my own motions. With a flesh graft and a few modifications, there's no reason that guidance cannot be provided by a transplanted human head."

"Magnificent!" Griff breathed. "How old were you, Miss Nijam, when you created this?"

"Barely twenty," she said, with a shrug. "It's a clumsy piece. The automaton I make for you would be far more nimble."

"Splendid, splendid!" Griff rubbed his hands with delight. "Miss Nijam, you are a woman after my own heart. What a fortunate thing that we happened to meet!"

"I *ought* to have said—the automaton I *might* have made you, had you held up your end of the bargain," Nijam added, with dry satisfaction. "But yesterday you attacked Alphonse Schmidt, and now the bargain is void."

The smile left Griff's face; he reddened. "Listen here," he blustered, stepping towards her.

Nijam did not wait for him to approach her; she made a quick pounce. The automaton moved at the same moment. Under Nijam's direction, it seized Griff from behind and drove him against the wall, an arm stiff like a bar at his throat. Griff shouted and coughed and extended his whip-arm, but Nijam's automaton caught it by the wrist. He slashed at the automaton with the blade in his right arm, but she was ready for that, too. The automaton got hold of it and forced the blade upwards, inch by inch, until the razor-sharp edge was at Griff's own throat.

"Now," Nijam said, panting a little with the exertion of guiding the automaton, *"you,* Vandergriff, will listen to *me.* I would advise you to listen very carefully indeed, for I can think of no one it would be a greater pleasure to do away with.

Here is the moment; here is the means. If you die here it will look exactly like a suicide, and no blame will attach to *me*. Do you understand?"

Griff snarled. "You're bluffing."

"I assure you that I have never been in greater earnest in my life," she said, with perfect tranquillity repelling another of Griff's attempts to struggle free. "I made it clear that I would help you only if you left Alphonse Schmidt in peace. Now you have broken your word, which was very foolish—as you are now aware. Perhaps you thought to defy me with impunity. Well, this time you will have no excuse. Here is our new bargain, Warren Vandergriff. I will allow you to depart this room alive. In return, you will leave Heidelberg and expunge from your memory the name and face of Alphonse Schmidt, and of his companions."

If looks could kill, the gaze which Griff fixed upon her should have reduced Nijam to ashes on the spot. But she only smiled and released him.

"Go," she said.

Griff did not approach her; but his face had gone almost purple, and he pointed a trembling finger at her.

"You haven't heard the end of this, Miss Nijam!" he snarled. "If you won't do as I want, then I shall simply have to find someone who will!"

Nijam only smiled—and such a smile it must have been, too! Griff flinched as though she had struck him; but then, gathering up his shreds of outraged dignity, he stalked from the room.

Nijam, after a moment, reached into her pocket to switch off the automaton. Griff would certainly not obey her orders, but she was now at such a pitch of emotion that this did not particularly bother her. Let him try to fight her: she would welcome the chance to crush him.

In the meanwhile—she took a deep breath. "You can come out now," she said. "He's gone."

Alphonse Schmidt emerged from the shadows at the back of the room. He had not entirely disregarded Nijam's orders, for he had concealed his face within the thick purple scarf which my sister Lilias had made him. He must have seen and heard everything; he unwound the concealing muffler and turned a solemn gaze upon her.

"I thought you would do it," he said. "Kill Griff, I mean."

That made Nijam smile again. "But I *have* killed him," she said, light and hard. "Only he doesn't know it yet."

Alphonse's throat worked. "Please," he said. "You mustn't say such things, even in jest."

He ought to know her better by now, than to believe her capable of jesting on such a matter. But let him believe her to be joking if it left him more at ease.

"All right," she said, although she knew that she was still grinning like a death's-head. "Enough talk of killing. We have a machine of our own to build. You can help me draw the plans, if you like."

He did not come at once to the table on which she now un-rolled a sheet of paper. Instead, he lingered by the automaton, running a finger along the cables that held it together.

"I remember you making this," he said. "Stefan told you it would never work, but you refused to listen."

"Well, at the time, he was correct," Nijam said. "I had to invent the necessary optical instruments, if you recall."

Alphonse gave half a smile, but it was evident that he was barely listening. After a hesitating moment, he said: "Yammu wants to have it."

"What for? It isn't as though he can transfer to an automaton, since an automaton cannot eat a brain. Or is it?" The intensity of Nijam's hope made her suddenly dizzy. *It's been lying to us. We* can *get it out of you—without cutting out your brain.*"

She and Alphonse stared at each other for a moment; and then Nijam turned and threw open a drawer.

"There's a paint-brush in here," she said. "We can try marking the Dunwich Signature on the automaton. Then—"

Alphonse's hand closed gently upon her wrist. "No," he said. "That would give it everything it wants."

Nijam went cold and stiff. What did that matter? "I can find a way to stop it once we get it out of *you.*"

"How? How do we *get it out,* Patty? How do we stop it ever coming back, or holding me hostage again?"

For a long moment she only looked angrily into his eyes, willing him to think of something, willing him to admit that there was hope. But he did not. There was no hope.

She opened her hand, and the brush fell back into the drawer.

Alphonse drew her into his arms. She must feel to him like an image of stone, but Nijam could not be the yielding warmth he wanted, not even in his arms. Not when she was in the midst of such a struggle.

But Schmidt was warm enough for both of them. His great hand rose to smooth the ruffled hair back from her brow, and for a moment, that was enough.

"You were always right about me," he said with a sigh. "I gave my conscience into the keeping of others. That was my sin, all the time. And now I must suffer for it. I'm willing to die, Patty, if that's what it takes."

"No," she said, but his confession had made it harder for her to speak with the passionate force of will that had carried her for the past few days. There was a crack in her voice, and a crack in her armour, and then everything she felt poured out.

"Stop saying that you'll die. You have to *fight*—you have to *win*. I can't—I can't lose you again, but you're already telling me that you've given up."

"Giving up? Is that what you think this is?" he asked, gently. "I'm *trying*, Patty. But it's possible that I may not be strong enough to do this; not on my own. You have to be ready to let me go, if that's what it takes."

"There are *answers*." Her hands were clenched in his lapels and white as death. "I'll find them. I ought to have found them years ago, but don't worry. I'll find them this time, and I'll do whatever it takes—"

"Patty—"

"I'll do *whatever* it takes," she repeated, overriding him. "But you must understand. Nothing I do can help you, if *you won't help yourself*."

"Patty," he repeated. "There was nothing you *ought* to have done. My fate is not in your hands. *None of this is your fault*."

Those words stopped the merry-go-round in her brain. Nijam looked up at him in something like hope. She had not known how badly she needed to hear him say such a thing.

"No," she said, drawing a deep breath. "I suppose it isn't. Only I—"

"My fate may not be in my hands either," he added.

Nijam drew breath to object, but he forestalled her. "You never used to be like this."

"Like what?"

"So anxious." He paused. "It was me. I did this to you. I

abandoned you out of my own weakness, and now you fear me doing it again. Can you believe how sorry I am?"

Nijam was speechless. Alphonse, she recalled, had *always* been like this; there were moments when he saw straight to the heart of things. It was one of the things that had, at first, terrified her about him.

Anxious, she thought. Perhaps he was right. Perhaps she was trying to control things, to control *him,* because she was so afraid that he would abandon her again.

She put the thought away to look at later, in solitude. She forced a smile; a real one, this time.

"It won't help either of us to lose our heads, I suppose."

He returned her smile, and it struck Nijam that it had been a while since she had seen such an expression on his face. She had been hard on him, she thought. She would have to change that.

"Help me," she said softly.

His smile broadened. "Help you with what?"

Nijam took his head between her hands, wishing that she could hold him to life by main force, and kissed him.

"We will find the Auberlen papers," she told him. "We will rid you of this creature, and then we will go back to Paris, and we will have a laboratory of our own where we can make—we can make—"

"Prosthetics," he said, "for boys with feet that do not work."

"Something like that," Nijam said, returning his smile. But there was too much sorrow in his eyes, and too much fear, still, in her heart. "We had better begin."

They settled in to their work. By the time Nijam had drawings and measurements for the contraption she meant to build, delivery-boys began to arrive with the things Vasily had purchased.

At any other time, Nijam would have been wonderfully happy to be back in her old laboratory with her beloved Alphonse at her side. Today, although she felt as though an old wound had finally begun to heal, the future still hung over her with a sense of dread.

Her betrothed had returned, but there might still be nothing she could do to save him.

Chapter XIV.

I, meanwhile, having returned home with the children, was surprised to find a visitor waiting in the study.

"Oh, thank goodness you've returned, Fräulein Dark," said the tractable Fräulein Angermeyer, when I entered the house. "Herr von Entzen doesn't like to be kept waiting."

"Brother Otto?" I asked, not missing the way all three of the children huddled a little nearer to me. "Why is he waiting for me?"

"Not for you," the housekeeper elucidated. "For Cosine. The doctor wants to see her."

At that, poor Heidi locked both her arms around my waist and stood up on tiptoe to whisper in my ear.

"I don't want to go! Please, Fräulein Dark, don't let him take me away!"

Fräulein Angermeyer clucked her tongue. "Now, then, Fräulein Cosine, don't be afraid! Your poor father has been in hospital all this time, and he wants to see his little girl!"

I put an arm about Heidi's shrinking shoulders. Peter had a fistful of my skirts locked in his hands, and Clara gazed up at me, anxiously shaking her head.

"Thank you, Fräulein Angermeyer—will you let me have a word with the children, alone?" She went away as obligingly as ever, and I let myself down onto the bench seat that stood in the hallway, whereupon Heidi, despite her size, climbed into my lap and held tightly to my neck.

"All right," I said gently, patting her back. "Don't be afraid; I won't let him take you away. But it isn't the first time something like this has happened to you, is it?"

Heidi shook her head where it was burrowed into my neck.

I asked: "What does your father do to you? Peter?"

Neither of them would answer me—and of course I could not force them to speak. "Very well," I said. "Off you go, upstairs to the nursery, and I will send Otto away."

They were reluctant to let go of me, and I am sure they did not retreat much further than the upper landing. Clara, meanwhile, stopped just short of the top of the stairs and sat down with her arms folded and a look of terrified resolve in her eyes, as though she meant to keep watch. I sent her a comforting smile and then went into the study, where I found Brother Otto sitting in an armchair, absorbed in a book.

He looked up when I approached. "And where is Cosine?" he demanded.

I folded my hands demurely before me. "I'm afraid she has been sent to bed; she isn't feeling well."

"How's that?" Otto demanded, throwing the book aside, and rising to his feet. "You didn't buy her sweets, did you? The doctor has strictly forbidden them."

I remained silent. If he thought I *had* been feeding the children forbidden sweets, then so much the better.

"It doesn't matter, anyway," Otto added, when I refused to speak. "The doctor needs a blood transfusion, that's all. A few too many *marzipankartoffeln* won't incapacitate her."

"A blood transfusion?" I asked, startled out of my dignified silence. A flicker of movement at my side caught my eye, and I found Clara gazing solemnly up at me. She nodded her head. I swallowed and added, "Why does the doctor need a transfusion? He had only a broken bone or two, and Cosine is only a little girl."

Otto flushed, looking uglier than usual. "You weren't hired to ask questions," he said in a harsh voice. "Bring the girl."

"I was hired to *care* for the children," I told him, "and that's precisely what I mean to do. If the doctor needs blood, isn't there someone else who can provide what is needed? It isn't right to take it from a child."

"It must be the right sort of blood. A woman like you would not understand."

"I daresay I wouldn't," said I, keeping my calm with an effort. "But I do understand what is best for the children, and I'm sure the doctor will understand, too. No doubt there will be someone with the right sort of blood at the hospital."

I turned to leave; and at that moment the young man seized my wrist with a grip so fierce that I almost cried out in pain.

"How dare you refuse?" Otto demanded. "The doctor himself—"

"How *dare* you offer me violence?" I retorted. "Mind your manners, young man!"

Had he been a werewolf, or a vampire, or even a mere Baron who had been brought up by an imposing English governess, Brother Otto would have curled up on the spot. But his education must have been lacking, for he only laughed in my face.

"You cannot stop me," he hissed. Then he stormed from the room. Clara fleeted after him, and I hurried after Clara to find Otto already upon the stairs, surprising the two living children, who had stolen halfway down to watch.

He pounced upon a fleeing Heidi and scooped her up. She neither shouted nor fought—she only turned as white as a sheet—and that somehow was the final straw. How I wished I had one of Nijam's little Stunners to hand! Instead I seized the sword-stick from the umbrella-stand and placed myself squarely at the foot of the stair. As Otto turned to descend, he was arrested by the sight of a narrow blade pointed directly at his heart.

I have never seen anyone so taken aback. For a moment he could only sputter in disbelief. As for me, I was not quite sure I believed it myself. I am no Alphonse Schmidt, and even Nijam was more use in a fight than me. Yet, at that moment, there seemed nothing else that I could do.

"Is this what happened to Tangent?" I asked him now, softly. "Did you carry *her* off, too, to drain her blood?"

Whatever Brother Otto had been about to say faded from his lips.

Upon the stair, Clara nodded sadly, and for the first time I understood that I had stumbled upon the truth. So surprised was I, and so distressed, that I allowed the point of my blade to drop.

"Really?" I asked the little shade-girl. "They drained your *blood?*"

Otto moved, and I threatened him again with the tip of the sword. "Is this true?" I demanded.

He paled. I do not know whether it was the knowledge that I had arrived at his guilty secret, or merely the sight of me conversing like a madwoman with the thin air. Heidi must have sensed his fear, for she squirmed free of him at once and ran to my side, burying her face in my ribs. I put an arm about her and stepped to the side, with an imperious sweep of my sword offering Otto a path to the door.

That young man breathed stertorously for a moment or two; and then he raised a shaking hand and shook his finger at me.

"You!" he hissed. "You'll be sorry for this!"

Then he threw open the door and left the house. Dropping the sword-stick, I bolted the door behind him and then collapsed, trembling like a larch, on the bottom stair. Heidi remained latched to my waist, and now Peter stole downstairs too, and hid his head in my lap. Even Clara curled up against me; I felt her only as a shivery sort of feeling at my side.

We were all still sitting there in a heap when my transmitter chirped in my ear.

"Molly, are you there?" Vasily cried in English.

I tapped mine to awaken it. "Yes," I said wearily, "but for heaven's sake, speak German!"

Vasily muttered something in French which I understood but pretended, for the sake of propriety, not to. "Listen," he said in German. "I know what is happening to the children. Schwab has been *drinking their blood.* The veiled woman—she told me. That's how the little girl died. Molly-my-love, you mustn't let them out of your sight for a moment."

"No indeed," I agreed. "I have just thrown Brother Otto out of the house!" And I hiccoughed for pure amazement.

"You what?"

"Never mind—I'll tell you later. Go on—what else?"

"He does it to stay young!" Vasily cried. "Can you believe it? Who does he think he is—a vampire? A Russian Grand Duke?"

"My God, Vasily," Mimi put in—she was evidently listening. "How is *that* the thing that offends you?"

"Of course it isn't the main thing," Vasily began. "His own children, besides! I beg my family's pardon. No Grand Duke would be so depraved!"

He might have gone on, but he was interrupted in turn by Nijam.

"Never mind about that," she said in a jubilant hiss. "We have him now—Dr Schwab, and all his henchmen. Who told you this?"

"Ah!" Vasily drew a deep breath. "That is a discussion for later. Tonight, we hold council. Tomorrow, we raid the library!"

* * *

Mimi is always telling me to get to the point and not drag my stories out too long. So, instead of telling you everything that was discussed at the council of war that night, I will say only that Vasily had excellent reason for haste. Brother Otto had informed Fräulein Angermeyer that the doctor would be returning from hospital in the next day or two; and when he did so, our freedom of movement would be greatly curtailed. With all our plans laid to our satisfaction, therefore, it seemed best to make our attempt upon the Library the following day.

That morning an urgent telegram was received by a certain archivist, calling him to the bedside of a dying grandmother in Württemberg. Dispatching a message to the Library, which was intercepted, he promptly took the train to that city and comes no more into our story.

Meanwhile Vasily donned spectacles and a muffler and went to the Library in his place, letting himself into the building with a key from the archivist's ring, which Mimi had filched the night before. "Bad cold," he told Karl Zangemeister hoarsely, when the Head Librarian greeted him. From there Vasily mounted the steps to the third floor, tried another of the stolen keys on the archive-room, and was soon safely ensconced within.

The morning dragged by. This was the dangerous part of the plan, when it was possible that another librarian wanting something in the archives might explode Vasily's disguise. Yet the hours passed uneventfully. By the early afternoon, when the Library opened its doors to the public, our man inside was still at large.

It was then that Alphonse followed in Vasily's footsteps. I could tell from Nijam's manner, as she directed affairs via the transmitter, that she was ill at ease with this arrangement. Yet he, too, made his way through the streets without incident. Once within the Library, he made himself known to Zangemeister, who could be relied upon to conceal him from most inquirers.

He, too, quickly ascended to the third floor; where, unbeknownst to Zangemeister, he and Vasily began work in earnest. The archive having been organised and catalogued with traditional German efficiency, Vasily had already quite easily located the Auberlen papers, together with both the Schmidts'. He then amused himself inspecting the rest of the sealed books, some of which he could see at a glance were highly valuable.

Some loose papers were kept in large boxes; these Vasily now began to empty, replacing their contents with the books we intended to steal. Alphonse hung back, glancing through the pages of one of his old journals.

"Seen something useful?" Vasily asked, as Alphonse went

still and silent for a moment.

"No," Alphonse replied, returning to the present with a visible effort. "I have only the faintest idea what I am looking for."

Vasily beheld his former valet with some anxiety. Schmidt appeared distracted; his face was wan and drawn like a man who suffers constant pain.

"Is something the matter?" he asked.

"It's Yammu," Alphonse confessed, unable to repress a shudder as he uttered the name. "I can always feel him clawing at the back of my mind. I am always struggling to hold him off."

"But then it's good news, if you still have the upper hand of him," Vasily pointed out.

"He keeps making me promises," Alphonse said, after a moment passed in silent work. "He tells me that it will leave me and never return, if I only allow him to transfer to Miss Nijam's automaton. But we must have something better than his word to rely upon."

Vasily shrugged. The offer did not seem a bad one to him, but no doubt Schmidt was right to insist upon a bargain which he could enforce. He emptied another box of its papery miscellany.

"Are we not finished?" Alphonse asked, startled, as Vasily began to pack the new box with books from an altogether new shelf. "Are we taking more than just the Auberlen-Schmidt papers?"

"Undoubtedly," Vasily answered. "If they are the only thing missing, old Zangemeister will know at once who to blame. We must muddy the waters at least a *little*."

The Auberlen-Schmidt journals and various other related

201

papers had filled three archive boxes; by the time Vasily was satisfied, they had nine more filled with unrelated but, he thought, interesting and valuable items. They stacked the boxes by the southwestern window. It was now nearly four o'clock, with the sun low in the sky and the closing-bell due any moment. Schmidt set to work opening the window, which had been bolted shut, and Vasily congratulated himself upon a job which had hitherto gone as smoothly as possible.

It was then that his transmitter crackled.

"Can anyone hear me?"

My voice was quite steady. Vasily, in his ebullient mood, did not hold back.

"Molly-my-dear!" he cried. "The very person I wished to speak to! Little mouse, only one thing remains to make this day complete. Will you marry me?"

"Yes," I said, without hesitation.

Vasily was so shocked that he went into a frightful coughing-fit.

"Are you joking?" he asked, when he had recovered himself somewhat.

"Why should I be joking?" I retorted, and thereby reduced him once again to confusion.

"But—*Gospodin,* Molly! Won't you regret it, in the end? I only meant—that is to say, I meant every word of it, but—"

From Vasily's transmitter there came the sound of rustling and fumbling; and then a new voice interrupted him, this time in English.

"Herr Dunkel—" said Warren Vandergriff, "—or perhaps I should call you Mr Nicks? –and company. Your friend was kind enough to let me have her transmitter for a moment. Now..." He drew out the word with relish. "Now, I should

202

advise you all to listen very carefully indeed, for I can think of no one it would be a greater pleasure to do away with."

Chapter XV.

Now that I have your attention, I ought to explain how this unfortunate situation had come to be.

As usual, I spent the day with the children. We were in the midst of our English lesson, painstakingly learning to ask after the pen of the gardener's aunt, when the doorbell rang—jangling like a fire-alarm, not once, but two or three times.

A few minutes later, Fräulein Angermeyer rapped on the nursery door. "It's the Herr Vandergriff, the American gentleman," she told me. "He wants to see you, Fräulein."

Proper governesses do *not* receive gentleman callers, and this, I thought, made a useful excuse. "I'm sure *I* don't wish to see *him*," said I, virtuously. "Ask him to go away."

"That's what I told him, Fräulein," said the housekeeper, distressed. "But he refuses to go away until you see him—and he threatened to search the house for you if you did not come down at once."

I reflected sadly that it was unlikely I could send *Griff* packing with just a sword-stick.

"Wait here, children," I told them.

"Is it the bad man again?" Peter asked, with a wrinkle between his brows.

I ruffled his hair. "The very worst man I know—so mind

204

you keep out of sight!"

Then I went downstairs to find Griff waiting in the drawing-room. I knew the moment I saw him that he was on the war–path, for he was on his feet and his eyes glittered with tightly-controlled fury. When I entered—Fräulein Anger-meyer behind me—he turned and ushered her out of the room saying, "What I have to say to Miss Dark is private, ma'am. Thank you." Then he closed the door. Griff and I were alone.

No—not quite alone. Clara had accompanied me; and when I saw the look of determination on Griff's face I felt oddly grateful to have another person in the room, even if she was a little ghost whom only I could see.

"Shall I send for tea?" I asked him, as winsomely as I might.

"No," he snapped. "Sit down, Miss Molly."

I did so reluctantly. As I suspected, he had only offered me the seat so that he could hover ominously above me.

"We must vary our agreement," he said, looming assiduously. "The old one will not do. That Nijam woman is impossible to work with."

"So she is!" I said, fondly. "But really, Griff, don't you remember our agreement? Nijam was to help you, certainly—but only so long as you left Alphonse Schmidt in peace. If she refuses to do so now, it is because you chased him halfway across Heidelberg. You can't expect us to respect an agreement if you do not."

"I never agreed to it," Griff corrected me. "I wanted to work with *both* of them in exchange for not marrying you. Now, if Miss Nijam won't come to the party, Schmidt must, and *you* must."

"But I'm not going to marry you," I told him, patiently. "Why should I? There's nothing in it for me."

"I've explained this before," Griff said, testily. "You and I can merge and enlarge our trade in the Pacific. You won't have to be a thief anymore, and I can shield you from prosecution. Or, certainly, you can refuse me, and throw it all away!"

"I *have* refused you!" I said. "Five times, one of them at gunpoint!"

He flushed. "That's enough! Open up that transmitter and tell your friends that if they ever want to see you again outside of a German gaol, they must hand over Alphonse Schmidt. Why are you laughing?"

Sooner than give up her Alphonse, Nijam would cut my throat herself—but I did not think that Griff would listen if I told him. He had not listened to anything else I said.

At that moment, a scuffle distracted us, and the drawing-room door opened. It was (of course) the children—Heidi and Peter.

"Go away," Griff told them.

"Go away yourself," Heidi informed him. "We don't like you. You're a bad man."

"And you're a very disrespectful little girl," Griff said, closing the door firmly. He turned back to me, unaware that Clara remained in the room and was pulling an extremely rude face at him. From this moment on, the little shade remained by the door, disappearing through it at intervals—no doubt in order to communicate with her brother.

"Call your friends," Griff demanded, returning to loom over me. Seeing that he was in earnest and would not be fobbed off, I switched on my transmitter.

"Can you hear me?" I asked, in German. Whereupon Vasily, of course, asked me to marry him.

It had occurred to me that he might do so, and it had

206

moreover occurred to me that if I assented, it would be so unexpected—so far out of character—that he must infallibly perceive that I was in very great danger.

"Yes," I said.

I could not quite avoid the little thrill of delight that went through me when I said this. It occurred to me that under less exigent conditions, I might positively enjoy saying *Yes* to such a question. Vasily's emotions, however, were not so favourable. For a moment it sounded as though, like the late Aunt Dete, he had swallowed a fly.

After a painful moment he asked me whether I was joking.

I pressed a despairing hand to my forehead. "Vasily," I said, willing him to understand me. *"Why* should I be joking?"

He went into another gargle of terror. Griff reached out and seized my transmitter without so much as a by-your-leave. "Nicks and company," he said, "Your friend was kind enough to let me have her transmitter for a moment. Now, I should advise you all to listen very carefully indeed, for I can think of no one it would be a greater pleasure to do away with."

He was, of course, repeating Nijam's own words, with ironic relish. I did not hear Vasily's response. The answer must have been lengthy and heartfelt, however. Griff's face changed.

"Look here! If you want to speak to Miss Molly you'll have to give me Schmidt."

There was a brief silence. Then Griff said, "Wait!" He sent me a furious look and returned the transmitter to my ear.

"Vasily? What did you tell him?" I asked, in German.

But it was Alphonse, to my surprise, who answered. "I told him I knew why he wanted the automaton, and that if he didn't want me sabotaging it, he'd better do as we asked."

"That's my boy," I said. "Have you finished at the Library?"

"Nearly," Schmidt answered.

But Vasily said, "Hang the Library. I'm coming to fetch you."

"No!" I protested. "Do the job—I'll keep Griff occupied."

"Molly," Vasily pleaded. "He's threatened you. In Hong Kong he came within an ace of forcing you to marry him. I can't leave you with him."

"Yes, you can," I said, closing my eyes to escape the suspicious glare with which Griff had intensified his looming. "Do not forget, my love, that we are something more than lovers. We are conspirators—and conspirators must be able to trust each other."

Vasily muttered something under his breath in his own native tongue. "Don't let him hurt you," he said, and then the transmission cut out.

"Well?" Griff demanded.

I sat back, trying not to look as nervous as I now felt. Somehow it was harder to put on a brave face when I knew that Vasily feared for me, too.

All the same, I thought I could take care of Griff. He was the kind of man—and it is always a man—who will take all the time in the world if it means hectoring a woman into agreeing with him.

"Well," I said, "it sounds as though we will have to make a new agreement, after all. But you'll need to offer us something better if you expect us to give up Schmidt to you. For one thing, what assurances will you give that you mean to keep your word?"

"I beg your pardon!" said Griff, clearly offended. "Of the two of us, Miss Molly, *I* am not the thief. I believe that if anyone ought to provide assurances, it is yourself."

"*If* I am a thief," I said, "then what are you? You have

attempted to entrap me into marriage, prison, and a lunatic asylum, and now you are using me to extort services from a bionic chemist."

"Don't be dramatic," he said. "It's not as though you are a saint, yourself! Besides, you must face facts, Miss Molly. You hold no cards. Do you think you can win? I know precisely what you and your friends are doing in Heidelberg."

"I am quite certain you don't," I told him, which was entirely true.

"You mean to recover Alphonse Schmidt's memories," he said, "and with them the secret of revenant-making, which you mean to sell to the highest bidder. Naturally you don't like to give the man up; that would be like letting go of the golden goose. But really, you ought to consider selling him to *me.*"

"He's engaged to be married to Miss Nijam," I protested. "Would *you* sell *your* fiancée?"

"Of course not," Griff said. "You're worth a fortune to me. But I'm willing to *pay* a fortune for Alphonse Schmidt—and not just for my own benefit, either. Let's say you sell the revenants to Russia or France. They'll be sure to keep the secret to themselves, or else they'll sell it at vast cost to their allies. In either case, every other Great Power in the world will hunt you for the rest of your lives, in hopes of getting what their enemies are keeping from them. That's the cost of keeping the secret, and that's precisely what I mean *not* to do. Knowledge like this belongs to the world, not to a single government. I'll make a gift of it to everyone; there'll be revenants in every nation by the time I'm done."

I did imagine it—and shuddered. But I stiffened my upper lip. "All right. How much did you think of paying us?"

"That's not important."

"I'm pleased to hear it," said I. "For a little thing like eliminating all the crime in the world, I think that four million pounds would be a pretty reasonable sum."

Griff raised his eyebrows. "Four million! You must be joking!"

I pointed out that he was the one to suggest paying a fortune, and that four million would divide nicely among the four remaining members of our crew once Alphonse had been handed over. Griff did not like this. I allowed myself to be bargained down to two million—a loss I took philosophically, given that I did not expect to see a shilling of it.

"Well," I said at length, "two million doesn't sound fair to me, but I'll admit that you've already given us two million for the Noor-Jahan. I shall have to discuss it with the rest of the crew."

"Why wait?" Griff asked, rising to his feet. "Where are they now? At the Library?"

I was speechless. Griff laughed—rather nastily, I thought.

"I may not speak German," he told me, "but even I know what *Bibliothek* signifies. What are they doing there?"

I shrugged, regaining my composure. "What do you think? They are looking for a way to reverse poor Schmidt's memory loss. Wait until tomorrow, and we shall have an answer for you, I'm sure. In the meanwhile, I ought to be giving the children their English lesson."

I rose to my feet, with a sweep of my arm that invited him to depart. If only he would go away!

But he did not.

"The library has no books about siren-induced memory loss," Griff declared. "I asked old Zangemeister myself."

"The working of the human brain is very mysterious," I agreed. "I doubt the answers we seek are labelled so clearly."

But Griff's eyes had narrowed. "Why would an attorney like Basil Nicks be reading brain-science at the library?" And then he guessed.

"It isn't the memories you're after at all," he exclaimed. "It's the Auberlen papers!"

Before I could speak another word—still less think of warning my crew—he reached out and tore the transmitter from my ear. At the same moment he touched his own.

"Jones? Yes," he said, tersely, to an unseen interlocutor. "It's me, Vandergriff. Listen: some funny business is happening at the University Library. A theft, I believe. Alert the German police at once. Yes, *and* our British friends."

"Wait a moment," I begged, but it was already too late. He caught my wrist.

"The birds will be caught in a trap," he exulted. "And as for you, Miss Molly—I'm going to put you where you can't make trouble."

I struggled in vain. Griff marched me out of the drawing-room and across the entrance-hall into Dr Schwab's study. With a twitch of his segmented arm he turned the latch on the sinister trap-door and threw it open. The cellar yawned before us smelling of chemicals and decay, of damp and of dread.

That smell dragged me back to the hideous minutes I had already passed in that room. My heart failed me. I threw all my weight against him.

"Griff," I choked. "For pity's sake, don't leave me alone down there!"

His only answer was to seize me bodily and sling me across

his shoulders. This in itself was quite frightening, for I am built rather upon Junoesque than elfin lines.

"Really, Griff," I said, in a voice from which I could not quite eliminate the tremor, "if you leave me down there I don't know what I may do. I might run into a panic, and break everything in sight, and what will the doctor say?"

Griff paid no heed to my pleas. My last view, as he descended into the darkness, was the three children peering through the study door with pale, horrified faces. It was then that the plan sprang into my mind. I had no time to ask myself whether it was a good one; only it struck me that it might save my friends.

Frantically I mouthed three words at the children, accompanying them with a demonstrative motion of my arm. The three heads went into a little huddle. Then Griff dragged me into the darkness. A moment later he lowered me from his shoulders onto that ghastly steel table!

"What are you doing?" I gasped, as he seized my wrists and drew them to the corners of the table.

"Lie still," he demanded. "I said I'd put you where you cannot cause trouble, and so I will."

The straps tightened about my wrists. "Griff," I pleaded, "you can't really mean it. Are you setting up as a pantomime villain?"

"You know what they say about desperate measures," said he, in that colourless way of his; and then above, there came a rush of small feet. The trap-door shut with an echoing boom. The latch clicked into place—and the whole cellar was plunged into Stygian darkness.

Chapter XVI.

Darkness was also falling outside in the streets of Heidelberg. At the library, the closing-bell rang. Obedient to the summons, Schmidt drew his scarf up to cover his face again and departed. A few minutes later Vasily, too, locked the archive door and descended to Karl Zangemeister's desk.

"Leaving early tonight?" Zangemeister asked, and Vasily, who had also muffled himself up, gave a nod and a hoarse grunt that might have come from anyone. "Merry Christmas," Karl said.

Stepping into the Augustinergasse, Vasily took a moment to turn up his coat collar, inspecting the street for any sign of yachtsmen. There were none in view, so he crossed the road to the quadrangle around which the University buildings were set. The nearest door opened at a tap and Vasily entered to find the hallways deserted save for Mimi, Schmidt, and Nijam—the latter two robed and hooded. They tossed Vasily his own robe and hood, helping him arrange them until he looked sufficiently grand and ominous to pass as a Black Templar.

"All ready?" Nijam asked, inspecting a cross-bow which she held on her hip.

"Yes; our friends are waiting with the baker's van at the nearest livery stable," Vasily said. "But Vandergriff has Miss

Dark."

"We know," Nijam said. "Let her be, Vasily. She knows what she's doing. Stick to the plan."

Vasily gnawed on his lip, for as he said later, it went sorely against every inclination. All the same, he trusted—falsely, as it happened—that I had a transmitter with which to call him if I wanted him. Accordingly, he went off to the livery stable to fetch the Black Templars. Mimi, judging that the night had become sufficiently dark, fitted her tiger-claws to her hands and went to assail the library. Nijam with her cross-bow, and Alphonse, carrying a large case, ventured upstairs.

They passed many lecture-rooms. All of them were dark and empty, for it was Christmas Eve and the last of the students had been sent home. Many of them must have gone directly to the Night Market, for from the distant square there went up a rowdy sound of singing.

Nijam and Alphonse reached the window which Mimi had marked for their use: it was on the third floor and gazed across the Augustinergasse diagonally towards the archive window. In the deepening dusk, Mimi was a grey blur against the pale face of the Library, at a spider-like crawl approaching the window which Vasily had left unlatched for her.

Nijam checked her cross-bow and laid the bolt in the groove. Alphonse opened the window and touched his transmitter. "Mimi, we are positioned."

"All right. Tell Nijam not to shoot her little siege engine yet," Mimi panted, hoisting herself to the window-sill.

"If I wanted to kill someone," Nijam said coldly, winding the mechanism, "I would use something far more deadly than a cross-bow bolt."

"And what might that be?" Alphonse asked in a morbid kind

of fascination.

Across the way, Mimi's dark form slid within the window.

"A little of the wrong sort of knowledge," Nijam said, raising the bow. "Mimi, say the word when you are ready."

"Now," said Mimi, and Nijam shot her bolt. The missile flew with barely a whisper and vanished into the darkness. A bobbin of fishing-line mounted on the crossbow jumped and thrummed for a moment before stopping. Nijam put the cross-bow down, snipped the thread, and fastened it to the paired ends of a thin but strong steel cable, and a lighter, thinner rope, which were coiled together on a spool which Schmidt had extracted from the big case he carried.

Meanwhile Alphonse was hard at work fixing a clamp to the window-lintel. Mimi's shape was visible at the other window, following suit. Nijam fitted the cable into the pulley and fixed it to the clamp.

"Ready," she said softly, and Mimi drew on the fishing-line, pulling the cable and its rope silently across the space between the buildings.

By the time Mimi's end of the cable was secured to its own clamp, Nijam had her small trolley ready—a sturdy steel tray in each corner of which she had bored a hole, so that it could be hung securely from a third pulley. She attached the trolley to both cable and rope and stood back, observing her invention with pride.

"Trolley ready," she told Mimi, who at once began to draw upon the rope. Running smoothly on the pulley, the trolley vanished into the darkness. A minute later, the cable thrummed with tension. "Box away," said Mimi; and Alphonse drew on the rope. The trolley rolled back across the street, now laden down with the first of their purloined books.

"It works like magic!" Alphonse observed, admiringly.

Nijam gave a catlike smile. "Everything I do works."

"Save your flirting for when the job is done," Mimi cut in, via transmitter. "What if the whole thing falls apart three boxes in?"

"It won't," said Nijam with dignity. "Also, I was not flirting; I was making a statement of fact."

"Liar," murmured Alphonse.

Nijam pretended not to hear this; she was busy helping him get the box off the trolley and in at the window. Then she went down on her knees, her hands trembling with eagerness. Opening the shutter of the dark-lantern Alphonse had brought with them, she tore off the lid and peered at the contents.

"What's this?" she demanded, peering at the book within. "Goethe's *Faust*? Vasily, what the *blazes* is *this* doing here?"

"It's an eighteenth-century first edition," Vasily told her, via transmitter. "Absolutely priceless, I assure you."

Nijam rubbed her eyes. "Look, it wasn't a bad idea to muddy the waters by taking more books than we need. But couldn't you have at least stacked the Auberlen boxes at the top? What if something happens?"

"What if something happens to Miss Dark?" Vasily was heard to mutter. "Don't worry," he added. "There are only twelve boxes."

To and fro, to and fro went the trolley, high above the darkened street. To and fro went librarians and students in the street beneath: some to their homes, and others to the the beer-gardens where they would sing and drink until the night was old. Soon Vasily arrived with a dozen Black Templars, who at once whisked the first few boxes downstairs to the baker's van. Despite their very solemn robes and the fact that most of them were whiskered professors, Nijam thought that they behaved rather like schoolboys out on a lark. They whispered and chuckled as they carried the boxes away and generally looked thoroughly pleased with themselves.

Only nine of the boxes had been drawn in and carried downstairs to the waiting van when a carriage came pelting down the Augustinergasse. It drew up before the Library, and then four or five German policemen hurried out of it and went pelting up the steps. A second carriage followed hard on its heels.

"No, no, *no!*" Nijam protested, as though by saying the word she could forbid the policemen to enter. "How did they find us?"

Vasily bounded to the window, glanced at the gendarmerie, and knew at once what had happened. The voices of the Black Templars could be heard on the stairs as they returned for the next box. Shutting the door in their faces, he tapped his transmitter. "Molly!" he called. "Molly-my-dear, give us some sign if you're there."

There was no answer.

"Molly Dark can keep," Nijam hissed, opening her own transmitter. "Look sharp, Mimi; they're onto us."

"I saw, thanks. There are still three boxes left."

"We need to buy time," Nijam muttered. "Mimi, can you set off a fire alarm?"

"There's no time to find it," Alphonse said, hauling on the rope that guided the trolley. He snatched a tenth box from the tray and practically flung it at Vasily. "You must send me across. I'll lead them away from the archive."

Seizing the trolley, he stepped up onto the windowsill.

"Absolutely not!" Nijam practically shrieked. "Alphonse

Schmidt, don't you dare!"

"Don't I dare *what?*" he flung back at her. "Go to the aid of my friend? *Do* something to repay her for the horrible risk she is running for me?"

Nijam swallowed a jagged lump in her throat. "Don't throw your life away," she said, huskily. *"Please* don't."

All the indignation faded from his eyes. Then he reached out and laid his hand gently to her cheek.

"It's me they're looking for," he told her. "I'm the only one who can divert them from Mimi."

"He's right," Vasily put in.

Nijam caught his hand and kissed it. "If you die," she hissed, "I'll bury you in unhallowed ground."

"I would expect nothing less," he told her. Then he cried, "Mimi, *pull!*" and setting his foot in the tray, and gripping the pulley with both hands, he launched himself from the window.

He was too heavy to make a quick journey. Nijam watched with her heart in her mouth as his weight dragged the cable into a deep depression at the middle point of his journey. But he twisted himself upon the tray and dragged himself towards Mimi hand-over-hand. At last he vanished within the far window, and she breathed a sigh of relief.

"Quick," she heard Mimi say, over the transmitter. "Don't let them see you leave the archive."

"I'll try," he said; and that was the last they heard of him. Vasily was reeling in the eleventh box of books when a commotion erupted within the library—a distant shouting and the ringing of a bell. Lights blinked out from other windows. Vasily whistled for a Black Templar to take the box; back the trolley went, and returned with the twelfth box.

"All done," Mimi said, and they saw her unclamp the pulley

from the far window and stow it into the light knapsack she carried with her. Released, the rope and cable slithered into the street. Frantically, Nijam began drawing them in at her own window lest they be spotted by a chance wayfarer.

"What are you doing, Mimi?" Vasily objected, as the window across the way closed. "You must get out of there!"

"I *am* getting out," Mimi said, breathlessly. "But I'm going after Alphonse."

Her transmitter closed. Nijam stood vacillating by the window as Vasily gathered up the coils of rope and cable.

"Oh, *Gospodin!*" he said, after a moment. "I cannot rush to Miss Dark's defence, but Alphonse Schmidt is another matter, I suppose! Well, off you go! But do ask the Templars to step in and help me with all this gear!"

That decided her. Nijam turned without a word and fled the room.

Vasily heaved a deep sigh. Then the Black Templars were about him, and he was calling orders, hounding them downstairs to the waiting van.

Chapter XVII.

The slamming of the trap-door sent echoes rolling about the cellar. For a moment Griff and I were plunged into absolute darkness. Then I caught a glimmer of light. Turning my head, I saw Clara standing at the head of the steps, looking terrified but determined.

I sent her a smile much braver than I felt. The children, bless them, had done as I asked; but at what cost?

Griff said a quiet, frozen, *"What,"* which was somehow more frightening than if he had blasphemed. Then a match flared up and he lit the nearest gas-lamp before brushing past Clara to pound at the trap-door with his brazen fist.

"Open up!" he bellowed, when the trap resisted him. It must have been very solid; so solid, that I wondered whether I was the first prisoner to be kept here. "Open up, you little devils!"

There was no answer.

"Release me, and I'll speak to them," I suggested.

"Speak to them first," Griff panted, sliding me a distrustful glance, "and then I'll think about releasing you."

I sighed. Well—it had been worth a try. But if Griff refused to release me, he could jolly well stay put. I turned to Clara.

"There's a packet of *spitzbuben* in the top drawer of my dresser," I told her, "right underneath my stockings. Tell your siblings that they may go up and eat every single one of them, so long as they leave this trap-door shut and not open it for anything—do you understand?"

Clara gave a wide-eyed nod.

"Who do you think you're talking to?" Griff demanded, but Clara had already gone. A moment later Peter and Heidi could be heard crossing the floor above us, and then more faintly galloping up the stairs.

Silence fell. I knew that I could trust Clara; she of all people must know what horrible things were likely to happen in this cellar to children who made trouble for people like Griff. Somehow she would convince her siblings to stay upstairs, where Griff could neither cajole nor threaten them to release him.

Griff, who was now locked in here—with *me*.

At first he merely attempted to force the trap-door. When that failed, he tapped his own transmitter and called upon some confederate.

"Jones, what are you doing? What news?" There followed a moment's silence as he listened to the answer. "No, proceed to the library with the police," he ordered. "I've run into some trouble, but it's nothing I can't handle."

With that, he descended the ladder and began to pace the room. In the glare of the solitary gas-lamp he was like a great grey wolf stalking to and fro; from time to time I caught the sulphurous gleam as the light reflected from his eyes, and a nasty little shiver ran up and down my spine.

"It would serve you right," Griff said, at last, "if I ran an experiment or two on *you*, Miss Molly. This is the third time you've tried to thwart me."

"But I didn't come to Heidelberg to thwart you," said I,

repressing a shudder. "Nor to Hong Kong, for that matter. If you don't like to be thwarted, then you might consider giving me a moment's peace."

"You can have your moment's peace," Griff retorted. "All you have to do is give up your life of crime, and consent to become my wife!"

"Griff," I said, with a choking laugh, for how much longer must I bear this persecution? —"Griff, you are quite aware that I will never consent to be your wife."

He was now trailing a finger along a row of dusty jars and bottles on a high shelf. "No, you won't," he said.

This, I had not expected. "There! Was that so difficult?"

"I can offer you everything," he said bitterly. "Money. Power. Immortality. But you'll throw it away because you're still infatuated with that renegade vampire, Vasily Romanov."

My stomach twisted a little with worry. "Vasily is dead."

He took down one of the bottles and scanned the label. "Oh, I know. But I still haven't got a chance, have I? I'm a nice man, and he was a blood-sucking fiend who meant to ruin you. I guess he succeeded."

I felt another quake of fear. In most men of the class commonly called gentleman, there is a certain self-conceit that forbids them offering violence to a lady. But if Griff had convinced himself that Vasily had indeed *ruined me,* as he put it—why, then I was no lady; and he was under no obligation to be a gentleman.

"No one has ever dared to insult me like this," I said. "If I were a man I'd call you out."

"Don't be foolish," Griff said. "If you were a man you wouldn't be making a fool of yourself over a Russian gigolo. Women! You'd rather a scoundrel like Romanov than an honest, decent fellow who only wants to make you happy."

As little as a year ago, perhaps, he might have succeeded in shaming me. Vasily *was* a scoundrel, and Griff *was* law-abiding and respectable, and young ladies from Brixton were *supposed* to prefer the latter to the former. But there are bad men who know that they are bad and wish to mend; and there are bad men who do *not* know it; men whose badness consists in pride—in the keeping of laws, and the whiting of sepulchres. And whatever Brixton might have to say about it, I knew with absolute certainty which *I* preferred.

"Griff," I said, swallowing my indignation and terror, "I am trying to be kind to both of us. Marriage would be a punishment for you and me alike. Why insist upon it? Why not find some nice, sensible woman who *wants* to marry you?"

"They only want my money," he said. "I've known a great many women, and there isn't a bit of real feeling among the lot of them."

Not wanting to goad him to greater excesses of wrath, I forbore from asking him how it was that most women of his acquaintance should find themselves incapable of loving him.

"Aha!" Griff exclaimed. Evidently he had found what he was looking for. He placed a very tiny vial of clear liquid on the table by my head. It was too near to read the label. Then he went rummaging in the cupboards and soon came out with a syringe.

"No," he said thoughtfully, as he retrieved the vial. "I want someone who will be useful to me—someone with the ability to interact with other consciousnesses. The doctor says that under the right kind of stimulus—lysergic acid diethylamide, for instance—it is possible to enhance these abilities; and from there, to refine and control them. At present, Miss Molly, you are no more than a spoon—but I'll make you into a scalpel. You will become an instrument for the salvation of humanity."

Never in my life had I heard such ominous words. Even when Griff and Sir Humphrey were conspiring to lock me up in a madhouse, at least I had known what to expect.

"What is that supposed to mean?" I demanded. "Do you mean to make me like poor Alphonse, possessed by another mind?"

Griff smiled. The gaslight flickered yellow in the depths of his eyes as he pierced the wax-sealed cap of the vial and drew the drug into the syringe.

"Yes," he said. "That precisely."

A cold sweat broke out upon my forehead. Perhaps it would have been wiser to let Griff run off to hound the others, rather than allow myself to be shut in with him. But the children were gone now, even Clara. There was no going back.

If nothing else, I thought, Alphonse would have companionship in his terrible plight.

Unless I could distract Griff from his plans.

"I don't understand," I told him, once again testing my restraints. "I was taught that the gift of eternal life belongs to God alone. Aren't you afraid of your own hubris? Don't you fear to snatch at divinity?"

"What a ridiculous question," Griff said. "My hubris, as you call it, is the very thing that sets me apart. It makes me what I am—the Christ of the future, who will lead humanity to eternal life. …Besides, I've succeeded this far, haven't I? There's been no bolt of lightning to strike me dead."

I was not prepared to comment on this. To my mind, Griff had succeeded at little but making a nuisance of himself; he certainly had not managed to transfer a mind from one body to another.

But I must say something. I was like Penelope, spinning out tales night after night in the hope of escaping death at the hands of the man who had married her.

"All the poets—" said I, "—all the philosophers have called death the great leveller; the one who visits kings and peasants alike without fear or favour. Before death surely all mortals must kneel and confess our weakness. Even the great emperors of the past, when faced with death, have developed a becoming sense of humility. The Ancient Egyptians would pass around a mummy at their feasts, in warning of what must come to all. The great King Canute placed his throne in the tide and commanded it to rise no further, merely to demonstrate his impotence in the face of Nature and Nature's God. But you—you alone believe that you might master Nature, and death, and God. Is this wise, Griff? Is it humble? Is it, in fact, *likely?*"

I might have gone on like this for a few pages longer, except that I had to pause for breath; and then Griff spoke.

"Of course it is," he said. "Take Caesar Augustus, for instance. He might have been a pretty fine fellow in his day, but he didn't have the capabilities *I* have. He only had armies, but I have knowledge."

"But do you?" I asked him. "Do you really? Miss Nijam says that we don't even know whether consciousness-transference is possible."

"Of course we do." So absorbed was Griff in the argument that—much to my relief—he put the syringe back in its case. "Rationally speaking, it's a certainty. There's no conceptual limit to scientific progress. Think of all the things we've learned just in the past decade or two. We know that germs cause disease, that electricity can be harnessed to generate light and heat, that messages can be delivered via radio-waves around the world. The more we learn, the longer we'll live; the longer we live, the more we'll learn, until at last we have eliminated death altogether. The logic is unassailable."

The logic *was* unassailable, I thought. I had been taught a little logic at school, enough to know that you could reason yourself into utter absurdity, however sound your logic, so long as you started from false premises. In this way Griff had reasoned himself from a belief in infinite progress, into a belief in eternal life.

And it was not that he meant to steal divinity: he *already* believed himself to be a god.

"Do you really wish to transfer yourself into someone else's body?" I asked, still scarcely able to believe it. "Do you mean to transfer yourself to *me?*"

Griff gave me an exasperated look. "Of course not," he said. "You'll make an excellent test subject, Miss Molly, but a female body would be utterly unsuitable for a first-class brain like mine. I'll have Alphonse Schmidt build me an automaton."

"An *automaton?*" I almost choked on my own surprise. "You—you want to be a *machine?* But *why?*"

"Why not?" he asked, as though it was the most natural thing in the world.

Feebly I shook my head. If Griff did not know how to value the warmth of a cosy blanket on a winter's night, the enlivening effect of a cup of tea, or the touch of a lover's lips— why, then, I did not know how to make him.

I thought again of poor little Clara, who could not eat any of the Christmas biscuits, and must make do with sniffing them instead, like a beggar child outside a bakery.

"What will you do with your body when you've left it?" I asked.

"I'm not sentimental. I expect I'll have it cremated and thrown onto the flower-beds."

"You're going to throw away a perfectly good body as though it's nothing more than the sweepings from the fireplace?"

"Why not?" he asked again. He was laughing this time— but there was a wild note in his laughter, which I had never heard from Griff before. "I've already sacrificed two perfectly healthy arms. It's this sentimental attachment to mere biological hardware, Miss Molly, that is holding us back."

"But your body is a *gift*," I objected. "Your body can *feel*—and taste—and smell!"

"My body is about to kill me," Griff said, and had I been paying a little more attention, I might have noticed the strain in his voice.

"Be sensible," I said. "You can't be a day over forty. Forty-five at the utmost."

"Even so," he said, fixing me with those glittering eyes, "That's why it's unacceptable that I should be *dying of cancer.*"

Any words I might have been about to say were dashed from my lips. Cancer!

"I didn't know," I whispered, stricken despite myself. Had I not thought that he appeared thin and worn of late? The ambition that seemed so ridiculous a moment ago now suddenly became perfectly comprehensible. Dying! at his age! In his place I, too, might be tempted to fight against God.

In the silence Griff took a long, shaking breath. "If it's unacceptable at forty-one," he said, "then it's unacceptable at ninety-one. You see that, don't you? That's why I have to solve this. If I die, then everyone dies. But if I find immortality, then the rest of the world will find it, too."

"So long as they can afford it, I suppose," said I.

"A rising tide lifts all boats," he said, with a hard smile. "It is as I said: I am the Christ of the future. And when I come into my kingdom, Miss Molly, I won't forget your ridicule."

I was sorry for him, but I still believed him to be mad—mad and blasphemous. "I prefer the Christ of the past," I told him, as he retrieved the syringe from the case. "He at least was gentle and lowly."

Griff made no sound, instead flicking the syringe with a finger.

"Don't do this," I begged, trying to keep the tremor out of my voice. "Didn't you hear Alphonse, before? If you lay a finger on me then he will never build you that new body you want. Let me go and I'll put in a word for you, I swear."

"I don't mean to give him a choice," Griff answered, pinching the inside of my elbow, seeking a vein.

"Do you really think the police will allow that to happen?" I asked. "You sent your man off to fetch them—"

"Only because *you* had me trapped here," he answered. "Don't worry, Miss Molly. I want steamer ships for my trans-Pacific trade, and both England and Germany would dearly love to secure the contract. Whoever captures Alphonse Schmidt, I expect we'll be able to work something out."

"In time to save your life?" I asked, watching that gleaming needle.

He laughed at me. "And *you* can guarantee anything better? —No, don't try to struggle. It'll only sting for a moment."

But before he could inject me with that sinister drug, he was interrupted by the heavy tramp of many feet in the study above.

"Who is that?" Griff demanded.

I grasped at any hope. "It may be the Black Templars. Do you think they'll be pleased to find you here?"

"They will when they see what I've found them," Griff declared, addressing the syringe once more to my elbow.

But just then, the latch on the trap-door opened, and light poured down from above. A heavy step trod upon the stair.

"Bring those papers to the study," Dr Schwab boomed as he descended. "and I'll find a place for them in the laboratory."

Although he moved stiffly from his injuries, he must have noticed the light burning below; for now he bent down and beheld Griff and myself *en tableau.*

"Herr Vandergriff!" said the doctor. "Just the man I wanted to see! But what are you doing down *here?*"

Griff hesitated; but then he threw the syringe back into the case with a clatter. "I'm passing the time, doctor," he said, "that's all. Your children thought it would be amusing to lock me in the cellar with Miss Dark, and so I was preparing an experiment. Now, if you'll excuse me, I have a man to hunt."

He leaped up the stairs—hot, no doubt, on Schmidt's trail.

"I want a word with you!" the doctor called after him, but Griff was already gone. Schwab scowled and returned his attention to me.

"Fräulein Dark! What were you doing letting yourself be locked in a cellar with a man? This is very compromising!"

"Herr Doctor," I said, feebly, "you don't really imagine that I came to be lying here, trussed up like a cat's dinner, of my own volition!"

"Fräulein Dark!" Vasily hurried down the steps; I could almost have wept for joy. "What does Vandergriff have you down *here* for?"

"Not now, Dunkel; you must help to carry those papers in," Dr Schwab protested—but it was no use. Vasily pushed past him and flew to my side.

"Molly-my-dear," he panted, now in French, as he tore at my restraints. "Are you hurt? What has he done to you?"

"Nothing, thank God," I answered in the same language. I do not think I have ever been happier to see him, and we had had some memorable meetings. "But what are you doing here? Why are the papers *here?*"

Vasily scowled.

"I couldn't stop him," he said, with a covert glance towards the doctor. "It was cursed luck! He was on the doorstep just as I returned from the library, and forestalled me before I could get the books carried into our own house."

A shadow fell across the opening of the trap-door. Brother Otto said, in his brisk, punctilious voice: "Where do you want them, Doctor?"

Schwab looked up. "How many boxes?" he asked. "—*That* many? Then leave them in the study; I'll sort through them at my leisure."

He turned to Vasily. "I don't know how I can thank you, Dunkel" he added. "I have been trying to get my hands on the Auberlen papers for *years.* Now that we have them, nothing will stand in our way!"

Vasily gave a rather forced smile. Indeed, I could not fathom how he was able to smile at all. I might have escaped Griff— but we had lost our plunder to the Black Templars. And somewhere in the streets of Heidelberg, our poor Alphonse was on the run with Griff himself on his tracks.

Chapter XVIII.

Having determined to follow her beloved, Nijam hurried through the icy streets with a beating heart and one finger to her transmitter.

"Mimi," she panted. "What news? Have you found him?"

"Alphonse is going east," Mimi informed her, "leading the police away from the town. I could try getting ahead of them, if you had any idea where he might be going—"

"The castle," Nijam said.

"He's already past the castle. The police are going up the road into the hills."

"The castle," Nijam repeated, stopping to regain her breath. Evidently she ought, some years ago, to have taken up dancing-lessons, or calisthenics, or tennis, or some other strengthening exercise. Well—it was too late now. She spotted a cab and hailed it. "The castle," she reiterated, hurrying towards the vehicle. "Alphonse will know to meet me there once he has lost the pursuit—which he can only do once he forces them to leave their carriages and follow him into the woods."

"And only if he is still in command of himself," Mimi muttered. "I will meet you at the castle."

A few minutes later Nijam alighted from her conveyance at the castle gates. As she counted out her fare, the cabbie sent a worried look about them—at the great frowning bulk of the ruined schloss, and at the dark night cloaking the steep wooded hills that rose about it.

"Should I wait, Fräulein?" he asked.

"Absolutely not," Nijam said, with a ferocious scowl. After that he seemed rather glad than otherwise to escape.

As the cab retreated, Mimi emerged from the darkness and opened the shutter of her dark-lantern. Nijam beckoned her to follow, and the two of them scrambled through the undergrowth and across the tumbled rock until they came to the ruined tower where she and Alphonse had taken shelter on a previous occasion. Mimi whistled when she saw the great rock-slide, which had demolished a wedge of the structure; but she scaled the ruins without difficulty, reaching back to help Nijam scramble after her. At last they both stood panting in the partly-open chamber.

"Now what?" Mimi asked, wiping dirt and snow from her hands.

"Now we wait," Nijam said.

"I don't like waiting," Mimi muttered, but she settled on her heels and closed her lantern. After that they were silent for a while.

The minutes passed like hours. Despite the cold, Nijam did not bother lighting a fire, for she did not wish any light to draw the policemen from the hills. For the longest time there was no sound; no sign of light or life—except for Mimi, who seemed incapable of sitting still. She chuffed and fidgeted and at last rose to her feet and began bobbing up and down, counting beneath her breath.

"Must you?" Nijam snapped.

"It's cold and I might as well do some pliés," Mimi grumbled;

but just then, in the distance, a ghastly shriek split the air. Mimi stilled.

"He has lost himself," she said.

Nijam pressed her lips together. That scream could have been caused by any amount of things.

"We should go to him," said Mimi.

Nijam found that she was rocking to and fro with impatience; she forced herself to still. "We can't help him if we're blundering about the forest in search of him."

Mimi muttered something in Finnish and went on with her pliés, her breath coming quick and angry as she counted. The air was cold, but Nijam felt suffocated. She found herself counting too, under her breath.

He should have known better than to hurl himself into a confrontation with the police, she told herself. Of *course* it would provoke Yammu to seize control of him. *She* should have known better than to let him. Why had she not insisted? Would it have done any good? Alphonse always was stubborn; he had always thrown himself into harm's way for the sake of the ones he loved, and now—

There was the sound of a large body forcing its way through the undergrowth at the foot of the tower. A dark figure emerged from beneath the bushes and began to scramble up the white, snow-clad rocks.

Raising the dark-lantern and sliding open the shutter, Nijam called sharply, "Who goes there?"

The only sound was a grunt like that of a large animal. Mimi rushed to her side as the shape came crawling up the slope; she fitted her tiger-claws to her hands. Nijam put a restraining hand on the ballerina's arm. Then the shape loomed up into the light and was Alphonse Schmidt, all spattered with blood

233

about the mouth and hands!

Acting on instinct, Mimi struck out with her claws. But Alphonse evaded the blow and threw himself to his knees at their feet. His arms wrapped tightly about Nijam's waist, and he pressed his head against the row of buttons that went down her front. With that touch, all the hard thoughts of her faults—of his faults—fled away.

"Stay back, Mimi!" Nijam cried, bending to shield him with her arms and body. "It's him—it's Alphonse!"

Mimi went still. Nijam held Alphonse as tightly as he clung to her. His shoulders were shaking. "Alphonse, Alphonse," she murmured, with a heart that sat in her breast like lead. "Whatever it is, it isn't your fault."

"It killed a man," he whispered in a muffled voice. "Yammu killed him—with these hands! Oh, Patty! I cannot endure this! Is there no relief?"

Nijam ground her teeth. She could not endure it, either.

"That does it," she said. "Come back to town with me, and I'll transfer Yammu to the automaton as he wanted."

"Nijam," said Mimi, doubtfully, "are you sure?"

"Of course I'm sure! Anything would be better than *this.*"

"No," Mimi said. "Are you—are you sure that's really Alphonse?"

Nijam's heart stood still. She could *tell* when it was Alphonse, she thought. She had only to look into the eyes—but she had not seen Alphonse's eyes, not in the darkness, not while she was trying to hold Mimi back.

She had only believed him when he claimed to have unseated Yammu.

The arms about her waist tightened slowly.

"Alphonse?" she whispered.

234

In the same moment, somewhere within the darkness at their back, there came the sound of a heavy blow against an echoing surface— a door. The blow was repeated, and the door ground open. A shaft of light shone upon them. For a moment both Nijam and Mimi were dazzled. Then they beheld the Englishman, Cakebread, with yachtsmen at his back!

"Alphonse Schmidt!" Cakebread declared. "You're surrounded. Give yourself up!"

Alphonse lifted his head, and Nijam looked down in horror to see that his shadowed face was split by a demoniacal grin.

"Alphonse," she whispered, as Yammu rose to his feet. Mimi caught her arm in an attempt to drag her away from him. But Nijam wrenched herself free.

She had promised not to be Alphonse's conscience, but how could she help it now? She planted herself squarely between the creature and its enemies.

"Go on, then, you fiend," she said. "Kill me, if you like. See what Alphonse Schmidt has to say to *that*."

Yammu never hesitated; not even for a moment. He hurled her at Mimi and sprang at the enemy.

* * *

Alphonse knew that no nightmare could ever be as ghastly as this. With each day that Yammu dwelt with him, it had observed and learned; until now it could deceive even his friends.

He himself was powerless to resist; he could only watch the hideous scene unfold. The violence he had been forced to commit in the woods—the deception of his beloved—the reappearance of Cakebread—and now, the renewed blood-shed that followed. He was dimly aware of his eyes remaining open, of his body moving with consummate violence. But he somehow contrived to distance himself from what was happening. In his mind he drifted amidst the flurries of snow and the numbing grey clouds, praying for a gleam of starlight amid the rack.

And then suddenly he was opening his mortal eyes and coughing. His whole body hurt horribly, as though he had been beaten all over, but at least he was once more in command of it. Everything was dark and the air smelled thickly of dust. With a sob of pain, Schmidt staggered to his feet and gazed about him.

He felt a sense of utter dislocation. The tower loomed above, but it was a different shape now than it used to be. He had evidently fallen to the foot of the rock-fall, but this was no longer covered in snow. Then he heard a trickle of falling gravel and again smelled the dust in the air; and he knew.

Somehow Yammu had brought down another wedge of the broken tower. The falling stones must have swept him from the room. Others had descended upon the chamber itself.

Alphonse uttered a sound of wordless horror. "Patty!" he cried. "Mimi! Where are you?"

He threw himself at the upward slope. Where the lower level of the tower had once opened upon the night, there was now only tumbled stone. His hand touched a lifeless foot which protruded from beneath the fallen stones—a man's foot, not a woman's; it was one of the yachtsmen.

"Patty!" he cried again, growing more frantic.

"Alphonse! We're here!" he heard her cry.

"Where?" he sobbed. The voice was so clear—so strong.

Had he imagined it?

"Here, behind you!"

He turned. The moon had struggled out from behind a cloud, and the snow had ceased to fall, perhaps only for a moment. At the foot of the rock-fall, two dark figures stood, one of them with long bright blades attached to her hands— Mimi with her tiger-claws. Evidently the pair of them had had the presence of mind to escape the tower when they could.

"Stop, Nijam!" Mimi hissed, as the taller of the two shadows began to clamber up the rocks towards Alphonse. "How do we know that it's really him?"

Alphonse swallowed. "She's right," he cried, hoarsely. "For God's sake come no nearer. I'm not safe!"

"It *is* him, Mimi," Nijam said, very gently. "Here, Alphonse. Take my hand. Let's bring you home."

Home! "I can't," he choked. "There is no home for me anymore."

Nijam hesitated. Alphonse took another sobbing breath. He could feel Yammu inside, oozing through his veins like a poison. The worst thing was that the creature had deceived even Nijam. The thought was unbearable that it might do so again—that it might kill her as it had killed so many others.

"Stay back," he repeated hoarsely. "You mustn't come near me again—not even if it *is* me."

"I'm not afraid of you, Alphonse Schmidt!" Nijam said, but the anguish in her voice cut him to the heart. She drew back, and he descended the slope warily, still keeping his distance.

"Don't follow me," he told her. "Don't look for me."

"What are you doing?"

"I'm going to end this," he said, and turned towards the path that led back to the road.

Almost at once he came face to face with a figure that had been standing there in the shadows, God only knew how long. The faint, sterile scent of metal told him precisely who it was: Vandergriff, the American.

"Alphonse Schmidt, I presume," said Griff, pushing away from the wall. "Well, well! You *have* had a busy evening."

"Stand aside," Alphonse warned him. Yammu was picking at his mind; he did not know whether he could hold on long enough to carry out his dreadful purpose. "Stand aside. I can no longer control this creature for long."

"Alphonse, you must endure a little longer," Nijam begged him, in a voice so sorrowful that it cut at his heart. "We will find a way. We will free you. *This isn't your fault.*"

"I'm afraid I agree with Herr Schmidt," Griff said, with grim enjoyment. "We can't have this happening again. Not even the consciousness-transference is worth this."

And he lowered his voice, turning again to Alphonse. "Come with me," he said. "I'll take you back to the *Akbar,* where you'll be in safe hands. Nothing like this will ever happen again."

"Don't trust him," Nijam protested.

"What else were you going to do?" Griff asked. "Make a hole in the river? What makes you think that thing won't drag you right out again? No, you must hand yourself over to me. I'll take care of you."

Nijam caught and clung to his wrist. "No—I'll *help* you. We'll do it together. We *promised.*"

Alphonse turned to look sadly into her shadowed face.

"It's too dangerous," he told her. "You must understand. It's this—or death."

He realised that Nijam was weeping. "But we're so *close!*" she protested. "We have the Auberlen papers! You aren't to think of giving yourself in!" But then he heard voices and lights not far away. Lanterns came swinging towards them along the wall.

"Here are my people now," Griff declared. "Hold still, Schmidt."

Alphonse turned, startled, to find the American with a syringe in his gloved hand. Before he could say or do anything more, Griff thrust the needle into the exposed skin of his neck and depressed the plunger. Everything went dark.

Chapter XIX.

At the doctor's house, matters were proceeding no more satisfactorily. While the Black Templars trotted to and fro carrying the Auberlen papers, the first edition of Goethe, and various other priceless treasures to the study, Dr Schwab marched me out into the hall and fixed me with a suspicious eye.

"You have not yet told me what you were doing in the laboratory!" said he.

"Really, sir," I protested, "you ought to ask Herr Vandergriff! *He* was the one who carried me down there and tied me to the table! I mean no offence, but there are much pleasanter rooms in the house!"

"I believe the children have something to say about it," Vasily put in. He had disappeared a moment and now came downstairs, pushing a nervous-looking Heidi and Peter before him. "Go on, children—tell your papa what you told me."

"We shut the trap-door and locked it," Heidi said defiantly. "We don't like that man! He was being horrible to Fräulein Dark!"

I held my breath, sure that the doctor would ask to know *why* they should have shut me up in the cellar with my persecutor. But it never occurred to Schwab to do so. Evidently he was not the sort of man to try to understand his children.

"He was running experiments, Cosine. A little girl like you would not understand." The doctor stroked his sizeable beard. "I take it he was about to inject lysergic acid diethylamide to test your capabilities, Fräulein. An interesting experiment. The female may respond differently to the male; may be more receptive. Not a bad idea!"

Peter sent me a terrified look. Vasily's hand tightened a little on the boy's shoulder, and he said, "Now then! It's one thing to run experiments on your own children, doctor, but you can't go experimenting on the governess!"

"Why not?" asked the doctor. He turned to me. "You don't mind, do you, Fräulein Dark?"

"I do, rather," I said faintly. "I would prefer not to go down that trap-door again."

The doctor waved a hand. "Nothing easier! We can perform the experiment in the sitting-room, if it makes you happier!"

"I'd really rather not!" I protested.

"I can pay you," the doctor insisted. But Vasily slid before me and took the doctor's arm.

"Look, my dear fellow," he said. "I know that it is a bore, but Fräulein Dark has witnessed things in this house that make it—shall we say—*advisable* to treat her well. Best not to give her any reason to complain, hmm?"

Brother Otto, who had been hovering beside his master with a scowl on his face, gave a snort of contempt. "What if we do?" he asked. "We do what we do for the good of Germany! If this woman persecutes us for such a noble cause, she will only cover herself in ignominy!"

"My dear Brother Otto!" Vasily protested. "You cannot kidnap young English ladies and expect to get away with it!"

"Where do your loyalties lie, Dunkel?" asked Otto. "To the Master of the Black Temple, or to an opinionated governess?"

"Gentlemen! Gentlemen!" the doctor cried, putting himself between the two men. "Otto, you have no right to discuss Order business before an outsider! Go and see that the laboratory is tidy and the lights turned out. As for you," he added, turning towards Vasily, "I must say that I have not returned a moment too soon. You have done excellent work at the Library tonight, Herr Dunkel, for which I must thank you. But I don't like the way you handled that business with Herr Vandergriff."

"You don't?" Vasily inquired, evidently uncertain as to what he meant.

"So he is of Jewish descent," the doctor elucidated, waving another hand. "Naturally we don't want him gaining immortality—but he meant to fund our work! Now I shall have to make explanations, and things will be awkward if we do not lose him altogether!"

Vasily looked rather relieved than otherwise. "Master, I do apologise."

"You must remember the great seriousness of our mission and how little we can afford to care for lesser things! Knowledge! Knowledge, at all costs! Thank you; there is your hat and coat. I shall send for you tomorrow."

Vasily found himself thus bundled hurriedly out the front door. As he went, he fixed his dark eyes upon me and then raised them meaningly upwards. For a moment no one was watching me at all; I saw my chance and took it. I gathered the children and hurried them up the stairs.

* * *

Meanwhile, as I later heard, Nijam and Mimi were descending the road from the Schloss; the former under the power of her own furious internal combustion.

"I *told* him!" she hissed. "I *told* him that it was useless, that I could not help him unless he was willing to help himself!"

Mimi said nothing. Nijam glanced at her and became aware that for once, she was receiving, and not giving, a disapproving look.

"I suppose you ought not to have wasted your kind words on him, then," Mimi said.

Nijam pressed her lips together, but there was no argument she could make in return.

"Look," Mimi added. "Perhaps Alphonse is right. Perhaps he's beyond human help."

"I'm not going to *give up*," Nijam hissed. Indeed, she was already fomenting a new scheme for Alphonse's liberation.

"Of course not," Mimi said. "But you could stop expecting to be able to do it all yourself. We can't pull ourselves out of the bog by our own bootstraps, Nijam."

* * *

It took me perhaps two hours to get the children fed, brushed, washed, and put to bed; during the whole of which time I felt rather on edge, expecting at any minute that the doctor or his acolytes might come upstairs to carry one or the other of us away to the laboratory in the cellar. But all went smoothly. The children were quite subdued after the evening's excitement. I left them cuddled up in a sleepy pile in the same bed, for Heidi insisted upon joining Peter and Clara; then I hurried down the corridor to my own room.

No sooner had I shut the door, than a dark shape came out of the shadows and put a hand over my mouth!

I stamped on the shadow's foot, eliciting a grunt of pain.

"Ow! Molly-my-dear! It's me!" Vasily hissed.

"I know!" I cried indignantly, pushing his hand away from my mouth. "Who else would be lurking in my bedroom, smelling like a Siberian pine-forest? *That* was for being overly dramatic!" And then, as I smoothed the flyaway hair back from my brow, all the day's awfulness seemed to loom over me. I took a breath that shook, and Vasily, sensing my distress, put his arms about me.

I clung to him with something like desperation until at last my sobs grew less violent.

"I ought to have come to you sooner," he said, ruefully. "My darling! Tell me everything."

"No, no—you did right in securing the papers," I said, breathing deeply. "Only I am *so* glad to see you again! I never imagined that I would say such a thing, but I am coming to detest this house nearly as much as Seton Castle! I keep thinking that that awful Brother Otto is going to come and drag me back to that cellar!"

"If he does that, you must call me at once," Vasily said, "and this time I'll come for you."

"But I don't have my transmitter," I said dolefully, "and that would expose us as allies."

"I think I have already done that by speaking for you just now. It's all very well to get people's trust by going to greater extremes, but I couldn't let him drag you back into that laboratory. Speaking of which, here is your transmitter. Griff must have left it on the bench down there."

I was glad to see it again, as you may believe. After that I told Vasily everything that had happened in the cellar, and the dreadful secret Griff had confessed to me.

"There you have it," I said. "He is dying, and as wicked as he is, I could not help feeling sorry for him."

"That's because you are an angel and far too good for any of us," Vasily said. "But I hope one day to have the pleasure of throttling Mr Vandergriff with my bare hands!"

"If you do, Nijam will never forgive you, for she considers Griff's neck to be her own rightful prey. Speaking of whom, where *is* Nijam?"

Vasily in a few words summarised events at the library. He had overheard Nijam and Mimi planning to meet at the castle to await Alphonse; but after that, nothing. I was about to open my transmitter to seek further news when there came the muffled sound of a knock at the front door.

"Who could that be?" I wondered, arresting my hand. "Vasily, I have a sudden awful premonition."

With that, I dashed out of the room. Heidi, Peter, and Clara (who were, of course, *not* in bed as they ought to have been) were peering through the balusters as voices—including Griff's—swelled and then died away in the front hallway.

"Children!" I hissed. "What is happening?"

Peter got up and tiptoed towards me. "It's Herr Griff, and he has your friend with him—Herr Schmidt! I think he is hurt!"

"Oh, *fiddlesticks*," I groaned. "Go to bed, children." I closed the door and turned to Vasily, who had already opened his transmitter.

"Mimi! Miss Nijam!" he called. "Where are you? Vandergriff has just returned to the doctor's house with our Schmidt!"

"I'm aware," Nijam replied, in a voice clipped short with fury. "Griff *got* to him. Persuaded him to turn himself in. There was nothing I could do."

"You might have used your little prong-shocker," Mimi was heard to grumble.

"Be sensible, Mimi! If I'd used my Stunner there would have been no hope of getting Alphonse down the hill again; not in his condition. No." Nijam heaved a deep breath. "I have a plan. Vasily, you must come to the old Auberlen laboratory on the Plöck. Dark, you must stay there and keep an eye on Alphonse."

"And Mimi must come too," Vasily announced. "Dr Schwab returned from hospital before I could get the Auberlen papers stowed safely at our headquarters. I'm afraid they're at present stacked up in his study."

"Vasily," said Nijam, in the soft, dangerous voice she commonly only used with *me*, "do you mean to tell me that the Order of the Black Temple has *the Auberlen-Schmidt papers* in its possession?"

"Afraid so," Vasily said, with commendable insouciance. "But Mimi can get them back—can't you, Mimi?"

"What, you want me to steal the same thing twice in a single night? Ski into hell, Vasya!"

"Can't, my dear," he retorted. "Miss Nijam wants me at the laboratory. *Auf wiedersehen!*" Switching off his transmitter, he passed an arm about my waist and kissed me tenderly. Then he threw the window open and let himself down softly onto the roof of the garden-shed.

Sighing, I closed the window again. I had better make sure that the children were properly abed, and then I would venture out in search of poor Alphonse.

I took hold of the door-knob—attempted to turn it, was thwarted, and then rattled the door in mounting horror.

It was locked!

* * *

While I was making this unpleasant discovery upstairs, Alphonse was coming to his senses downstairs. Upon opening his eyes, his first sight was that hideous image of the ancient god, which was painted upon the wall of the cellar. For a moment or two he thought that Yammu had somehow taken physical form and now hovered, gloating, above him. Then the ghastly vision resolved into a flat painting upon the wall; and he arrived at the scarcely less horrible truth.

Griff had misled him. Instead of being safely on his way back to the *Akbar*, he was instead back in the cellar of the Black Templars, strapped to the steel table. And Griff himself was speaking nearby, his voice echoing hollow within the cellar's darkness.

"Is this what you meant by *something to my advantage?*" he said, contemptuously. "Your friends insulted my grandmother. All I want from you, Doctor, is a place to lie low until I can move Schmidt out of Württemberg without the police catching us. I'll pay you for it, if you like."

"My people spoke hastily and without my blessing," Dr Schwab retorted in his prim, harsh English. "They have been reprimanded. I ask you to reconsider. We can work on Schmidt together; there's no reason for the police to know that he is here. I'll provide the Auberlen papers, and you can provide the funding for certain instruments we shall need."

Griff considered this a moment in silence.

"It will take time and trouble getting him to America," Schwab added, persuasively. "We can begin at once, if you like."

"All right," Griff said, coming to the decision suddenly. "Shake on it. But you'd best warn your people to speak civilly about my family."

This hasty alliance struck Alphonse into a welter of fear. If he must be a prisoner, he did not wish to be a prisoner anywhere in the vicinity of this haunted laboratory—or that ghastly image on the wall. He drew breath to speak.

"Don't do it—let me away from here!" he meant to say. But between breath and lip the words changed.

"It is a wise decision," Yammu said through his lips. "Know, Herr Vandergriff, that so long as you help to free me from this body, I will give you everything you need. All the secrets you desire for the ritual of consciousness-transference."

"Holy Moses!" Griff exclaimed, darting to the table. "It's the other intelligence! Stefan Schmidt, I presume?"

Alphonse felt Yammu's outrage coil through him like a whip, even before it reached his lips. "Putrescent fool! How can you believe that *I* am a mortal? Could a mortal possess this body at will? Could a mortal understand the secrets of life and immortality? Could a mortal perceive the malignancy that even now eats at your body?"

For a moment Griff looked daunted; then amused. "All right," he said. "I'll bite. What are you?"

"I am Yammu, the Ancient!" roared the creature through Alphonse's lips. "Yammu, the Calamitous! Yammu, the Mighty! Yammu, who will devour all things and bring back the age of blood!"

"Phooey!" said Griff, turning to Schwab. "Immortality has gone to the poor fellow's head, and he's confused himself with these spooks of yours."

"I am no spook!" Yammu protested. "When I am free I will stand revealed—and in your final shrieks you will call for madness to blot the sight from your shuddering memory!"

Griff clapped Alphonse on the shoulder. "Anything you like, my good fellow, so long as you're willing to share the secret of immortality with us." He turned to the doctor and lowered his voice. "The madness is worrisome. We must be able to transfer the consciousness *without* damaging it—although I suppose it's better to be alive and crazy, than dead."

"Wait a moment," Schwab said, approaching the table where Alphonse's body lay. "Herr Yammu? *The* Yammu, in fact, from the *Codex Actorum Atrocium?*"

"The very same," said Yammu in lordly tones—Griff rolled his eyes. "Do not blaspheme!" Yammu suddenly roared.

The doctor bowed, rubbing his hands. "Sir—my lord—allow me to tell you what a very great honour this is, a very great honour. Am I to understand that the terms of association remain the same as they were said to have been in ancient times? That is, to your worshippers is granted a stay of execution, and in fact the power of eternal life, together with supremacy over lesser peoples?"

"All who bow the knee shall earn the right to feast on blood," Yammu declared, to Alphonse's horror. He felt as though he was trapped on a runaway train—utterly helpless to put an end to the conversation. Yammu seemed not even to feel his feeble efforts to seize back control. "Do you bow the knee, mortal?"

The look that transfigured Schwab's face was reverent— almost fanatical. "I do," he breathed. "Tell me, my lord: what can I provide you?"

"A body," Yammu declared. "Free me of this presumptuous

mortal. Bring me the Nijam automaton!"

"The Nijam—yes, of course, my lord," said the doctor. "But where shall we find this automaton?"

"Sorry, my friend," put in a still unimpressed Griff. "That particular vehicle is not available. It belongs to *me*. The doctor will find you a fresh corpse or something, Schmidt."

"I can do better," the doctor said, trembling with eagerness. "I can offer you a living body, my lord. Young and healthy, with a long life before it, and the appropriate sensitivity to other consciousnesses. Allow me to make you the gift of my first-born son."

Numb with shock, Alphonse tried to grasp control of his body again; he was beaten back almost effortlessly.

A startled whistle escaped Griff. "Schwab," he said in a low voice. "Your son! Are you *certain?*"

"True worship requires sacrifice," the doctor cried, shrugging off the restraining hand.

"Of course—but don't tell me you *believe* this mumbo-jumbo."

"The sacrifice is acceptable," Yammu intoned. "Bring the child to me. And cease to struggle, slave!" it added, inwardly, to Alphonse.

He could not stand by and do nothing as a child was sacrificed to Yammu's madness and Schwab's greed. Alphonse made another titanic effort; to no avail. There was sharp struggle with the seething malice within him—and then, suddenly, a bewildering dislocation. For a moment, dizzily, the only thing he knew was that he no longer felt Yammu's oppressive presence like a weight on his soul. Then his vision resolved and he found himself drifting free. He was no longer watching out of his own eyes; he saw himself lying on the bloody table, his face a mask of gloating triumph.

Yammu had expelled him from his own body!

Chapter XX.

I, meanwhile, was upstairs mustering all my wits. With poor Alphonse downstairs in durance vile, the Order of the Black Temple was evidently preparing to get up to a strain of skulduggery so black, so horrible, that the governess must be locked safely into her room before they considered themselves safe to begin. One of them must have stolen upstairs merely to turn the key in my door.

I did not allow my shock to rule me for very long. I ran at once to the window and threw it open. Alas! with a single glance outside I knew that the thing was useless. There was a shed far below, and its sloping roof was covered in snow. I have no head for heights, and mine, as I know well, is not Mimi's gift for performing circus-tricks on a sheer wall, or Vasily's for breaking and entering at young ladies' windows. *He* might have been able to leave the house by this road without risking his neck, but I felt certain that I should break every bone in my body.

I closed the window and asked myself how I had best tackle the problem. Call my crew via transmitter? But they were all away upon pressing business of their own. Shout for the children? That was likely to attract not only my charges, but also the Order. —I might, however, try picking the lock. I was searching my dressing-table for hair-pins, letter-openers, or anything else that might prove useful when there came a soft, rustling scratch at the door. I turned and found Clara's disembodied head watching me solemnly from the dark panelling.

It is possible that I uttered a shriek. With my gifts it is always possible that I may see something uncanny or unsettling at any moment, but this never seems to temper the fright when it comes.

"Clara!" I exclaimed, when I had my breath back. "What is it?"

She beckoned with a shadowy hand before withdrawing from view. I flew to the door and put my lips to the keyhole.

"Children!" I hissed. "Are you there? What is happening?"

"Are you all right, Fräulein?" Peter asked.

"Perfectly! But they've locked me in my room!"

"They locked us up, too!" Heidi said, from the sound of it shoving Peter aside. "But they left the key in the lock, so we slid Peter's composition-book under the door and poked the key out with a hair-pin, and it fell on the book and we pulled it back in! So then we came to get you!"

In all likelihood, all the locks on the house's internal doors must open using the same key. "Where is that key, Heidi?" I asked. "Slide it to me beneath the door and go back to bed at once! You should not be up—it isn't safe!"

"But the nice man said to come to you at once," Peter said.

I could not imagine who this might be—unless, perhaps, Vasily had looked in at the nursery window on his way past. "Man? Which man?"

"He said to knock first and make sure you're decent," Peter told me. "Are you?"

I could scarcely believe my ears. Here we all were in danger of I-knew-not-what villainy, and someone was telling the children not to unlock the door of my prison lest I were in *deshabille!* "Yes, I am decent! *What* man, Peter?"

But the children did not answer at once. Instead—oh joy!—I heard the sound of the key turning in the lock. Then the door opened and there in the hallway stood the three children and our own Alphonse Schmidt!

"Alphonse!" I sobbed, reaching out to seize his hand. "I should have known it was you! Come in at—oh!"

This last exclamation was caused by my hand passing clear through him. The words died from my lips at the same moment that the hope died from my heart. Alphonse Schmidt was a shade—Alphonse Schmidt was dead!

"Miss Dark!" he said, earnestly. "You must take the children and lock yourself within. Barricade the door if you must! You are all in danger!"

"Oh, Alphonse!" I choked, but I retained sufficient presence of mind to whisk the children inside, snatch the key and lock the door again so that we might not be interrupted. "Oh, my poor Alphonse! What has happened to you? What am I going to tell Nijam! Quickly—we might not have much time!"

"I—" he began. But suddenly his face went the wrong shape and he covered his eyes with his hand.

I could not very well press him for more; not in that state, no matter how brief a time was left to him in the world of the living. Vasily had brought me a packet of *spekulatius*, which I extracted from beneath my pillow and doled out to the children in an effort to distract them. Then I returned to poor Alphonse.

He had by now mastered his emotions. "Miss Dark," he

murmured, "this might be the end for me. That creature has expelled me entirely from my body."

"Then it still has possession?" I inquired, feeling a gleam of hope. "Your body is not dead?"

He gave a hopeless shrug. "My body is well. But if it is beyond my reach…"

The gleam became a sunbeam. "Thank God!" I exclaimed. "Do you remember Mimi's friend Anna, for whom we went to Russia? Her shade remained at large in the world for as long as her body remained in a coma. Oh, I *am* relieved!"

"That's not all," Alphonse said, refusing to be comforted. "Yammu and the doctor have struck a bargain. Yammu will grant the doctor immortality, if the doctor allows him to transfer himself to…" He gave the children a worried look.

For a moment I could not divine his meaning: then I did, and put a horrified hand to my mouth.

"Then you will *both* be under his sway," I whispered. "No— worse. *You* will be dead. He will make the poor child eat a slice of your brain."

"That will be the least of it," poor Alphonse replied. "Yammu means to bring about the end of the world, and Doctor Schwab means to help him. My body is down there in the laboratory at this very moment, ordering everything Yammu needs."

"And Griff?" I asked, without much hope.

"He seems content to go along with it. He is desperate to solve the riddle of consciousness-transference."

"What can we do?" I whispered, pacing as far as the wardrobe and back again. The children, I noticed, had broadcast crisp *spekulatius* crumbs upon the carpet; yet it was one of the few times in my life I have ever felt that this sort of detail was unimportant. "Alphonse, you must stop Yammu.

You *must* get your body back."

"But I have *tried*. And Yammu threw me out. It's no use; I have done everything wrong, and now there is no hope left for me in this world." There was a silence. Heavily, he added: "Miss Dark, I must ask you—"

"No!" I cried, wringing my hands. I might have made the promise Schmidt asked of me, but I did not know how I was to keep it; I could not imagine harming my friend. "No *human* hope, perhaps. But that is a very different thing indeed from *no* hope."

"It would take a miracle," he said, bitterly.

"Then why not *ask* for one? How can we find help, unless we are willing to seek it?"

There came a flicker in his eyes. "That is what Patty said."

"There!"

There was a silence. Schmidt shook his head.

"I have done everything wrong, and there is no way back," he repeated, with soft finality. "I have always known it."

My heart bled for him. "Alphonse, my poor friend! I know what you must feel. I, too, had to learn that I was worth fighting for. I, too, had to learn that I was never meant to be trampled on."

There came another knock at the front door—an ominous, muffled rat-tat-tat that echoed through the whole house. The sound, coming so unexpectedly, made me startle and throw up my hands.

"It must be Patty," said Alphonse.

"I believe you're right," I replied, tapping at my transmitter, which until now had been neglected. "Nijam! Is that you? What are you doing?"

"Making a trade," Nijam told me, succinctly. "I'll give them my automaton if they'll free Alphonse."

"What?" I asked, blankly. Nijam's transmitter snicked off. "Vasily!" I appealed. "You can't let her do this! If Yammu gets the automaton, nothing will stand in his way!"

"It's all right," Vasily assured me. "We're casting the golden apple of discord, my love—that's all. A feint, merely!"

I bit my lip and switched off my transmitter. From the look of worry on Alphonse's face, I saw that he felt no more at ease than I.

"I don't like it," I said. "So long as we could keep Peter safe from them, there was a hope of confining Yammu to *your* body. But now she's brought the automaton. Whatever she intends, it's a horrible risk."

Alphonse ran a hand through his shadowy hair, and I knew what he was thinking: of Nijam's loyalty to him, which cared not whether the world drowned in blood.

A look of resolve came to his eyes.

"I don't know if we can save me," he said, "but, Miss Dark, we must save as much else as we can. Whatever Patty thinks, promise that you'll kill me sooner than let Yammu escape this house."

I did not like to say the words. I understood Nijam's fear: that Alphonse might despair too soon and neglect to avail himself of some escape. But what else could I say? If Nijam really went through with the trade, if Yammu and his confederates were able to gain everything they wanted, then there would be no choice. Alphonse must be permitted to make his sacrifice.

"*If* there is no miracle," I whispered, "and no other choice."

Alphonse sent me a grateful look and faded through the heavy panelled door.

Chapter XXI.

After Alphonse had gone away I did a little more pacing, for he had given me a great deal of food for thought. What a pickle we were in, to be sure! The children in danger—Alphonse unseated from his body—the doctor and Griff hand in glove with the ghastly Yammu—and Nijam ready to do heaven only knew what to mend things!

I told myself to slow down and think matters through very clearly. Alphonse would try to get back command of his body. Nijam, I thought, *might* bargain the world away to Yammu to save her beloved, but I did not think that she was capable of standing by and allowing Dr Schwab to sacrifice his son. Moreover, there was Vasily, who was a consummate distraction all on his own, and who would have a thing or two of his own to say should Nijam try anything rash.

I must have made a soft sound, for Heidi's fair curls suddenly intruded upon my field of view.

"What is it, Fräulein?" she asked. "What are you laughing about?"

"I suddenly realised that I trusted Herr Dunkel to take care of Miss Nijam for me," I explained, in wonder. "How the chairs turn, my dears!"

"Isn't it the tables that turn?" Peter asked.

I waved a dismissive hand, still thinking fondly of my lover. How had this come to pass? At what moment, in the past three or four months, had I come to rely upon him more completely than upon anyone else in the world?

I thought again of the doubts that had plagued me in recent days. Was there a risk in loving Vasily? Undoubtedly; but there is a risk in loving anybody. At this moment I thought loving Vasily far less of a risk than loving Nijam.

No: I did not think that Nijam would have brought Vasily with her if she meant to betray us all for Alphonse's sake. We were still a crew, and I could still rely upon my crew to carry out our plans. And with that, I knew what I ought to do. Likely Mimi would be downstairs stealing the Auberlen papers, and Nijam—no matter what she might do in her desperation—would know her task: to distract the doctor and his accomplices long enough to enable the rest of us to steal away everything we could.

"Did you enjoy the biscuits?" I asked the children—not without a pang at the sight of the torn and empty packet, for I was fond of *speekulatius* and had not eaten a single one of them.

All three of the children nodded—even Clara, who as usual had enjoyed no more than a wistful sniff of one of Peter's morsels.

"Good then," I said briskly. "Now, children, I'm going to put you to bed; but not in the nursery this time. You shall curl up in my bed, and then I must go away. But I will lock the door, and then, I hope, you will be quite safe."

The novelty of the arrangements pleased them, and I soon had them tucked up and whispering in my bed. I turned the key carefully in the lock and then slipped it beneath the door so that they could use it if they really needed it. If things went badly wrong, I did not like the thought of the children being trapped in a room they could not escape.

This done, I descended the stairs with the utmost care. The drawing-room door stood open, and a loud voice echoed within—Griff's, of course. As I stole past, I saw the Black Templars surrounding Nijam's famous automaton—a frightful contraption that looked like nothing so much as an animated clothes-mangle. Happily for me, it was taking up all their attention. Not even Nijam and Vasily noticed me as I flitted by and ventured towards the study—towards the laboratory beyond, where Schmidt would be fighting his terrible battle.

I did not particularly *like* the idea of intruding upon what must be a very unpleasant scene; only it had occurred to me that one last piece of the job remained to be finished. Moreover, perhaps our Alphonse might be glad of some moral support.

When I ventured into the study, I found Mimi in her circus-knickers, standing before the open window with one of the library archive-boxes in her arms.

"Dark!" she hissed, when she saw that it was me. *"Must* you jump out at me like a jack-in-the-box?"

"I'm sorry," I whispered, whisking into the study and closing the door behind me. "It just occurred to me that we ought to take the—the Atrocious Codex with us, too, or whatever it is called. It would do us no good to destroy Auberlen's work, and leave the book that inspired him."

"Fine," Mimi said, dropping her box without ceremony through the open window, where it must have fallen to the ground in the garden-beds. "That is the last of the Auberlen-Schmidt papers—all the other books are German literature.

Where is the Codex?"

"I'm afraid it's probably down in the laboratory," I said. "And I want your help, for the last time I tried to touch the horrid thing, I fainted dead away."

Mimi closed the window and the two of us approached the open trap-door with a certain amount of trepidation. The only sound that arose from beneath was a sort of muffled gasping—the sound of a man in deadly pain.

I drew a deep breath, wishing that I was a Catholic and might make the sign of the cross. Mimi showed no such hesitation. "Alphonse!" she cried, plunging down the narrow stair. I followed her, in part because I felt a responsibility to watch over her.

At the foot of the stair was a sombre scene. A single gas-light burned with a fretful flicker above the steel table. Here Alphonse lay, rigid in the grip of some involuntary spasm—his back arched, his head thrown back, his heels ground into the table-top.

To my eyes, moreover, a pulsating shadow hung about him, darkening his struggling body.

Mimi started forwards, but I caught her arm.

"Don't," I whispered. "Can't you see? They are fighting. If you release him now, who knows what may happen?"

She sent me a frightened glance—and *then* she made the sign of the cross.

"The Codex," she whispered.

I took her over to the glass case in which old Dr Auberlen's desiccated and lifeless corpse sat grinning cheerlessly at the sufferer. Mimi felt about beneath and then with a soft exclamation of satisfaction drew forth that ancient, wicked book, which I could never behold without a shudder.

"There!" said I. "Now—"

But I never had the chance to finish what I had been about to say, for just then the light went out altogether.

The cellar was plunged into darkness. Only a thin glimmer of light came down from the study itself. With a gasp, I caught Mimi by the elbow.

"Upstairs," she whispered, taking a step towards that promise of light.

But just then a weak voice spoke from the shadows.

"Miss Dark! Miss Laine! Is—is that you?"

"Alphonse!" I gasped, turning towards him. "Alphonse, you did it!"

A match struck and Mimi hurried to re-light the gas. It came back to life with a whoosh of blue flame that nearly scorched her. In the restored light Alphonse could be seen resting upon the table, his face mantled with sweat. He looked very pale and very weary.

"Thank God," I exclaimed, weak with relief. "One moment and I'll free you."

Even as I reached for the restraints, Mimi caught my wrist.

"Wait, Dark," she said. "Are you *quite* sure it's him?" —I stared at her without understanding until she added, "It deceived Nijam earlier tonight."

A cold hand seemed to clutch my heart, and I turned to gaze down upon my friend with slowly dawning horror. What nightmare was this, in which one who looked like a friend, and spoke like a friend, might not be a friend at all, but some inconceivable terror!

Alphonse gazed up at me with dark and shadowed eyes.

"Listen to her, Miss Dark," he begged me. "Leave me bound, or carry out your promise."

There was a long, frozen moment during which neither Mimi nor I spoke or breathed.

"I'll be hanged if I will!" I said. "Let go of me, Mimi. Of course it's Alphonse!"

"No niin," Mimi said, with brisk assent. I went to his hands; she to his feet.

"No—please!" Alphonse begged. He was almost sobbing. "Don't do this—you'll only free him—please!"

We tore his restraints free and for a moment he lay there, gasping.

Then his gasps changed—to laughter.

There was someone horribly chilling about that sound. "Alphonse?" I asked, touching his shoulder.

Like a striking serpent, his hand seized mine!

I recoiled with an involuntary shriek as Alphonse—or the intelligence that yet controlled him—rose from his cold couch. Mimi, her face white as paper, plunged her hands into her pockets in search of her tiger-claws. But Yammu was too quick for her. With one pounce he caught up a scalpel that lay upon the bench, and held it to my throat.

"Do you really think Yammu, the Elder God, incapable of such a trifling deception?" he demanded, even as footsteps sounded in the study upstairs. "How foolish! Now leave your weapons, small mortal, and go up the stairs before us. If you attempt to escape, your friend will suffer for it."

Mimi snarled, but she had no choice. Leaving her tiger claws in her pockets, she turned and climbed the stair. I followed after, watching the sharp blade of the scalpel with more attention than my own feet.

Brother Otto was at the top of the stairs. By the time my captor and I emerged, he had seized upon Mimi.

"The governess!" he snarled. "I ought to have known! But, my lord," —this to Yammu— "what does this mean?"

"That they freed me," Yammu said, throwing aside the scalpel now that Mimi was secured, "and for that I shall owe them a swift and easy death when the time comes. Bring me to your master, mortal. I would commune with him."

From the drawing-room, Dr Schwab could be heard demanding to know what the commotion in the study was all about. As Mimi and I were dragged within, Nijam and Vasily turned startled faces upon us; but Griff smiled a thin, grey smile.

"Miss Molly!" he exclaimed. "Naturally!"

Here I ought perhaps to summarise the conversation which we had interrupted.

At first, Vasily had entered the Schwab residence with something of the air of a conquering hero. "Herr Doctor," he declared, advancing to meet that gentleman. "I am delighted to introduce you to the famous Padma Nijam, who has consented to bring her ingenious automaton for your inspection."

"I know Fräulein Nijam," Dr Schwab said, exchanging a hostile glare with the lady in question. "She has wilfully intruded upon the sacred business of this Order and is no longer welcome in this house!"

"Now, now, now, be polite!" Vasily exhorted, as Nijam navigated her walking mangle through the front-door. "I have had a deal of trouble persuading Miss Nijam to come and offer her marvellous automaton for your experiments. Don't you *want* to transfer Stefan Schmidt's consciousness from Alphonse Schmidt to something else? Here is your solution."

Vasily patted the automaton on its iron shoulder. Nijam raised a hand, and the thing flicked him away with an unmistakable air of irritation.

"Good God!" the doctor exclaimed, much impressed despite himself. "This could be just the thing! What do you think, Vandergriff?"

"It's out of the question," Griff said. "I've already arranged to buy that contraption!"

"Excuse *me*," said Nijam. "I've already refused to sell it to Mr Vandergriff. Doctor, so long as you are prepared to purchase the automaton, it is yours."

I might have told her that it was no use telling Griff *no*. "Whatever he offers you, I'll double it," the American said.

Nijam paid him no attention. "I was thinking of asking three hundred marks," she told the doctor.

"I'll pay you six," said Griff. "Look here—Dr Schwab and I are in a partnership. If you sell it to him you'll sell it to both of us."

"Is that so?" Nijam asked. "Then I'll take my invention elsewhere. I'm sure there will be others eager to buy it."

"No, no, no!" Dr Schwab exclaimed. "I'm sure we can come to an agreement."

Nijam raised an eyebrow. "Excellent. I would accept two hundred and fifty and the opportunity to collaborate with you, doctor. Don't forget that I knew Auberlen and the Schmidt brothers personally. But you'll have to dismiss Vandergriff."

"This is persecution!" Griff protested.

Dr Schwab looked somewhat flustered by this very peculiar mode of bargaining. "A moment, a moment!" he exclaimed. To Nijam, he said, "*If* I agree to your terms and take the automaton, I cannot pay you at once. I shall have to raise the funds."

"Nine hundred, ready cash," Griff said.

Nijam said, "Give me ten per cent. now, doctor, together with your signed and written promise to pay the rest within a year, and we have a deal."

"Within a *year?*" said Griff. "You can't be serious!"

"I'm afraid she can," Vasily murmured, but this earned him another menacing gesture from the automaton.

"Well?" Nijam demanded.

The doctor opened and closed his mouth rather in the manner of a landed fish. "Give me a moment to think," he begged.

"Yes," Griff put in. "Let's discuss it, doctor."

"Yes, but I must ask His Lordship first."

"You're crazy," said Griff, losing his temper altogether. "He's crazy, Miss Nijam. He *believes* all that hocus-pocus about the elder gods. No; trust me, you're better off selling the thing to me."

"Excuse me, Vandergriff," said Dr Schwab, with dignity. "The lady is selling her automaton to *me.*"

"Until you appeared, he was about to make a human-sacrifice of his own son!" Griff told Nijam, in boundless indignation. "And he calls himself a man of science!"

"I beg your pardon!" the doctor protested. "How is it unscientific to accept what the evidence is telling us? Besides, it's ridiculous to refer to consciousness-transference as human sacrifice! If you were one of my students, I should mark you down for using such emotive language!"

It was at this juncture, more or less, that Yammu made his appearance as part of a procession consisting of Brother Otto, Mimi, myself, and what had until recently been Alphonse. At the sight of Dr Schwab and Griff standing at loggerheads over Nijam and her automaton, I caught a fleeting breath of hope.

The golden apple of discord, it seemed, had had some effect.

But now Yammu himself had come.

"Kneel!" he proclaimed, emphasising the command with a sweep of Alphonse's arm. "Kneel before Yammu, you contemptible weaklings! I have come to assume command!"

The doctor went down on his knees at once and so, after a moment, did Otto, Vasily, and the other Templars present. Griff threw up his hands and subsided into an arm-chair. Only Nijam and the automaton remained defiantly on their feet.

"*Kneel*," Yammu repeated, pointing an accusing hand at her.

"I'd rather keep the automaton standing, thanks," Nijam said coldly. "Its joints are a little stiff."

Yammu made a sceptical sound, but Dr Schwab now suddenly seized upon Alphonse's hand.

"My lord!" he cried. "We have found you a new vessel—one that will never tire or age! We are ready to transfer you into this automaton at once!"

Alphonse's eyes swept the room with a magnificent detachment. "That won't be necessary," Yammu announced, in a voice no less wintry than the scouring north wind that rattled the drawing-room shutters. "This body has been ceded to me, and is now fully and forever my own."

There was an involuntary clank from Nijam's automaton, and a hiss of horror from Mimi. Other than that—only silence.

We had failed, thought I, in a dreary kind of despair. We had failed, and now I—I had vowed to destroy Alphonse's body. But how would I do that when I was wholly without a weapon, and not only Nijam but the entire Black Temple and Yammu himself were here to prevent me?

Nijam was the first to recover the wits to speak. "Alphonse would never do such a thing," she whispered. "He would die sooner."

"Alphonse Schmidt could do nothing to stop me, even if he wished! But I offered him a bargain. His body as my vessel forever—in exchange for one last word."

Nijam's face had gone grey. "And that word?" she asked.

"This," replied Yammu, releasing me, and stepping towards her.

Then Alphonse's arms went about her, and Alphonse's lips whispered four words into her ear—words which made Nijam go still and cold with shock. Alphonse's mouth pressed one last kiss upon her lips.

"Alphonse!" Mimi cried out. "If you give in now I shall never forgive you! —Oh, keep your hands to yourself, you milk-beard." This last, to Brother Otto's attempt to silence her.

Alphonse released Nijam, who still stood as if deep in thought. Then he turned from her to the rest of the room and was Yammu again.

"There," he cried, "I am free, and this vessel will be mine forever!"

"Allow me to congratulate you, my lord!" said the doctor. *"Hag sithmugsk Yammu!"*

"Hag sithmugsk Yammu," intoned the Black Templars. Had I not been so distraught I might have laughed to hear that solemn chant in a chintzy drawing-room.

Griff rose briskly from his arm-chair. "Yes, yes, very touching!" he said. "And now, since I believe you will no longer be wanting the automaton, I shall take it off your hands."

"But I *do* want the automaton!" cried the doctor. "Not for my lord's use, but for my own! Tell me, my lord," he added, turning to Yammu. "The secret of consciousness-transference!

Between you and me, it is a brain transplant, isn't it? Not, in fact, *consuming* the brain?"

"That is correct," said Yammu; and had I had any doubts as to whether our poor friend was truly gone, this would have laid them to rest.

"I had my suspicions!" The doctor's face was transfigured with excitement. "Now I shall be immortal!"

"Listen," Griff said, losing his temper for a second time, "if you think I mean to leave this house without the automaton, you are sorely mistaken!"

"Lord Yammu will grant the automaton to the one who best deserves it!" said the doctor.

"But *I* am the one who best deserves it! *I* am the one who captured Alphonse Schmidt—twice! *I* am the one of us who is dyi—hrrrrgh!"

This last exclamation was due to Yammu, who for some reason that I did not quite understand—whether because Nijam had made a gift of it under better circumstances to her beloved, or because he had taken advantage of their embrace a moment ago to pick her pockets—now proved to be in possession of one of Nijam's little Stunners. One moment Griff was gesticulating angrily at the doctor; the next his eyes rolled back in his head, and he sank gracefully upon the hearth-rug.

"There," said Yammu, with satisfaction. "Now we can carry out our consciousness-transference experiments in peace. This one will be of more use to us with a reliable intelligence piloting him." And he prodded Griff's unconscious body with a toe.

I do not think that any of us were expecting this. I let out a muffled shriek, and Vasily cried out, "Alphonse! For the love of God, I *know* you can hear me!"

He stepped forwards, but Nijam put out a hand and the automaton arrested him with a crushing grip to the shoulder.

"Leave him, Vasily," Nijam said, in a very soft, very menacing voice.

Vasily cast a horrified glance at her. "Then you must stop him, for we cannot!"

"I said I'd not let anyone raise a hand to him," Nijam said, still very soft. "What about it, doctor? Down to the laboratory?"

"Yes, yes!" the doctor agreed. Then he turned and sent me a wondering look, as though he was trying to determine what to do with the rest of my crew.

"Shall we throw them out?" Brother Otto asked.

"Yes—all except the governess," Schwab said; but Yammu interrupted.

"Keep the men," he growled, in that voice that bore such an unholy resemblance to Alphonse's own. As he spoke he bent over Griff's body and quickly drew a pair of gleaming steel hand-cuffs from his pocket. "We're in need of spare bodies. Best not to test the procedure on yourself, doctor."

Schwab looked a little dubious at this. "Is it so risky, then?"

"Not with my help," said Yammu—and the way he adjusted the buttons on his cuffs seemed for a moment horribly like our poor Alphonse. "Only you'll want to supervise the procedure closely the first time it is performed, rather than being helpless under the knife."

"So I do," the doctor admitted. He turned to Brother Otto.

"Throw the small woman out of the house, and keep the others," he announced. "Then, if you like, Brother Otto, yours shall be the honour of being transferred into Vandergriff!"

Otto looked dubious. "But his *grandmother*," he began.

"It is a very great sacrifice," Dr Schwab said, putting a comforting hand on the young man's shoulder, "but it is necessary for the cause that the Vandergriff millions should remain at our service."

The mention of the millions seemed to do the trick. Otto straightened. "It would be my highest honour. –One moment."

He seized Mimi and dragged her into the entrance-hall.

"Stop it, you backwoods idiot!" she could be heard protesting. "They're talking about *scooping out your brains!* Can't you hear them?"

The front door slammed, cutting off Mimi's protests. I exchanged a look with Vasily, for I was utterly at a loss. Dr Schwab seemed unable to contain his glee. "Prepare the ritual!" he cried out, rubbing his hands together. "We're going to cut open a pair of skulls!"

Even as two of the Black Templars leapt to seize Griff, that gentleman came to with a gasp. He struck his own temple. "Help!" he gasped into his own transmitter. "Help me—they're trying to kill—"

"Not so fast," Yammu breathed, using Nijam's gadget to administer another shock. Griff convulsed and fainted. Away he went, carried by his captors; and Vasily and I were left staring after them in horror. Nor were we long left to our own devices. At a word from Yammu, Vasily and I were marched into the front hall and with Griff's handcuffs were shackled to the banister.

We were near enough the umbrella-stand that I was able to stealthily possess myself of the doctor's sword-stick; and yet my hands were clammy upon its brass fittings, and the umbrellas rattled as I drew it from the stand, as though chattering with terror.

Nijam folded her arms. "I'll keep an eye on them, my lord," she told Yammu, "until you're ready for me and my automaton."

Yammu gave her a careless pat upon the head as though she was a pet, and he her master. "You've done well," he told her. "One day I will grant you a boon for this. Come, Doctor!"

With that he and the remaining Black Templars vanished into the study. Vasily and I were left in the entrance-hall, both of us regarding Nijam with mingled reproach and alarm.

"Nijam!" I burst out, when the study door had closed between ourselves and the Templars. "Oh, *Nijam!* This is no way to have your revenge upon Mr Vandergriff!"

Her only answer was a look of withering scorn.

"No time for recriminations, Molly-my-dear," put in Vasily, rattling the chains that linked our hands through the staircase. "Quickly, Miss Nijam! Didn't you see that Griff got a word through his transmitter? He has called upon his reinforcements, and the police will be here at any moment! Can you imagine the disaster, if they find poor Schmidt in the hands of that monster? You must bring him to his senses—you are the only one who can save him now!"

Nijam scowled. "How can *I* save him? I told him I wouldn't be his conscience!"

"Then for heaven's sake get us out of these handcuffs," I begged her. "Can't you see what will happen if any of the Great Powers gets their hands on Yammu? We have to stop him in any way possible."

"Do you think me so incompetent?" Nijam said, apparently offended by this. "They're not *going* to get their hands on him— and I'm not letting either of you out of these cuffs, unless you promise you don't mean to hurt him."

That was a promise I could not make. I felt the tears start to my eyes. One way or another it would all be over after this. If we did not stop Yammu, then it was the end of the world. And if we *did* manage to stop him in what seemed the only way left to us, then there was an end to our fellowship. Nijam would never forgive me. Nijam would hunt me to the ends of the earth. No—I would not resist her. If I killed Alphonse I would simply let her do her worst, because I would have the heart for nothing else. Then I wondered what would become of Vasily...

At least, thought I gloomily, while Nijam and Vasily were locked in a feud to the death over the loss of their respective loves, Mimi was likely to move to Argentina or Australia and begin a new and uneventful life teaching ballet and stealing anything that was not nailed down. And I hoped very much that she would find a better family than we had been.

It was Mimi, in fact, who pulled me out of my funk. My transmitter crackled, and she said, "The Auberlen papers are safe at home, but you ought to get Alphonse and leave at once. The street is full of yachtsmen, and there are more arriving by the minute."

"I have it in hand, Mimi, but we need your lock-picks," Nijam said, tersely. Then, closing her transmitter, she turned to us with an imperious gesture. "Your word that you will not harm him!"

"My word of honour," said Vasily at once. "Molly-my-dear, tell her you don't mean to hurt Alphonse!"

Mimi was right: we must leave at once, and we must take not only Alphonse, but also the children with us, for I could no longer trust their father with their lives. And yet—there

273

were larger things at stake.

"Oh, Nijam!" I exclaimed, goaded beyond bearing. "I cannot! He begged me to promise, and I did!"

"Well, he's not begging you *now*," she said. "Is that a *sword-stick?*" and she swooped down upon me, and divested me of the weapon.

The front door shook suddenly beneath an onslaught of fists.

"Open up!" a voice cried in very bad German.

"The yachtsmen," Vasily said, in desperation. "Really, Nijam, you *must* let us go. Molly won't touch Alphonse. She has never hurt a living thing in her life!"

"Lies," said Mimi, who now appeared from the back of the house, apparently having let herself in from the mews. "Molly once threw a bowl full of salted punch at some German werewolves. What are you all doing? Where is Alphonse? Haven't you brought him to his senses yet?"

"But what if we *can't?*" I wailed. "Yammu said—"

"Molly-my-dear, we can't trust a *thing* that creature says," Vasily put in. "Miss Nijam, I will answer for Molly."

There was a renewed pounding at the door. It sounded now as though the yachtsmen were attempting to break in. Startled, Nijam turned towards it, and her automaton put up clenched fists in an attitude of battle. Mimi, muttering under her breath, produced a lock-pick and seized the hand-cuffs. She was thus occupied when Fräulein Angermeyer appeared upon the scene.

"Lord save us!" she exclaimed. "Why has no one opened the door?"

"Open it, and you die this instant," Nijam hissed, turning upon her. Poor Fräulein Angermeyer thus received the full brunt of Nijam's wrath, and a threatening motion not only from her, but also from the automaton. She gave a faint gasp and sat very suddenly upon the bench-seat beside the umbrella-stand.

And there we all were. The police were about to break open the door. The Black Templars were downstairs intoning abominable hymns in an ancient tongue, preparatory to cutting open Mr Vandergriff's skull. Mimi was trying to open a pair of handcuffs with a lock-pick, Nijam stood with a drawn sword-stick in hand, preparing to pilot her automaton into battle; and we had no notion whether any of us should ever see our poor Alphonse again.

The handcuffs gave way. Vasily seized my hand.

"Now for Alphonse," he said.

"First the children," I protested. "They're still upstairs in my room!"

"Alphonse first!" Vasily insisted.

"Leave Alphonse to me and *go!*" Nijam cried.

"How?" Mimi asked. "There are yachtsmen in the mews, too. I'd suggest the roof, but Dark would never manage the climb."

At this moment a childish voice piped up. "We'll show you the way out!"

I threw up my hands as the three children descended the stairs. Of *course* they had not remained safely in bed. Perhaps that was for the best.

"There's a loose bit in the fence," Heidi said, coming to a breathless halt at the foot of the stairs. "If we can climb out the study window—"

Whatever she had been about to say next was interrupted by a dreadful shriek which arose from the bowels of the house.

Fräulein Angermeyer let out a sob and pulled her apron over her head. Then we heard a slow, heavy tread coming from the direction of the study. The children quailed and hid themselves behind me; and then all that was left of Alphonse Schmidt stood framed in the study door.

His back was to the light, and his face in shadow; but I, with that unlucky sight of mine, could see the streamers of darkness that flowed from him, twisting and writhing like sea-weed in submarine currents. There he stood, blocking our escape. Behind us the front door splintered—gave way—and then burst open.

German police, accompanied by Griff's yachtsmen, poured into the hallway. Evidently, this Christmas Eve, peace on earth meant that for once, the Great Powers were for once working together.

Then Alphonse staggered forwards with a moan.

"Thank God you're here," he gasped; and had it not been for the writhing shadows that I alone could see, I might have believed this to be in truth my old friend. "Quickly, this way! They're about to kill a man down there!"

The gendarmes—there must have been a dozen of them—rushed past him and plunged down the staircase into the cellar. But the last of them, a navvy with a thick Russian accent, seized Alphonse by the arm.

"One moment!" he cried. "I know you! You are Alphonse—"

Before the words were quite out of his mouth, Nijam moved; her automaton sprang forward and fastened its iron hands upon the Russian's neck. There was a brief and silent struggle before the policeman folded up and descended onto the carpet.

Alphonse adjusted his cuffs in quite his old manner—in fact with such an air of purely mortal satisfaction that I suddenly

276

doubted everything that had seemed so sure a moment ago.

"Why, yes," he told the fallen policeman. "I *am* Alphonse Schmidt. You guessed better than the Black Templars, at any rate."

Mimi's mouth dropped open, and I am sure I looked no less foolish. But Nijam now reached into her pocket and disconnected the battery that kept the automaton's movements synchronised with her own; it gave a little electrical sigh and leaned gently back against the wall.

"Gloat later, Alphonse," she said briskly. "Let's go."

"Let's," Vasily chimed in. Somehow he gathered up me, and Mimi, and the children, and swept us all into the study, past the trap-door from which sounds of shouting and even blows were now arising. Nijam threw the window open, sheathed the sword-stick, and went through with a flutter of petticoats. Mimi followed, dragging Alphonse with her. The children insisted on jumping through themselves, which they did with commendable alacrity. Then I followed, sliding with some trepidation into the arms which Alphonse held out to catch me.

"It's really you?" I gasped. "I was convinced—that is, what were you *thinking*, Alphonse? I thought I was going to have to kill you!"

"It may yet come to that," he murmured, in my ear alone; and then he released me and I was left with a new sense of dread.

But Vasily had followed me through the window, and we were all free. He reached up gently to close the casement, and then we hurried along the fence that divided the Schwab garden from the one next door, to where the children were busy kicking at a pair of loose boards. Alphonse bent down and forced his way through, pulling the boards after him as he emerged on the other side, and then replacing them once the lot of us had followed.

There was a moment's silence, employed by Vasily in brushing snow and earth from his once-shining boots. Mimi turned to Alphonse.

"What do you mean by it, Alphonse!" she cried, wrathfully. "Were you fibbing when you said you had bargained yourself away to Yammu?"

"I had to tell them *something*," he protested, raising his hands. "I had to protect the children!"

"But why didn't you *tell* us, instead of scaring the lights out of us?"

"He told *me* when he kissed me!" Nijam put in. "I tried to explain, but no one listened!"

I did not know how to tell her that she had not tried very hard. "The children are shivering," I said, instead. "Let's discuss it inside."

Vasily let us in at the back-door, and within a minute or two was in the front drawing-room stirring up the fire whilst Nijam peered through the window into the street. Three carriages were drawn up outside the doctor's house, and dimly through the wall that separated us could be heard the sounds of muffled voices and heavy footsteps as the police completed their raid.

"I'm sorry," Alphonse said in a more subdued voice. "I wanted to tell you, but there wasn't time; and I thought that it might be more convincing if you really believed me to be Yammu."

He looked very pale and tired, as though the nervous energy that had keyed him up to his terrible imposture had now dissipated, leaving him exhausted. And the shadows that emanated from him had become darker and longer, their tendrils thicker. I exchanged a look with little Clara, and when I saw the look of mute terror on her face, that sense of dread increased. Something new was happening to Alphonse; the ghastly intelligence was waxing in strength.

Before I could say anything, Nijam pointed.

"Look!" she cried. "They are coming out! The police have all the Black Templars!"

Crowding to the window, we saw that this was in truth the case. As we watched, Dr Schwab was led from his house in cuffs and put into one of the waiting carriages. His robed acolytes followed. One of them had to be carried. As he was brought down the steps, the yellow gaslight shone from the hallway upon a ghastly red splash daubing the cloth which had been thrown over his head.

Hurriedly, I put a hand over the children's eyes. "I suppose that is the last of Brother Otto," I breathed. "What a horrible way to die!"

"Is he *dead?*" Heidi asked, shoving at my hands.

"Yes," Nijam answered. "But Griff isn't. What a shame!"

In truth, the American emerged from the house in triumph, bearing aloft, like a prize, Nijam's wonderful invention.

"Oh, Nijam! He's got your clothes-mangle!" I said, ruefully.

"As planned," Nijam said with grim satisfaction. "I'll finish him yet, Dark. Don't you worry."

Somehow, this was not comforting.

Griff had the wild and dishevelled appearance of a man who has barely escaped death at the hands of a sinister cult; his voice could be faintly heard haranguing the policemen as he gesticulated towards those who a moment ago had been his captors. More policemen now appeared from the house bearing boxes—the last remnants of our raid on the library. But they had failed to retrieve all of them. Three battered archive-boxes were stacked right here in our drawing-room beside the fireplace.

"Well," said Mimi, with a sigh, "all's well that ends well!"

Just then the clock struck six.

"It's morning!" I exclaimed in surprise. The night had been such a busy one that I had scarcely noticed the passage of time.

"No—better yet, it's Christmas!" Vasily declared. "Merry Christmas, everyone!"

"Merry Christmas!" Heidi shouted, leaping up and clapping her hands. But Peter sent a sorrowful glance around the drawing-room.

"There's no Christmas tree," he said sadly. "You *promised* us a Christmas tree, Fräulein Dark!"

"I *am* sorry, children," I told them, but I was sorrier for Alphonse. He had not joined us at the window. Instead he was standing with bowed head before the fireplace, his hands clasped before him. I wondered whether he was praying.

I did not have the heart for Christmas cheer. I almost hated how cheerful Vasily sounded when he proclaimed, "Who says there's no Christmas tree? I deny the charge! There *is* a Christmas tree, but it's not here."

"There *is?*" Mimi asked, sounding almost like a child herself. "Where?"

"You'll have to put on some warm things and follow me," Vasily declared. "We can't stay here, in any case. In another minute, Griff will recover sufficiently to send the police after *us* as well, and then we shall be for it. Come along; I've already sent our luggage ahead of us."

Chapter XXII.

Vasily might have sent most of the luggage ahead, but he had kept back warm coats for everyone, even—to my surprise—for me.

"If there's anything in the Schwab house you can't do without, I suppose that Mimi can go and steal it back later," Vasily offered.

"My book," I said at once, as I buttoned up the nice new winter coat I had bought in Paris and left behind me when I once more assumed the role of the humble governess. *"Can You Forgive Her?* I'm so *very* close to the end. But perhaps Mimi is tired of stealing books?"

"Oh, I am used to it by now," declared Mimi. *"Forth, said grandmother in the snow!* But, Nijam, what did Alphonse tell you, that convinced you it was really him?"

Nijam primmed up her mouth with undeniable satisfaction. "He told me that he'd be hanged if he let me hand over the automaton to Schwab."

"But that doesn't sound like anything Alphonse would say!" Mimi said.

Nijam's satisfaction only deepened. "Indeed. Had Yammu been impersonating him, it would never have thought to say such a thing."

"But *we* believed him when he asked us to leave him in the cellar and save ourselves," Mimi said. "Only that was Yammu—or no. It was Alphonse *pretending* to be Yammu pretending to be himself! Alphonse! Who knew you had such a talent?"

Alphonse had not put on his coat. Sunk in lethargy, he stood before the blazing fire, seething with darkness. I reached out and put a gentle hand on his shoulder; it was cold, but he did not shiver.

"Alphonse," I said softly. Dread had me in its grip: if I did not speak, then I would scream. "You told me, tonight, that you could no longer keep Yammu at bay. What happened? Did you really drive a bargain with him?"

"What are you *saying*, Dark?" Nijam demanded. "That was part of the trick!"

"No," Alphonse said in a hollow voice. "It was the truth."

A horrified silence settled upon the room as Alphonse turned to face her. The darkness radiated from him like the nimbus of a deadly saint—so strong that by now, perhaps everyone else could feel it, too.

"It was the only way I could get my body back," he whispered. "I promised to cede everything I owned if Yammu allowed me the undisputed use of myself until dawn on Christmas morning." He glanced at the clock, whose hands now pointed to fifteen minutes past six. "I have perhaps five minutes left."

Nijam said nothing; only I saw the hope die from her eyes. Then she turned to Mimi.

"The Auberlen papers," she said, fiercely. "Where are they?"

"Right here," Mimi said, pointing to the boxes, which were stacked by the fireplace. Nijam swooped upon the nearest—and then upturned it with a cry of horror.

"Empty!" she exclaimed. "Where are they? What have you

done with the journals?"

"They're gone, Patty. They're burned."

"What?" For a moment Nijam stared at Alphonse in horror; then she understood, and her gaze went to the fireplace, where stacks of papers and journals were even now consuming into white flakes, that shot up the chimney with a rush!

"What?" Nijam repeated in disbelief, and now there were actually tears in her eyes. *"What?* Do you *want* that creature to win, Alphonse? Do you *want* me to have to kill you?"

"No," he said, softly. "I want to live. I want to grow old in a lab. somewhere, studying and learning and discovering with *you.* But first—"

Alphonse's words faltered, and he reached out to steady himself against the mantelpiece. At my side, Clara shuddered as the darkness first unfurled and then drove itself with shocking violence deep within him. I think I must have let out a little sob as Alphonse fell to his knees, his hands clenching into fists with a groan of pain.

"What is happening?" Nijam hissed. "Dark—tell me!"

There were no words that seemed sufficient. I made a despairing gesture. Nijam saw my face; and the calm of absolute despair settled over her.

Without a word—without a plea—she drew the blade from her sword-stick, and advanced upon the man she loved.

I suppose that it had to be Nijam, after all. No one else could have done it. Vasily could not allow himself to kill, and Mimi and I did not know how.

As Nijam drew back her hand for the thrust, Mimi made a wordless sound of horror; Vasily put his hands over the children's eyes. But I caught her arm.

"Wait a moment," I said. "Look! He means to fight it."

Indeed, it was very like the scene in the cellar: I saw the shadow trying to force itself within him, and being repulsed. The struggle went on for a time that felt both fleeting and interminable; and then the darkness withdrew and coalesced into a horrible man-shape. There before my eyes was the hideous shape from the *Codex*—the jelly-like head with its waving tendrils, the man-like body, smooth and misshapen and coated with a poisonous slime.

Alphonse fell on his hands and knees before it, his breath coming in little labouring sobs. Nijam, unable to see the apparition, whispered his name like a plea.

"We had an agreement!" —I cannot possibly describe what the Voice was like; only it communicated not so much in words as in thoughts—thoughts that struck one like a bludgeon, thoughts that imposed themselves by pure violence. "You vowed me your body, mortal! Beware! Do not seek to resist me, or your soul as well as your body shall belong to me forever!"

Alphonse drew another gasping breath. "I didn't," he whispered. "I didn't vow you my body."

"No?" the creature demanded, with loathsome laughter.

"No," Alphonse repeated more firmly, pulling himself upright with an effort. "You demanded my body, and I vowed you *everything I had to give.* Which, as I see it, is *nothing at all.*"

"Insolent!" Yammu roared, but Alphonse cut him off.

"What is your only comfort in life and death?" he asked in a dreamy, sing-song voice. *"That I am not my own, but belong with body and soul, both in life and in death, to my faithful Saviour Jesus Christ...* Begone, you fiend. I give you *nothing.*"

The tendrils lashed; the darkness seethed. "Insolent thief!" the creature hissed, reaching out a cruel talon towards its prey.

"Give yourself up! You know that you are mine by right; you have been mine ever since you first let me in!"

"That's what you always told me," Alphonse said, with gentle doggedness. "But I think I've had enough of those lies. I revoke the consent I once gave you. I will hear you no longer. Begone."

He swept out a hand as though flinging a door shut; and all at once Yammu was gone.

My knees gave way; I found myself sitting on the carpet, close to tears. The whole room seemed to have lightened in a way that could not be accounted for by the dawn. Mimi and Vasily glanced at each other with a startled look, as though they had just emerged from some dreadful trance. Alphonse knelt still before the fire, a hand outstretched, as though he could not quite believe that the ghastly creature was truly gone at his command.

Only Nijam seemed still to be in command of herself.

"Is it gone?" she asked, seizing Alphonse by the shoulders and giving him a little shake. "Is it really gone?"

"Yes," he said, looking with bewilderment at the naked blade in her right hand. "Yes, it's really gone."

Nijam drew a shaky little breath and let the sword-stick fall to the carpet. Such was her emotion that her eyes filled with tears.

"This," she said after a moment, "is compelling evidence for the existence of miracles."

Alphonse was still staring at the blade. "You were going to kill me," he said.

"Who else could have done it?" she asked.

He looked up at her, and rose to his feel, and pulled her into his arms. *"Thank you,"* he said, and then there was silence for a moment. Vasily and Mimi and I looked out into the street with great interest.

Mimi made an exclamation and struck her forehead.

"I *knew* I had forgotten something!" she exclaimed. "I dropped the *Atrocious Codex* in the laboratory when Alphonse grabbed me! Now the police will have it!"

"No—Griff had it," said I, suddenly recalling how he had emerged from the house with the automaton over one shoulder, and a book in his hand. "He brought it out of the house, and heaven knows where it is now."

"Don't worry about Griff," said Nijam, behind us. "He won't be a trouble to us much longer. But if we don't leave now, he may be quite enough trouble as it is."

"Oh, yes," said I. A great weight had rolled from my mind, and I felt twice the woman I had been. "Vasily promised us a Christmas tree. Lead us to it, Vasily."

We left at once by the back mews—Vasily and Schmidt carrying the two living children, who had come away without any shoes.

I walked beside Vasily, thinking how unusually handsome he looked carrying a child.

Evidently, there were heavier things weighing on Vasily's mind. His voice was hushed. "Schmidt made you promise to end him?"

I nodded.

"But Molly-my-dear, you didn't *tell* me!"

"How could I?" I asked, in a voice equally soft. "Had you agreed to help him, it would have meant more blood on your hands, and that would have been intolerable. But had you refused, it would have been too much like ordering him about; and that, too, is something you have tried to leave behind you.

Was I wrong?"

He gazed at me in something between wonder and adoration. "No," he said. "You were entirely correct on both counts. How well you understand me!"

"I chose, instead, to wager that we would not be left without our miracle," said I. After that we went on in silence; but I could not help thinking, again, how much Vasily had changed. I had not known him in the days when he was a vampire and a Grand Duke; and yet his loss of his fangs and his title had been but the beginning of a slow rebirth.

Ten minutes' brisk walk brought us to a little block of tenements, rather shabby but quite respectable. On the third floor Vasily paused before one of many identical doors, letting down Heidi to the floor.

"There's not just a Christmas tree waiting behind this door," he said. "There's something far, *far* better. Why don't you knock for us, Heidi?"

She laughed with pleased anticipation. For a moment there was no answer to her knock. When the door opened, the woman who stood there was fully dressed, but her eyes were tired; she seemed to have been sitting up all night. She did not see the children at first. Instead, her gaze fixed upon Vasily, and her lips parted with a look of mingled terror and hope. Then—

"Mama!" Heidi shrieked.

The triplets locked their arms about her. Only Clara hung back, but she raised a wistful little face to me, and there were tears in her eyes.

"Oh, my little bears!" the woman cried, drawing them close to her heart. "Oh, my little bears! Oh, you have come home to me!"

It was too much; I dove into my pockets, but found nothing. Vasily, seeing my plight, offered me a handkerchief.

"Merry Christmas!" he said, to no one in particular.

"Oh, come in! come in!" cried Frau Schwab, drawing aside and motioning us to enter her little room. We ventured in to find the place quite crowded: there in the narrow space between stove and window was a Christmas-tree all done up in tinsel, with an array of brown-paper parcels set out beneath it. There, too, were our band-boxes and carpet-bags piled upon the little table; for Frau Schwab, of course, was the woman in black with whom Vasily had spoken the previous afternoon!

"It is a fairy-story!" Mimi cried, wiping the tears from her eyes. "Isn't it *just* like a fairy-story, Nijam?"

"I don't know," said Nijam, with a sniff. "I don't read a great many fairy stories. Nonsense, all of them." But I had never seen her look so happy. She was holding Schmidt's arm as though she meant to make him into a sort of prosthesis, and to carry him about with her forevermore.

"How can I ever thank you?" Frau Schwab now asked through her tears. "But can I really keep them? Will the doctor let us go?"

Vasily had already related to us what he knew of Frau Schwab's sad history. For some time she had been unhappy in her marriage, knowing that the doctor was carrying out experiments on the children without her consent. When Clara died, she had resolved to dare everything the law could do to her, and rescue her two remaining children. Alas! she had been betrayed, and the doctor, retrieving the children, had prosecuted his wife as a kidnapper! Not even the fact of Clara's death was enough evidence to remove the children from his care. Frau Schwab's term of imprisonment was shortened by her good behaviour, and upon her release she had come at once to Heidelberg with a wild idea of attempting a second time to spirit herself and her children away to France. It was while she was still formulating these plans, of course, that she had come to our attention.

"The doctor will almost certainly be convicted of murder," Vasily said now. "And in that case, the law should put little obstacle in the way of your obtaining either a divorce, or the care of your children. But I have written to a certain wealthy benefactor of ours, ma'am, and I am certain that he will engage you an able attorney, so as to remove all doubts of your victory."

"Are we going to live with you now, Mama?" Peter asked.

"I hope so," she said, in a tremulous voice. "Are you going to thank Herr Dunkel, children?"

Detaching themselves from their mother, they seized upon Vasily with zeal. "Thank you! Thank you!" they cried.

"Thank you for the most wonderful Christmas in the world!" Heidi added.

Vasily laughed, ruffling their hair; he sent me a rather shy glance, as though half ashamed of his own enjoyment. "But Christmas has scarcely begun," he said. "You can't say that until you've opened your *other* presents—over there, under the tree."

Then, to all our surprise, we found ourselves sitting in a little circle upon the bare floor as Frau Schwab made tea and Vasily, on his knees, dealt out brown-paper parcels. The children had jumping-jacks and toy soldiers and carved and painted wooden swords; and also a magnificent, colossal, very hairy tarantula-spider to replace Aunt Dete, together with a beautiful new cage to keep her in. Frau Schwab had an enormous box of *Mozartkugeln.* Mimi had an ornament of coloured glass to hang in her window, which made her squeal with delight. Schmidt received a beautiful embroidered waistcoat and Nijam several pairs of thick, soft, woollen socks, which she declared to be exactly what she had always wanted. It really does take all kinds to make a world! Mine was a book in three volumes.

"*Phineas Finn,*" I read, "by Anthony Trollope. But I haven't finished *Can You Forgive Her?!*"

"You will soon," Vasily declared, "and then you can go straight on to what is next! —That is," he added, "if you are *ready* to begin a new part of the story."

"I think I might be," I told him, with a smile. "But what about you, Vaska? Please tell me you bought yourself a present, for I wholly forgot to give you anything."

"But you could," he said, kneeling before me. He reached into his pocket and drew forth a small pasteboard box. "Molly-my-dear, you could give me the very kindest Christmas present since the Christ-child himself."

I opened the box—and there, to my surprise, lay the wedding-ring which I had believed left behind in Paris!

I bit my lip. Mimi groaned. "Not *another* proposal!"

"Hush, Mimi!" said Vasily. "I am trying *very* hard to be serious! Well, Molly? You will always have my heart, but won't you take my hand into the bargain?"

Until now he had only asked me in a flippant, off-hand manner, and at inconvenient times, as though he expected me to refuse and meant to soften the blow to himself as much as possible. But now there was a ring of sincerity in his words.

I am very bad and wicked, I know.

"How can you ask me such a thing?" I said, plaintively, "when I have already said yes?"

He blanched.

"But that wasn't serious!" he protested. "You weren't *supposed* to say yes!"

"Oh! I beg your pardon. Am I supposed to say yes now?"

"Yes!" he cried. "No! Only if you like to—Molly, must you drive me to distraction at *every* turn?"

"Yes," I said, and leaned forward to press a swift, soft kiss upon his lips. "I really must, and therefore I will certainly marry you."

"Then it's settled!" he cried, with a return of the old ebullience. "Molly-my-dear, you and I are going to run the Paris Opera, and we shall be the talk of Europe. Nijam and Schmidt will set up a laboratory and make marvellous gadgets that astonish the world. Mimi will be a ballet-mistress and the despair of all hearts. And we shall steal some things occasionally, when Herr Haber calls upon us, or when we find some wrong to set right. Yes—indeed I think that God's in his heaven, and all's right with the world."

"Not quite all," said Alphonse. "We haven't heard the last of Griff, after all. *And* he's got his hands on the *Codex.*"

And poor little Clara, I thought, looking about me for the ghost-child. *She* had had no Christmas at all. But I could not see her anywhere. I got up and looked behind the Christmas-tree, and behind Frau Schwab's skirts as she warmed the tea-pot; but there was no sign of her.

Peter slipped a hand into mine. "Clara went away," he whispered, sadly. "She kissed me goodbye and went. I don't think we'll see her again."

I put a comforting arm about his shoulders. "She has gone

to something ever so much better than Christmas, my love." And in my heart I sent up a prayer of thanks that she had been allowed to remain for so long—just long enough to keep her siblings company until they could find their mother again.

Then the tea was ready, and the sun rose high enough to peep in at the windows, and Frau Schwab, who had been amply equipped by Vasily on the previous day, brought out all manner of good things for breakfast that were not *Mozartkugeln*. And I found myself in perfect agreement with Heidi. It really was the best of Christmasses.

* * *

Alphonse was correct: we had not yet heard the last of Griff.

By the time we bade Frau Schwab and the two remaining triplets farewell at the train station a day or two later, Griff was all over the papers congratulating himself on foiling the great Heidelberg Library robbery. This crime had been plotted and carried out by that odious malefactor, Dr Hermann Schwab—the leader of a dangerous cult, which murdered one of its own members in the course of a ghastly occult ritual! The paper made no mention of Miss Molly Dark or her crew. Vasily thought that Griff must be reluctant to admit that he had not single-handedly solved the case. Mimi thought that he was embarrassed by our having escaped him a third time. I suspected that he still planned to get his hands on my shares in the Hong Kong shipping venture, and therefore preferred not to smirch my name. Nijam said nothing; only she smiled thinly at the final line of the article, which stated that Mr Vandergriff would shortly embark at Hamburg on his long voyage to America.

Nijam took to reading the *New York Herald* until one day late the following January when she drew our attention to a notice in the obituary section. *Suddenly, at home on Long Island, the prominent and well-respected businessman, Mr Warren Henry Vandergriff.* A news item in the following day's paper shared the conjecture that Mr Vandergriff, who had been severely ill for some time, had in fact perished in the course of an attempted cure.

"An attempted cure!" exclaimed Vasily. "That's a nice way to say *a botched head transplant.*"

"So you committed your perfect murder after all, Nijam!" said Mimi, with undisguised admiration. Alphonse choked on his tea, but Nijam gave a shrug.

"I told you that a little of the wrong sort of knowledge could be deadly," she said. "But *I* didn't force him to cut off his own head."

Griff was thus no longer a danger to us; but the *Codex,* it seemed, had survived him. It was, of course, not long after this that the revenants began to reappear in America, where they were employed once again in police work, and in repressing the coloured population. So in a way, our quest had been a failure.

"We can't blame ourselves, Dark," said Nijam ruefully, when the news came out. "We did what we could. People are the scum of the earth, and you can't stop them getting what they want. At least Alphonse is himself again."

"And the world didn't end," I said, clinking my tea-cup against hers. "Don't forget that, for a little while, that was a distinct possibility."

Alphonse *was* himself, although I believe that he will always be haunted by the old memories. He is, in addition, no longer being chased by the policemen of Europe. I believe that they are over in America these days, trying to wheedle the secret of revenants out of the Americans.

It seems likely that Frau Schwab and her children will soon be legally free of the sinister doctor; although that prudent lady has withdrawn with her children to Strasbourg, safely beyond the reach of the German law.

As for my crew and I, we have been settling into life in Paris, where Alphonse and Nijam have found employment at the great University. Mimi is both teaching and dancing, and Vasily and I—well. Since fashionable Paris already believes us to be man and wife, we are planning to be married very quietly in London in May. Herr Haber has promised to attend; my sisters are excited to be my bridesmaids; and Alphonse is to be the best man. For our honeymoon we are to visit Ruritania, one of those pretty little Balkan kingdoms, which Vasily says is just like a fairy-tale. It will be just the two of us, and for a few short weeks neither of us is to worry about stealing *anything,* he says, but kisses.

I wonder what we shall find to do with ourselves?

S. D. G.

Unhistorical Note

We come—for now, though perhaps not forever—to the last
of Molly Dark's adventures. This book, to a greater extent
than perhaps any other in this series, has managed to remain
largely free from historical fact. While there has of course for
many centuries been a famous university in the German town
of Heidelberg, I cannot say for certain that it ever played host
to a secret society of scientists seeking to achieve eternal life.

Some travellers' accounts of travel in nineteenth century
Germany did, however, inform my story. The British hu-
mourist Jerome K Jerome, better known for the classic *Three
Men in a Boat,* also wrote a hilarious and engaging account
of travel in 1890s Germany, *Three Men on the Bummel,* which
provided me among other things with a number of details on
the laws governing the use of perambulators. Mark Twain
in *A Tramp Abroad* recorded his experiences in Heidelberg
itself, complete with some fascinating details on the student
duels, or *Mensur,* which decorated so many young Germans
with facial scars. This tradition, I'm told, continues at some
German universities today.

The early years of the twentieth century saw the rise of a
number of secret societies in Germany, many of them with
occultist and far-right leanings: the Thule Society, which
sponsored the creation of what would later become Adolf
Hitler's Nazi Party, and the Order of the New Temple, founded

in 1900 by the fascist agitator Adolf Joseph Lanz, were two that inspired the secret society in this book. (As a self-taught crusader history buff, I could not refrain from giving Molly Dark a number of acid comments on the difference between the Templars of reality, and those of popular legend). An even greater influence on Griff, Dr Schwab, and the Black Templars, was the contemporary transhumanist movement, as portrayed in Mark O'Connell's very entertaining book *To Be a Machine: Adventures Among Cyborgs, Utopians, Hackers, and the Futurists Solving the Modest Problem of Death.*

Dr Auberlen is fictional, but his decision to have himself mummified after death is partly a homage to the eighteenth century English philosopher Jeremy Bentham, whose (poorly) mummified remains are still on display at the University College London. Eagle-eyed readers will recall that the second volume of Miss Dark's memoirs largely took place at the UCL. Sadly, I missed the chance to allude to this unusual decoration at the time. With Dr Auberlen, I hope this sad oversight has been addressed.

As ever, I would love to thank my wonderful beta and sensitivity readers for their time, help, and insight: Catherine Ko, Claire Trella Hill, Rosamund Hodge, Christina Baehr, W.R. Gingell, and Karen Scharff. In addition, I would like to thank Christina's ten delightful children, for providing me with far more material for hilarious childhood shenanigans than I could possibly use in this short book.

Suzannah Rowntree
September, 2025.

About the Author

Suzannah Rowntree lives in a big house in rural Australia with her wonderful family, drinking fancy tea and writing historical fantasy fiction that blends real-world history with legend, adventure, and a dash of romance.

You can connect with me on:

🌐 https://suzannahrowntree.site

Subscribe to my newsletter:

✉ https://subscribepage.io/srauthor

Also by Suzannah Rowntree

The Miss Sharp's Monsters Series
  The Werewolf of Whitechapel
  A Study in Sirens
  Anarchist on the Orient Express
  A Vampire in Bavaria

The Miss Dark's Apparitions Series
  Tall & Dark
  Dark Clouds
  Dark & Stormy
  Dark & Dawn
  A Stab in the Dark
  Dark Secrets

The Watchers of Outremer Series
  A Wind from the Wilderness
  The Lady of Kingdoms
  Children of the Desolate
  A Day of Darkness
  A Conspiracy of Prophets
  The House of Mourning
  A Stranger in the Land

The Pendragon's Heir Trilogy
  The Door to Camelot
  The Quest for Carbonek
  The Heir of Logres

The Fairy Tale Retold Series
  The Rakshasa's Bride
  The Prince of Fishes
  The Bells of Paradise
  Death Be Not Proud
  Ten Thousand Thorns
  The City Beyond the Glass

Non-Fiction
  How to Write a Fantasy Battle

www.ingramcontent.com/pod-product-compliance
Lightning Source LLC
Chambersburg PA
CBHW071920130726
47909CB00014B/2213